Peabody Institute Library
Peabody, MA 01960

The Door

The Door

ANDY MARINO

SCHOLASTIC PRESS | NEW YORK

Library of Congress Cataloging-in-Publication Data

Marino, Andy, 1980– author.
The door / Andy Marino. — First edition.
pages cm
Summary: Twelve-year-old Hannah Silver can sense things that other people cannot, and living in Cliff House she is surrounded by secrets and the voices of people who are not really there — but when she finds her mother murdered she will have to confront the secret of a mysterious door that may lead to another world.
ISBN 978-0-545-55137-3 (jacketed hardcover) 1. Future life — Juvenile fiction. 2. Children's secrets — Juvenile fiction. 3. Mothers and daughters — Juvenile fiction. [1. Future life — Fiction. 2. Mothers and daughters — Fiction. 3. Secrets — Fiction.] I. Title.
PZ7.M33877Do 2014
813.6 — dc23
2013032039

10 9 8 7 6 5 4 3 2 1   14 15 16 17 18

Printed in the U.S.A.   23
First edition, May 2014

The text type was set in Garamond Classico.
Book design by Christopher Stengel

For my parents

Chapter One

The spiral staircase to the top of the lighthouse was full of invisible traps. Hannah Silver ascended by skipping the odd-numbered steps. At step sixteen — halfway up — she planted both feet in a decisive hopscotch landing and wiggled her fingers and toes. No pain. She examined her arms and legs.

You're fine, Belinda said. If Belinda were to appear in real life, instead of in Hannah's head, she would smell like beef stew and wear a cream-colored floral housecoat. *Walk normally. You're too old for this game.*

"I know, I know, I know," Hannah said, but the rule was hard to defy — even though, at twelve years old, she knew better.

Take them one by one, urged Belinda. *Seventeen, eighteen, nineteen. All the way up, just like that.*

"Chalkdust!" Hannah said, stamping her foot. The old iron staircase protested with a metallic groan. *Chalkdust* was a swear in Muffin Language, which she had been developing since she was old enough to talk. She was the world's foremost expert on its grammar and vocabulary; a fact she had verified on the library computer.

That's because you're the only person in the world who speaks it, Belinda reminded her.

"Crepuscular slurp," Hannah muttered. Belinda backed off. Hannah rested her hand on the railing in her best imitation of a normal person on a staircase. The odd-numbered steps before her were like dark things lurking in the corners of a dream. If she squinted, she could make out all manner of medieval torture devices, dangling leather straps and rusted screws the size of baseball bats, waiting to ensnare her limbs.

Hannah reminded herself that she was never going to make it through her new school if it took her twenty minutes to climb a few steps. The junior high school in Carbine Pass was four stories high, and the elevator was teachers-only. She shuddered at the memory of her recent tour. The assistant principal had ushered Hannah and her mother inside the elevator and pressed the button for the top floor. The button was instantly surrounded by a thin circle of yellow light, like a tiny eclipse, while the others were rimmed in darkness.

Hit two and three, urged Nancy, Hannah's mischievous inner twin. *Light them up or the cable will snap and the elevator will fall!*

Hannah's left hand trembled. "Grenadine magnetism," she whispered.

"Come again?" said the assistant principal.

Hannah's mother put a reassuring hand on her shoulder, but it wasn't enough. Hannah punched the buttons with desperate urgency.

"Huh," said the assistant principal, writing something on a notepad.

Her mother must have worked some kind of magic, because Hannah wasn't kicked out on the spot. One week from today, she would be homeschooled no longer. She had gotten her wish, and now she had to learn how to navigate stairs. Outside, waves battered the rocky cliffs. The sound was a foamy murmur inside the thick walls of the lighthouse; it helped. She lifted her right foot —

"Hannah!"

— and froze. Her mother was calling from the mossy garden path that connected the Silvers' backyard to the lighthouse.

"Come meet our guests!"

Hannah turned the word over in her mind. *Guests.* It was practically meaningless. The few kids she knew from the Carbine Pass library were never allowed over. And anyway, with no TV, no computer, and no cell phone reception, Cliff House wasn't exactly a prime hangout spot.

With a shameful blossoming of relief at the interruption, Hannah turned and descended the stairs, skipping fourteen, twelve, ten. . . .

On the way down, these steps were trapdoors to a bottomless pit.

Chapter Two

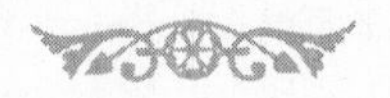

Hannah and her mother received their guests in a room with a big round window overlooking the sea.

"Hannah, I want you to meet Patrick." Hannah's mother introduced a tall, sandy-haired man with pale skin, friendly wrinkles at the corners of his eyes, and dark symmetrical blotches on his earlobes. He was dressed in a fine suit.

"Are you a lawyer?" Hannah asked, wondering if she was supposed to shake his hand, give a formal little bow, or just stand still.

"Retired," he said, flicking his eyes toward Hannah's mother and back to Hannah before indicating the boy at his side. "This is Kyle."

Kyle was a year or two older than her, a teenager, with dark hair that swept in a perfectly accidental way across his eyebrows and along the tops of his ears.

"I'm not a lawyer, myself," Kyle said, smiling at Hannah. "Anyway, hey."

"Hey," she said. Then she looked quizzically at her mother, who was wearing a bright orange dress that seemed to reflect light upward, bathing her face in a tropical glow.

"Patrick was a friend of your father's," her mother explained. "From a long time ago."

That much was obvious — her father had died before she was born. Hannah studied Patrick's face and tried to imagine a younger version of it. Hadn't she seen a picture in one of her mother's albums? Patrick and her father sitting on the porch, empty bottles cluttering the wicker table between them.

Quit staring! Belinda said.

Patrick's earlobes weren't stained by birthmarks, Hannah realized — they were tattooed with black ink. She transferred her gaze to Kyle and found that his lips were pressed together in a funny half smile. She felt like everyone was waiting for her to say something, which made her want to run away. At the same time, she felt helplessly rooted to her spot on the carpet.

Ask him what's up with those marks on his ears, suggested Nancy.

"They are pretty weird," Hannah agreed — and winced at having said it out loud. Being around guests was going to take some getting used to. Her mother settled a familiar reassuring hand on her shoulder and added a light squeeze.

"Patrick's in Carbine Pass on a business trip," her mother explained.

"Isn't the point of being retired not to be in business anymore?"

"Yes and no," Patrick said. "I'm no longer a lawyer, but I still have work to do."

"My wild and crazy uncle Patrick is a *consultant*," Kyle said.

One who consults, Nancy explained. *They mostly work in outer space, I think.*

Kyle went on. "It means he gets to travel around a lot, and sometimes if I don't have school, I get to come."

"My work affords me the freedom to visit old friends once in a while." Patrick smiled at Hannah's mother. "It really is wonderful to be back at Cliff House." He took a deep, satisfied gulp of air. "I missed that smell. Sea and rocks and . . ." He flared his nostrils and inhaled gently, as if he were sniffing a glass of expensive wine. "Good memories. The strangest part about coming back after so many years is that it doesn't really feel strange at all. Do you know what I mean?"

"No," Hannah said. "I'm always here."

"I guess in a way, so am I," Patrick said.

Hannah looked at Kyle, who shrugged and seemed to roll his eyes without moving them very much at all. Hannah tried to make her own eyes say *I know what you mean*. Her mother's vague pronouncements were often followed by a long, wistful glance out over the sea, and Hannah watched with satisfaction as Patrick and her mother both turned toward the window at the same time.

Patrick and Kyle stayed for dinner, and after the meal, it was left to Hannah and Kyle to clean up.

"I've never been this close to a real lighthouse before," Kyle said, pulling a white plate from the landscape of steam and bobbing dishes that filled the sink. He scrubbed with a thick sponge while Hannah's towel-draped fist made listless circles on a serving tray. She counted each revolution of the towel: *six, seven, eight.* Kyle worked at a smudge of stuck-on cheese, frowning with effort. Leanna Silver's lasagna could be stubborn.

"I guess not that many people have them," Hannah said.

As dinner had progressed through salad and bread and lasagna and ice cream, Hannah had found herself speaking almost nonstop to Kyle. He was much nicer than anyone she knew in Carbine Pass, and he seemed really interested in her life, rather than just waiting for his turn to talk. He didn't ask how on *earth* she lived without TV and the Internet. He watched her eyes while she answered his questions, and seemed to file away her words in an important place in his head.

Even better, Nancy and Belinda hadn't chimed in once. Usually they steered her conversations. That was a good sign. Maybe she *was* ready for public school.

"So is it really, like, *yours*?" Kyle asked.

"Before Cliff House was even built, my great-grandpa was the lighthouse keeper. He lived in this tiny little shed. It's a whole story."

Kyle scraped the last piece of cheese off the plate and handed it to her for drying. She set the tray on the counter and took the plate, resuming her lazy circles, starting her count over at one.

"I think we've got time," he said, eyeing the pile of dirty dishes.

Her mother's boisterous laugh drifted in from the dining room, where she and Patrick were having coffee. If the first surprise of the night was the sudden appearance of guests in the house, the second was the incredible change in her mother's mood. Leanna Silver existed within a mild but steady gloom, as if the gray desolation of the North Atlantic had long ago seeped into her bones.

"That's the old shed, right there." Hannah pointed out the window above the kitchen sink. The whitewashed exterior of the lighthouse had soaked up darkness from the evening sky, and the forlorn shed at its base looked defiantly squat.

"Is there somebody in it?"

"Not for a really long time. We don't need to warn boats away from the rocks anymore because radar got way better, and anyway they changed the shipping lanes. That's part of the story."

You're telling it out of order, Belinda reminded her. Hannah jumped, fumbling the plate, catching it just in time. Belinda had been silent for almost two hours, and it startled Hannah to hear the old woman's voice.

"He asked a question . . . shut up," Hannah murmured, turning her head away from Kyle and setting the plate on the counter with a porcelain thud. She froze momentarily, trying to remember if she'd wiped the plate twenty-seven times or if she'd messed up and gone over.

Fifty-two! Nancy said. One of her favorite games was to yell random numbers when Hannah was trying to count in her head. *Thirty-eight! Four hundred ninety-three!*

Hannah closed her eyes and chased Nancy away.

Kyle said, "I can't believe somebody lived in that little shed."

"His name was Jackson Silver, and he really only slept there, because he spent all his time up in the lighthouse. That was back when lots of ships were sailing down the coast and smashing into rocks. Then after he got married he started building the main part of Cliff House. His son, Abraham, my grandpa, learned how to be a lighthouse keeper, too."

"Is it really that hard?" Kyle asked. "I mean it's just, like, turn the light on, turn the light off, right?"

"No, it's — I don't know. But there weren't as many ships to watch out for anymore, so when Abraham was old enough he added more rooms to the house so he could start his own family. By the time Benjamin, my dad, was born, there was like no traffic out on the water at all, so he and my grandpa spent all their time working on the house. Then just my dad worked on it. By the time I got here, Cliff House was pretty big."

Kyle had stopped washing dishes and was leaning against the sink, watching her tell the story. "That's funny," he said. "It's like your family built this huge house because they were bored. You wouldn't think part-time lighthouse keepers would have the money, you know? No offense."

"They didn't *pay* somebody to build the house."

"You know what else is funny?" Kyle used his fingers to tick off names. "Jackson. Abraham. Benjamin. Your mom. Then you. You and your mom are probably the first girl lighthouse keepers." He grinned. "I bet the ones before Jackson were all dudes, too."

"I'm not going to be a lighthouse keeper. And I don't think it's been here that long."

"You'd be surprised." He plunged his hands back into the sink and came up with a spatula, made a face, and traded it for a fork. "Maybe when we're done with the dishes, you can take me up there. I bet the view is awesome."

"Take you to the *lighthouse*?"

That was absurd. Out there, the no-guest rule counted double. And getting past the traps was hard enough without dragging along some staircase rookie. Flustered, she picked up the plate she had just dried and was about to decline, as politely as possible, when her mother came through the door carrying two coffee cups with handles like flower stems.

"Here are some more, if you wouldn't mind."

Behind her came Patrick. Hannah felt herself turning red. The fact that Kyle had even mentioned going to the lighthouse made her feel like she'd just been caught stealing from her mother's purse.

"We were just talking about the lighthouse," Kyle said. "About maybe checking it out, if it's okay." Hannah stared at her featureless reflection in the plate. Did Kyle even realize what he was asking? She braced herself for her mother's mood to plummet, for the chilly *absolutely not* to smack Kyle in the face like an arctic wind.

But her mother did something curious and completely unexpected. She turned to Patrick and raised an eyebrow. He looked at her for a moment, then nodded very slightly, just a quick bob of his head.

Leanna Silver practically beamed. "I'm sure Hannah would love to take you once you've finished with the dishes."

This time, Hannah really did drop the plate.

Chapter Three

The garden path was enclosed by a tunnel of trellises woven with flowering vines. On sunny days the light came through in millions of tiny patches that made a mosaic of white and yellow on the ground. At night the tunnel made the darkness deeper and blacker, blotting out the nighttime sky and any stars that happened to peek through the clouds. Hannah could sprint blindly back and forth to the lighthouse — she'd been doing it all her life — but her mother had insisted she take a flashlight to escort Kyle.

When they were almost to the end, Kyle stopped walking and took a deep breath through his nose.

"I've never been to the ocean before. It's definitely got its own smell."

"Brine," Hannah said. Whenever she read a book that took place near the sea, people were always calling it *briny*. In English, she guessed the word meant something like "fishy" or "salty." In Muffin Language, she decided, it would mean "the sound of a boy smelling the air."

That's a good one, Nancy said, genuinely excited for the new word.

Hannah had been enjoying the walk, but when she pushed open the door to the lighthouse, anxiety swelled. How was she going to handle the stairs? If Kyle didn't already think she was a friendless weirdo, wait until he watched her skip steps, perform self-checks on her limbs, and dodge invisible torture devices. And the password! Once they reached the landing, there was an entire sentence in Muffin Language that had to be spoken with authority. Only then could they climb the short ladder to the bell-shaped glass room where the lamp sat dormant.

Inside, she turned off the flashlight and flicked a light switch on the wall. There were no windows in the lower part of the lighthouse, just the metal staircase spiraling up the center of a gradually narrowing tube.

"We gotta go up if you want to see anything," she said, her voice cracking.

"Lead on, Miss Lighthouse Keeper."

Hannah turned and glanced at the bottom step. One: an odd number. Just above it, step two beckoned like a warm embrace. Both Belinda and Nancy began to chatter, the old woman urging her once again to disregard this game, Hannah's twin encouraging her to make it even more complex by adding math problems along the way. Their voices were impossible to ignore outright, but they could be shoved to the back of her mind. The problem was, this act of will made it hard to move her body. She lifted her foot with a jerky, robotic motion and placed it on the first step, conscious of the way she looked to Kyle, standing just behind her. He asked her something, but she barely heard him as she closed her eyes and moved to the next step. If she kept them closed, maybe she could pretend the traps weren't there. And if the traps weren't there, they couldn't hurt her. As long as she moved very methodically . . .

Something slammed into her back and she cried out in horror. *Searing hot pokers, sharpened hooks, the rack!*

"Sorry," Kyle said, backing off, embarrassed. "You slowed down all of a sudden and I — well, I didn't."

"It's fine," she heard herself say through clenched teeth. Now her eyes were open. She and Kyle were a little more than halfway up, and the rest of the staircase bristled with steel spikes and spinning pizza cutters with shark's teeth.

"Hey — are you okay?" Kyle asked.

She looked at him over her shoulder. Belinda and Nancy continued their onslaught inside her head.

"Shhhh!" she hissed.

Kyle nodded, as if this were a perfectly reasonable thing for her to say to him. There was nothing unkind about it, and the longer she studied the calm face of the older boy the more relaxed she became. It was hard to tell how long they stood on the staircase, looking at each other.

"It'll be easier if you let me take your hand," he said so quietly she had to strain to hear him. He blinked in what seemed like slow motion, his eyelashes like the tendrils of a carnivorous plant moving so slowly that she could pick out each individual lash. Suddenly, his hand was outstretched, fingertips brushing her own. Outside, the waves battering the rocks slowed to a dull, constant roar.

"Okay," Hannah said, giving in to how good it felt to have someone else lead her through the traps. Kyle seemed to know all about them, the precise location of each swinging blade and trip-wire chain, which was impossible, but somehow didn't strike Hannah as all that strange.

One minute she was paralyzed with fear and anxiety; the next minute they were standing together in the round room just below the glass chamber at the very top. Had she even said the password? It was as if someone had extracted sixty seconds of memory with the precision slice of a scalpel.

In the center of the room was the ladder. Behind it, clearly visible through the rungs, was a curious design flaw: a nondescript door in the wall. Hannah once spent a whole hour looking up from the ground outside, searching for clues in the shape of the exterior — a bulge, an outcropping — but there was nothing. As far as she could tell, the door went nowhere. There wasn't even enough space for a tiny storage closet.

If Kyle asked about it, she'd just tell him what her mother had told her: *I have no idea. Some ancient mistake.*

But Kyle climbed the ladder without giving it a glance.

The glass enclosure at the top was dominated by the hulking

black shell of the fog lamp. Outside, the base of the bell-shaped room was ringed by a narrow, off-limits balcony.

"This is unreal," Kyle said reverently, gazing out at the endless, darkened sea. A half-moon, partially obscured by wispy clouds, sent pale light rippling along the crests of the waves as they rolled in toward the cliffs. The sheer size of the emptiness that surrounded her, along with all that was hidden beneath the ocean, made her feel light-headed.

"Albert," she said, a sudden memory tugging at her.

"Um . . . it's Kyle, remember?"

Hannah could feel her face reddening. One week until school. Time to stop thinking out loud. Now she would have to explain herself.

"When I was little my mom would plop me in front of this window to look out. Albert is all that. . . ." She made a sweeping gesture across the glass. "The water and the air. The darkness. It's just so gigantic, all that empty space, going on forever. I was, like, six."

"Did you name other stuff, too?"

"Rooms," Hannah said. "But they don't have people names."

Kyle tapped a fingernail on the glass. In the vague reflection from the light that leaked up from the room below, Hannah caught his eye and wondered if he might be an actor, someone a person with a TV would recognize right away. The more she thought about it, the more it made sense: He could be a famous kid who made more money than his parents and was free to explore the world with his eccentric uncle Patrick whenever he felt like it.

"Yeah, right," he said. "I wish."

She froze, realizing what she'd done, again.

"Don't worry about it," he said.

Strangely enough, she didn't.

Chapter Four

Hannah squirmed in the passenger seat of her mother's pickup, which was idling in the horseshoe drop-off zone where the parking lot met the front steps of the rambling, old school building. It was a week later, her first day at the public school. Since no bus could make the winding drive out to Cliff House, Hannah was forced to endure a barrage of her mother's instructions, like *Look people in the eyes when you talk to them* and *Don't think out loud* and *Please use words to convey their proper meaning.*

While her mother wrapped up the lecture, students drifted into cliques before the first bell of the year had rung.

"Yep, okay," Hannah said, watching a circle of boys holding flipped-up skateboards.

"I know it's not easy for you to make friends when you can't have anybody over," her mother said, and Hannah looked — really looked — at her for the first time since they'd left the house. Her mother's hands were gripping the steering wheel as if she were about to change her mind and decide that another year of homeschooling was for the best. Her fingernails chipped at the ends where she picked and bit them — a habit that seemed to have flared up sometime in the last week. "I don't want you to think I made that rule to mess up your life."

"I don't think that." Hannah returned her mother's odd, lingering smile, then opened the door and lifted her new backpack from the floor between her feet. She shifted her right leg outside. "I gotta go."

"Hannah," her mother said, a little too loudly. Her forehead was creased with concern. Hannah transferred her backpack to the pavement outside the car. There was a sudden urgency to the way other kids were streaming in from the parking lot. Even the skaters, so unhurried a moment ago, had vanished inside the front doors. The last bus was pulling away.

Hannah made her eyes flash an angry, impatient *What?*

"I love you," her mother said.

The morning passed like a very mild nightmare: scary but still kind of fun, thanks to the parade of unexpected things. There was a musty, old library-book smell that seemed to invade every classroom and hallway; a boy in social studies with facial scars that might have come from a knife fight; and a math teacher who wore tan bell-bottoms and a mustache that was surely fake. Hannah found that moving from class to class among an ever-changing throng of kids made her feel at once overwhelmed and happy to be part of the everyday blur. The chatter of Nancy and Belinda was easy to ignore.

There was only one problem: The cafeteria was in the basement.

When it was time for lunch, Hannah found herself gripping the railing at the top of the stairs. Her backpack felt stuffed with bricks. She tried to keep calm and take deep breaths . . . even though, in her eyes, the staircase was being consumed by roaring flames and sulfurous fumes. All around her, Hannah's new classmates descended into the pit, excited for lunch, only to disappear into the black smoke. There was no game to avoid the trap here; the blaze flowed like lava, creeping up the walls, licking the ceiling.

This is not the behavior of a sixth grader, Belinda said. *Now go eat your lunch.*

Save them! Nancy pleaded. *Get them out of there. Warn them!*

Hannah shut her eyes tight. She could feel the heat on her skin. Nancy was right — some had already been lost, but she could save those who hadn't yet gone to lunch. Distantly, she knew this was a bad idea and felt shame begin its burn, hot as the flames. But then two of the skaters from the parking lot began to descend, somehow oblivious to the pain, their jeans turning to ash. . . .

"Get out of there!" Hannah screamed. People stopped, confused. She was suddenly aware of just how invisible she'd been this morning, until this very moment, when she had made herself impossible to ignore. But she couldn't stop. The skaters were lost, but others approached the steps. Hannah turned to face them, extending her arms to block the way.

"Get back!" she ordered.

Yes, said Nancy. Belinda's disapproval was silent.

From the stunned and bewildered gathering before her emerged two older boys. Hannah was breathing hard. One of the boys leaned forward and began imitating her panting, his entire body heaving, beefy breath hitting Hannah in a potent wave, as the boy next to him giggled.

A girl stepped up to join them.

"What's your problem?" she asked Hannah.

Another girl ducked under Hannah's outstretched arms before she could stop her, muttering, "Psycho."

Behind her, Hannah felt the flames roar in satisfaction as they claimed their newest victim. She cried out. The boy stopped imitating her and cocked his head curiously, then moved his neck like a snake, trying to meet her faraway gaze.

"Dude, this girl is *damaged,*" he said.

"Leave her alone," a familiar voice warned. There was a sudden presence at Hannah's side, gently pushing down on her arm. "Everybody go ahead; it's fine."

Hannah blinked, turned, and saw Kyle standing beside her, facing down the boys.

"Psycho chick's got a boyfriend," said the giggler, his eyes darting to his friends, drinking in their approval.

"Freak," said someone else as she passed. Hannah turned, wanting to reach out and pull her back from the pit, and was surprised to see the flames receding, shrinking down into embers.

"It's okay," Kyle whispered, his hand still resting on her arm, warm and reassuring.

"It's not," Hannah said, leaning against the wall. With the show over, most everyone headed for the cafeteria, chattering excitedly. All except the two boys, who were watching Kyle, sizing him up.

"One second," Kyle said to Hannah. He stepped toward the boys and said something calm and quiet that she couldn't hear. The boys nodded in unison, their faces blank. Then they slunk down the stairs past Hannah without giving her another look. She watched their feet stamp the last remaining embers into ash.

"What did you say to them?" she asked when Kyle returned to her.

"Doesn't matter. Come on."

Without another word, he led her back into the day.

And without another thought, she followed.

Chapter Five

That night, her mother made her favorite dinner, crispy fried chicken and long grain rice. They ate in the dining room instead of at the kitchen table. From here, they had a view of the ocean as it changed from blue to steely gray, reflecting the setting sun in colors that spread like ink along the waves.

"So," her mother said, pouring what she called a big-girl glass of red wine, "how was school?" She looked as if she were about to laugh at some private joke that had just popped into her head.

"What's so funny?" Hannah asked.

"I guess it's just that I've never had to say that to you before, because I always knew exactly how school went."

Hannah summed up her day, leaving out the episode on the stairs, but mentioning that she'd seen Kyle.

"I don't understand how he goes to the same school as me, if his uncle was only here on business."

"Patrick called me today — he rented an apartment in town. It turns out that he's got steady work in Carbine Pass for a while, so Kyle enrolled in the eighth grade here."

"That doesn't make sense. His parents just let him do that?"

Hannah noticed that her mother's fingernails were a mess, even worse than this morning; cuticles raw and torn, as if she'd spent the entire day nibbling at them.

She's lying, Nancy proclaimed, before her mother had even answered the question.

"They thought it would be good for him to try a new school. Get a fresh start."

"So he's in trouble."

That made more sense than her actor theory. The way he deflated those two boys today — that was the talent of a boy accustomed to threatening and fighting.

"I don't really know the details, Hannah."

Ha! Nancy said. *Told you. Total lies.* Hannah chewed her lip to keep from shushing her twin out loud.

"Okay, but it's definitely weird to randomly be allowed to move in with your uncle and start school in a new place."

"First of all," her mother swirled the remaining wine in her glass and eyed the uncorked bottle, "there was nothing *random* about it. You say things are random all the time, when in fact they fit into patterns of behavior, or correspond with actual decisions and plans. What is it with you and that word?"

Hannah hoisted a fat chicken thigh and began gnawing. Her mother drained her glass and poured another.

"Anyway," she said after the first sip, "the point is, I'm happy to have them here."

Hannah paused. "Will they be allowed over again?"

"Of course."

"So they are, but nobody else is."

"Rules are rules."

"Except when you break them."

"My house, my rules."

Hannah remembered something else she'd been meaning to ask. "Well, if you're already changing the rules, I think we need to get Internet for the house. For homework and research projects and stuff."

"What's wrong with the computers at the library?"

"They aren't here."

"You never minded going there before."

"I can't go to the library every day just to do my homework, Mom. It's *home*work. I'm supposed to do it here."

Leanna Silver stared down at the untouched food on her plate, then at Hannah. "I'll have to talk to the principal. I'm sure your teachers can make an exception for you if they understand the situation. Give you alternate assignments, or something like that."

This was too much. It was completely unfair and ridiculous. Outside, a gull squawked angrily. Hannah wished she could communicate with such alarming directness. She pictured herself jumping onto the antique oak table, flapping her arms, and letting loose with a few high-pitched birdcalls in her mother's direction. Instead she said, as calmly as possible, "What exactly *is* the situation? It's the Internet. It's everywhere in the whole entire world except here."

"I just don't like the idea of letting all those people in."

Liar, Nancy said again.

"What people?"

"Strangers," her mother said decisively. "Pretending to be people they're not, or adults pretending to be people your age. You never know who's who unless you're talking to them face-to-face."

"Mom. That is so weird. What are you talking about? We can be careful."

"I caved on the public school thing, Hannah. I'm not sure you realize what a big deal this is for me, having you leave every day. So don't push me right now, okay?"

Her mother picked up her fork, and Hannah cringed. "You're bleeding."

Leanna Silver studied the long hangnail on the side of her thumb. Blood was welling up beneath the ragged skin, forming a bead as she gripped the fork.

"Huh." She frowned at the wound and wiped it clean with a napkin, leaving a long smear on the white linen. "So I am."

Hannah concentrated on her chicken and rice, finishing her meal in silence. Even the waves seemed calm tonight, gently sloshing like the wine in her mother's glass.

Hannah's bedroom was on the third floor, a big, old-fashioned hideaway with bookshelves built into the wall and a cozy alcove where the cushioned window seat offered a perfect view of the lighthouse. Rag dolls in overalls and brown shoes trooped across the wallpaper, performing a variety of strange chores like pushing wheelbarrows full of turnips and lighting the wicks of streetlamps. One wall was plastered with drawings of the lighthouse and the sea from her sketchbook, scribbly crayon pictures from when she was little all the way up to delicate pastels from this year. The four-post bed was positioned directly across the room from the alcove and its bay window, which meant that Hannah could lie in bed, propped up on pillows, and stare at the ocean until she fell asleep.

Good night, Hannah.

"Good night, Belinda."

Nitey-night, sis!

"Shut up, Nancy."

Just hearing Nancy's voice brought images of the fiery staircase flooding back — a memory Hannah hoped to banish for good so she could sleep. But there was no chance of that, at least not for a while. Her whole body grew hot as she thought about everyone at school watching her lose control. And when Kyle appeared, the scene moved fluidly from the top of the steps to the cafeteria. It was the same way they'd climbed the stairs in the lighthouse; as if they'd floated gently through a time warp, emerging into a better, calmer version of the world. How did he do that?

She stared out into the darkness for a long time. Words came and went inside her head, disconnected from their meanings.

Nancy translated them busily into Muffin Language for future use. *Internet. Cafeteria. Damaged. Freak.*

Over the years, Hannah had become skilled at picking out the silhouette of the lighthouse, a slightly different shade of black than the sky. She focused on it until the edges blurred, the blackness seeped into her bedroom, and her mind blanked.

Sometime later, kaleidoscopic bursts of light began swirling behind her eyelids. It was one of those nights where she'd slept so soundly that it was over in what felt like a second. Hannah opened her eyes, then sat up in bed, instantly alert.

It was still dark. The top of the lighthouse was illuminated by a spectral glow. She blinked, then rubbed her eyes. This couldn't possibly be happening: The great lamp hadn't been lit for decades. There was no way it actually worked.

And yet . . .

Hannah threw aside her covers and crept into the alcove, kneeling on the window seat. It took her a moment to realize what was wrong: The light wasn't a piercing beam, it was contained entirely within the glass. The light flickered once, twice, and was snuffed out, quick as a candle flame.

Hannah blinked away the afterimage and saw only darkness. Two figures emerged from the door at the base and began moving up the garden path toward the house. She traced their journey beneath the tunnel of vines by following the inky ripples of shadow that seemed to shroud them, until they were too close to the house and the angle made it impossible to see.

A second later, she heard the back door open and close.

Heart pounding, mouth dry, Hannah crept out of her room and down the hall to the back staircase. She tiptoed down to the second-floor landing, careful to tap her big toe twice against the edge of the seventh step, disarming the pendulum blade, the back stairs' sole trap. From the landing, she could look out over the Tree Room, which was furnished with mahogany, teak, and bamboo furniture from all over the world.

She heard shuffling in the back hallway, then the click of a small desk lamp that lit the far end of the room. Hannah could make out the shapes of two well-dressed men standing with her mother. They were conversing in gentle whispers that reached Hannah's ears as the barest hint of sound. Her own breathing seemed ragged and harsh in comparison. Still, she thought she was being quiet enough, until one of the men slowly turned his head so that he was staring into Hannah's hiding place on the darkened landing. Or at least, she assumed he was staring at her. It was hard to tell. He was wearing a formless hat that seemed to compel the shadows in the room to obscure his face.

She froze. Who was he? Did he see her? Why was she so afraid, if her mother was there, too?

The man's eyes flashed out of the darkness with the predatory gleam of a coyote. Hannah sat, transfixed, as the second man slowly turned his head, too. Together, the pair's eyes lit the room like the glass atop the lighthouse, brighter and brighter as if they were turning a dial, until Hannah shielded her face with her hands and screamed for them to —

"Stop!"

— and she was sitting upright in bed, panting as if she'd just run a four-minute mile. She untangled her legs from sweat-soaked sheets, and squinted at the morning sun shining through the alcove window.

Just a dream, Belinda said. Nancy snorted.

Hannah stumbled out of bed feeling dizzy and hollow, as if she hadn't slept at all.

Chapter Six

Hannah squinted at the board, on which the social studies teacher, Mrs. Adams, had neatly written and underlined the word APPEASEMENT.

It was real, said Nancy.

"Shut. Up," Hannah whispered.

"Hannah," Mrs. Adams said, "how kind of you to volunteer."

Most of the class swiveled to stare at her. Panic dulled her thoughts. She had no idea what was going on.

Conciliation, Belinda said. *Pacification.*

Hannah repeated those unfamiliar words out loud. Mrs. Adams opened her mouth, said nothing for a second, then turned to the board and wrote the words beneath *appeasement.*

"Very good," she said. "Two excellent synonyms. But who can define the term?" She made a show of looking around — one of the funny things all Hannah's teachers did — before choosing the one girl with her hand up. "Go ahead, Alicia."

The rest of the morning was full of close calls. When she wasn't haunted by the blinding eyes in her dream, she was mentally rehearsing a plan to sneak into one of the empty classrooms and eat lunch alone, avoiding the stairs.

Except she didn't have a lunch. She had to buy one in the cafeteria.

Was it worth going hungry to avoid those stairs?

When fifth period rolled around and her stomach was tying itself in knots, she decided to risk it, plodding along with the crowd of students. To her amazement and relief, Kyle was waiting to escort her. They didn't talk once they got to the cafeteria. He left her alone to join a table of eighth graders, a table that included the two boys from yesterday.

Hannah assumed her staircase incident was kind of a big deal, so she kept looking around, expecting to catch mean glances directed at her, but there was nothing. It was as if Kyle had taken everyone aside, one by one, and given them a dose of whatever he'd said to the two boys. Maybe nobody cared, after all, about some new girl's first-day jitters.

Maybe she was invisible now.

The ride home was a silent echo of the ride to school. Her mother drove with her eyes glued to the road, jabbing her finger into the radio's SEEK button, station-hopping through pop, country, news, and talk before settling on silence. Hannah pretended to be immersed in the trees that lined the road from the outskirts of Carbine Pass all the way up the long, winding driveway of Cliff House. After twelve years of living together, Hannah was a tuning fork when it came to her mother's bad moods. This one had familiar elements — extreme nail-biting, radio indecision, fast driving, silence — but there was something else, too: a damp, clammy aura that seemed to surround her. Hannah thought it might be fear.

At home, Hannah took the back way upstairs, pausing in the Tree Room, setting her bag down next to the cherrywood desk where the figures from her dream had been standing when they'd spotted her.

She ran the tip of her finger along the wood and studied the particles of dust. Then she knelt to pick fibers and crumbs from the carpet, and examined the sides of the doorway. Nothing was out of place. It wasn't until she began climbing up to the landing that she noticed it. The air had changed. It was normal here, on the steps, but in the Tree Room it had been heavier — moist and oppressive, as if the molecules were pregnant with some new energy. Slowly, she went back down and crossed the room, taking deep breaths. There was a slight sweetness, too.

Told you, Nancy said. *Also, "appeasement" means the weird new smell in a room.*

"Feeling okay, Hannah?"

She whirled around to see her mother standing, arms crossed, watching her.

"Fine."

"You're up on your tiptoes, sniffing the air."

"I know."

"Did something happen at school?"

Hannah thought for a moment. There were plenty of secrets within the walls of Cliff House. What was one more? The school year was just beginning. She could leave it alone, move on. Make friends. Have a life.

Just ask her what's for dinner, Belinda agreed. *Let it be.*

Before Hannah could stop herself, her voice ran away with her thoughts.

"There were people in the house last night. Two men. Standing right here."

Her mother laughed. "Sounds like somebody was dreaming." She brushed some nonexistent dirt from the front of her jeans and recrossed her arms.

"I thought maybe it was a dream, but now I can sort of smell them. The air is all wrong."

Outside, a deep rumble made them both look to the window. Dark clouds were pushing in from the ocean.

"Storm's coming," her mother said. "You know how nasty they can be this time of year. That's what you smell. You're sensitive to the weather, just like me."

"No way," Hannah said. "I know what a storm coming smells like, and this is different." She sniffed the air. "It's like . . . cotton candy."

"Come on, help me layer the noodles. It's lasagna night."

"Mom!" Hannah surprised herself by yelling. Raised voices weren't often heard at Cliff House. When they were mad, the

Silvers just sulked and slunk about. Her mother turned to a cabinet and extracted a glass, along with a bottle of amber liquid. Then she sat down on a sofa made of knotty pine, upholstered with thin green cushions. She poured a tiny bit in a glass and set both glass and bottle on the matching coffee table.

Hannah wondered if she was in trouble. Her mother drained the glass, poured another, then patted the cushion next to her.

"Come sit with me."

Hannah did. There was another long silence, during which they both watched clouds cover every inch of the sky. Thunder rumbled twice, with a sharp, punctuating crack. Then Leanna Silver spoke.

"I'm going to tell you something that you're not supposed to hear until you're older."

Hannah must have been staring, wide-eyed, because her mother gripped her shoulder and gave it a familiar squeeze.

"If you're lonely right now, you have to understand that it's not half as lonely as you'll feel for the rest of your life, once you know what I know. So I'm only going to tell you if you're sure you want to hear it. Things are happening — there are reasons I should tell you. But once I do, there's no going back."

Yes! Nancy screamed. Even Belinda agreed.

Hannah thought about school. She could smell the musty hallways, hear the murmur of droning chatter. That was the life she wanted. Wasn't it? Not shut up in Cliff House, keeping secrets, puttering around.

She closed her eyes.

"Tell me," she said before she could think about it anymore. "I want to know."

"Oh, Hannah" — her mother was hugging her, pulling her close — "my baby girl."

CHAPTER SEVEN

It was after midnight by the time Hannah went to bed, but she wasn't tired. In fact, she wondered if she'd ever be able to sleep again. She sat on her alcove cushions, watching the rain pummel the glass. Every few minutes, a flash would light up the choppy surface of the sea, freezing the dark shape of the lighthouse in photographic stillness against the backdrop of the storm.

Albert, she thought. *Waving hello.*

Hannah lost herself in the downward slashes of water on the glass. Her eyes blurred, and her mother's words played over again, as if she'd recorded them.

The city of the dead has no beginning and no end. Just as there are no edges, there is no center. The city simply exists in every direction. Pick a street and follow it for centuries. You'll meet billions of souls, but you'll never reach a gate to the countryside or a road to the suburbs. The city is the temporary home to everyone who has lived and died in our world.

I know — it's a lot to take in. It was a lot for me to take in, when your father told me. But bear with me. Just try.

Beyond the city lies Ascension. To help souls travel from life on earth through the city and onward to Ascension, there's a government of sorts, an eternal ruling body that maintains order. The lower branches are called the Watchers. To be eligible for a trip to Ascension, a soul must follow the rules. Watchers enforce these rules and make sure nobody jumps the line. That sort of thing.

The only way into the city is death, except for a single tiny exception — an exception you've been living next to your entire life. You know the door in the lighthouse that seems to lead to nowhere? Well, for most people it will lead to nowhere. But for a few, it will lead to the city of the dead. Think of it as an emergency portal. For humans, of course, it's strictly off-limits and completely secret.

Long ago the city appointed a Guardian to monitor the door, to remain close to the threshold at all times. To keep its secret. Over the last century the Guardianship has been passed down through names you'll recognize: Jackson Silver. Abraham Silver. Benjamin Silver.

Me.

And after me, Hannah: you. It's not so outlandish a proposition. I thought, once, that I would never have to worry about it. I expected your father to carry the burden into old age, at which point it would be passed on to you. But after your father's accident, I became the Guardian. You and I are part of the order, Hannah, tasked with protecting the door to the city of the dead. Patrick is the one who taught me the rules. Patrick, as you might have guessed, is one of the few Watchers to live as a human on our side. Kyle is his apprentice.

* * *

Hannah didn't know how much time had passed while she'd zoned out at the window, but after a while it was no longer just the lightning flashing outside — it was the lighthouse, too. The same flickering as the night before, pale and misty in the storm. Did that mean more visitors from the dead city?

The rain intensified, battering Cliff House like the waves upon the rocks below. Water trickled into her room around the corroded iron windowpane. Was her mother actually out in this storm, opening the door, tending to the threshold? Hannah slid off the window seat, standing on tiptoes to stretch her cramped legs. Then she went out into the hallway to listen for the arrival of more bright-eyed strangers.

Watchers.

She waited for a long time, but the house remained silent. Unable to stay still, she moved down the hallway — very quietly, even though she was pretty sure she was alone in the house — and down the back stairs to the landing above the Tree Room.

Go back to bed, Belinda said.

"You don't get to tell me what to do anymore."

I could get used to this Guardian thing, Nancy said.

Hannah waited for the click of the lamp. It never came. She headed down the stairs and crossed the Tree Room — there was the shape of her mother's empty glass on the table — and into the back hallway.

She was not quite scared, but she was hyper with nerves.

She stepped out the back door, fighting a gust of wind that

almost knocked her over. As she walked down the garden path, her bare feet squelched. At the base of the lighthouse, it took her a moment to realize what was out of place: Off to the right, no more than ten feet away, was a lump that could have been a gathering of rocks, a mound of dirt, a large tree limb taken down by the storm.

Hannah stopped breathing. She must have started running and slipped, because she found herself crawling across the soaked ground — it wasn't rocks or dirt or a tree branch, it was a body, twisted unnaturally, as if it had fallen from a great height. The body's eyes, her mother's eyes, *her mother's eyes*, were open. Any blood had been washed away by the rain.

Hannah cried out. Shook her. Tried to wake her. Felt for a pulse.

She couldn't believe this was happening.

No twitch beneath the skin, no heartbeat, no breath.

It was happening.

Her mother was —

Hannah looked up. Hidden somewhere in the darkness was the narrow steel walkway that encircled the top of the lighthouse. Built for emergency maintenance, too dangerous to use as a balcony.

Why had her mother been up there in weather like this?

How had her mother fallen?

Or had she died some other way?

Hannah cried out again. Where was Patrick? Kyle? Where were the Watchers? Surely they could revive her mother with their powers. Hannah felt manic, full of live-wire energy rather than grief. She had to find the Watchers. They would know what to do.

She slid her along the wet grass until she reached the dry interior of the lighthouse. She bounded up the steps and stopped at the landing. There was no sign of the Watchers.

She was alone.

But the door in the wall . . . it was open.

Many years ago, there was a breach. Not from our world into the city — that's never happened, not even once — but from the city into Ascension. A group of rebellious souls found the second doorway hidden deep within the city and tried to ascend before their time had come. But trying to sneak through either one of these doors is a good way to summon an army of Watchers. The rebels were caught and banished to earth, with no hope of ever getting back into the city, much less Ascension. They will never be allowed to move beyond our world.

When you cheat at the game of existence, your punishment is eternal.

For a while, everything was quiet on earth. The banished souls scattered and lived peacefully among us, beaten and humbled. But now there are rumors, alarming reports from Patrick's network. For the first time in centuries, the banished are inspired. They're beginning to emerge from the shadows. Organizing. Patrick thinks they're preparing for an assault on the city — an assault that would have to be launched from our door. There's no other way in for them.

We're preparing for the worst without knowing what it might be. That's why I've been a bit crazier than usual. It's not just you going to school. And then last night, with the Watchers from the other side . . . I didn't even know they were coming. It's a rare event — no one has visited since I've been the Guardian. Crossing over can be disruptive. But they'd heard the rumors, too.

I'm worried that I won't be strong enough, when the time comes. If it comes. Worried that I won't recognize it for what it is.

There's more, of course. Much more. But now you know who I am. Who we are.

And what we must do.

We must guard the doorway.

It was only open a crack, like someone hadn't bothered to shut it all the way. Hannah crossed the landing and placed her hand on the doorknob. The churning in her mind drowned out the raging storm, the pleading of Belinda, the frantic encouragements of Nancy. She had listened to her mother tell the story, had seen the Watchers with her own eyes, and still it was hard to believe. What if her mother was crazy? What if they were *both* crazy?

If they were crazy, there'd be nothing but a blank wall behind this door. And her mother really would be out of reach, forever.

But what if opening the door meant that she could see her again? She didn't know how the city of the dead was supposed to work, exactly, but if it was a place where people went after they died, then her mother was already there.

There was no way to bring her back to life in this world. On this side of the door, death was the end.

But maybe on the other side, it was just the beginning.

My mother is dead, she thought, abruptly choked with grief so potent that it almost made her pass out. She fought it, crying, swallowing air in gulps, and never took her hand from the doorknob.

Desperate to find her mother, Hannah Silver opened the door.

Chapter Eight

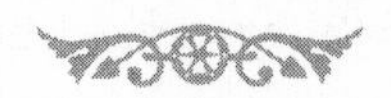

The world creaked beneath Hannah's feet and she pitched forward. Every portal-crossing, time-traveling, dimension-hopping story she'd ever read came back to her at once. She prepared to be dissolved and rocketed through a tunnel of stretched-out stars.

Some otherworldly force, solid and unyielding, struck her hands, elbows, and knees. In a panic, she pushed back. After a disorienting struggle, she realized that her palms were resting against floorboards gouged with burnt-looking knotholes. She had merely tripped, and now she was inside an empty attic. A melancholy afternoon leaked through a soot-darkened window. Shapes in the dusty floor gave the impression of absent furniture.

When Hannah stood up and brushed off her jeans, she felt a queasy tug in the tip of her pinky. A tiny sliver had lodged itself just beneath her skin. She pinched it between her nails.

"Salamander," she muttered, wincing at the odd sensation of an object sliding out of her finger. It was much larger than she could have imagined, and Hannah was astonished to be holding a thin wooden spike the size of a toothpick. Before she could flick it aside, the sliver burrowed into her thumb — the pain was barely a pinch — and disappeared completely. She examined her hand in disbelief, prodding and poking, but it had left no trace.

Okay, Hannah thought, allowing herself a shudder of revulsion. *That happened.* She was going to have to accept it and move on, because there was no retreating back into the lighthouse: The doorway had vanished.

Mom, you have to be here, she thought.

A *thump* from below made her freeze. Had she stumbled into someone's house? Was there a family of dead people having lunch a few rooms away? She imagined a skeletal hand pulling a cobwebby jar of peanut butter from a cupboard. The sound of muffled voices sent her to the window, the only possible escape route. There was no way to open it. She could probably break it with her elbow — she was wearing a long-sleeved flannel shirt — but after the odd behavior of the wooden splinter, she wasn't keen on introducing her skin to shards of glass.

Thick grime around the edges of the window faded to a filmy coating in the center, giving the world outside the look of an old photograph. The house across the street was a dreary mansion bristling with chimneys. It belonged near a manicured garden, a hedge maze, and a pond full of geese, yet here it was shoved up against its next-door neighbor, a decrepit palace whose balconies seemed to be spawning tendrils of creeping ivy. Candlelight flickered in an upper window. A woman sat down and began combing her hair with slow, leisurely strokes. Hannah rapped on the glass, trying to get her attention.

"Hello!" Hannah called out.

Hannah could tell that the woman wasn't looking in a mirror; she was gazing out across the street.

"Over here!"

Now there were distinct footsteps in the room below the attic, and Hannah remembered her mother's words: *Trying to sneak through either one of these doors is a good way to summon an army of Watchers.* She turned away from the window. Getting scooped up by the Watchers was the best possible thing that could happen. Once she explained her situation, they could check their files, or government database, or whatever system kept track of new arrivals. She imagined waiting in an office while a Watcher sat at a computer and scrolled down to a highlighted name: LEANNA SILVER.

The Watchers would know where she was. After all, she'd just gotten here.

Someone began pounding against the floor of the attic like an angry neighbor with a broomstick. Hannah remembered a helpful phrase from one of the playground games at yesterday's recess.

"Same team!" she called out, stamping her foot.

A square panel in the floor opened, pointed straight at the ceiling, then collapsed flat, sending a plume of dust swirling into her eyes. She coughed and fanned the air with her hand. She felt sluggish, as if she were stirring an impossibly thick stew. A man joined her in the attic. His features were indistinct, shadowed by his shapeless hat, but Hannah could make out his eyes.

It's not a hat, she realized. *It's more like a strange tattoo.*

"I need your help," she said in a faraway voice.

The silent man wore the attic's musty gloom like a cloak. Light from the window slunk away to cower in the eaves. *He's on my side,* Hannah told herself as she backed into the corner. The Watcher's face began to ripple in and out of a dark shroud, as if he were hiding behind a veil on a windy day.

"Let me just tell you what happened," she pleaded. Then the Watcher's eyes gleamed and she lost herself in the radiance.

Chapter Nine

Hannah's cell was a concrete sphere. If she sat on her cot and faced the sink, there was a steel door to her left. To her right was a bench the size of a baby-changing station in a public restroom. The only flat surface was the floor, which she had to cross to get from the cot to the sink. She could make this crossing in three steps, and had done so eleven times. Sixty-six steps in all (there and back) and yet she still couldn't figure out how to make the faucet work. It was shaped like the forked tongue of a lizard and had no handles or knobs.

Nobody came to give her food. And anyway, she wasn't hungry. This made it impossible to tell how much time had passed since the cell had taken shape around her as abruptly as the attic had vanished. The overhead light, a circular fluorescent tube, was always on. Bathed in its washed-out glow, she sat on the cot's thin cushion and studied her thumb. The fact that it didn't hurt was alarming.

The skin of her face felt the same as ever. Her jeans and checked flannel shirt (snaps, not buttons) still smelled like fabric softener. She couldn't tell if she was thirsty or not, but figured it had been too long since her last drink of water — her mother had given her a glass before bed, which might have already been days ago, for all she knew.

Three steps to the sink. Hannah ran her finger along the smooth curve of the faucet, tracing its sea-monster humps, tapping both forks of the tongue. She closed one eye and peered at it from every angle. No openings in the faucet, no drain in the basin. She waved her hand, hoping to trigger a sensor.

"'Lizard tongue,'" said a familiar voice, "means a sink that doesn't work."

"Nancy!" Hannah said, tapping the faucet with a fingertip. "Help me figure this out."

Now it was Belinda's turn to chime in. "Why don't you just sit still instead of fidgeting — I'm sure someone will be along to help if you'll just be patient."

Hannah scoffed at Belinda's school-teacher tone. The old woman's advice always involved acting mature and being polite.

"What if it's not even a faucet? Ever thought of it that way?" This new voice belonged to a boy. "Anyway, who cares."

Her hands were gripping the sides of the basin. The voices weren't coming from her head. They were echoing inside the cell, crisp and audible. It was as if Nancy and Belinda and the boy were —

"Maybe the metal thing under the sink needs to be hooked up," Nancy suggested.

Hannah turned. Leaning against the door was a girl who could be her twin — except this girl's acid-washed jeans were ripped at the knees and her hair was cut short and spiky. The cot was occupied by an elderly woman who sat with her legs primly crossed; instead of the floral housecoat that Hannah had always imagined, she wore linen pants and a long-sleeved blouse. A pale, hollow-cheeked boy was sitting on the floor, knees hugged to his chest, head tilted back against the wall, his half-lidded eyes focused on nothing.

"Who are you?" she asked.

Slowly, as if it required an incredible amount of effort, the boy raised the lids of his eyes and moved his head slightly to look at Hannah.

"Seriously?"

"That's Albert," Nancy said, jerking her thumb in the boy's direction. "He's new."

"He is not *new,*" Belinda corrected. "In fact, he's been around longer than you, Nancy. Isn't that right, young man?"

Albert sighed, closing his eyes. "Whatever." There was a sound like a faint coastal wind, and Hannah's shirt collar fluttered. She approached the cot — seventy, seventy-one, seventy-two steps — and reached out with an unsteady hand.

Belinda nodded. "Go ahead."

Hannah took the sleeve of the old woman's blouse, rolled a bit of fabric between her fingers, and was surprised to find that it felt like real clothing. Gently, she prodded the woman's arm — skin, with muscle and bone underneath. Hannah had always pictured the voices in her head as cartoons with a few basic characteristics. But Belinda's face bore the markings of an entire life — a *real* life — lived in full. Wrinkles and plucked eyebrows and a beauty mark just to the left of her nose. A bit too much concealer, cracking in places.

"How did you get here?" Hannah asked.

"Same way you did," Nancy said. "Through the lighthouse."

"You followed me?"

Nancy scratched at the exposed skin of her knee. Albert mumbled something. Belinda patted the cushion beside her and said, "Why don't you have a seat, and we'll chat."

Hannah was brimming with questions, but right now there were only two that mattered. "Can you help me find a way out of here? And do you know where my mother is?"

It occurred to her that the Watchers were probably spying on her. She wondered if they were gathered around a screen, laughing at the crazy girl talking to herself. Or maybe, in this place, Belinda and Nancy and Albert were visible to everyone.

"Eat the stuffing out of the cushion," Nancy suggested. "They'll have to take you to a hospital, and it'll be easier to escape from there."

"You'll do nothing of the sort!" Belinda said. "Bide your time. Watchers and Guardians are supposed to work together. This is just a misunderstanding, I'm sure."

Then came the unmistakable sound of a key in a lock. Hannah found herself alone as the steel door swung open.

"When did the banished ones first contact you?"

The Watcher sat on the cement bench. His voice was reedy and distorted, as if the words were swimming across a vast distance. Hannah could barely look at him; the fluid tattoo that slithered about his face reflected the overhead light, and the harsh glow veiled everything but his eyes.

"Years ago?" he asked. "Months? Weeks? Days?" His hands were folded carefully in his lap.

"I don't know what you're talking about," Hannah said. "Nobody contacted me about anything." She was hugging her knees to her chest, just like Albert had been doing before he vanished along with Nancy and Belinda at the sound of the door.

A second Watcher leaned casually against the sink, arms folded across the front of her evening gown. This woman's face glinted with silver as it picked up hints of her necklace to spin through its camouflage. Gaudy jewelry ringed her wrists and ankles, and her strappy shoes looked like they had come from an expensive vintage shop.

"I know we'd both appreciate it if you'd help us put together a little timeline of events, Hannah. Okay?" The woman's voice was slightly more pleasant than her partner's.

"When did the banished ones first contact you?" There was

no variation in the man's tone, as if he were playing a recording of himself.

"Chalkdust!" Hannah said. "Stop asking me that, I told you I don't know."

"There's no need to swear at us, Hannah. We're not your enemies."

The woman kept saying her name, which was almost as maddening as the man's broken-record question.

"I wasn't swearing."

The woman uncrossed her arms and said something to the man that was impossible for Hannah to make out. Their voices sounded like a sped-up song, chirpy and quick. Then they went back to normal — or at least as close to normal as their voices ever got.

"Crepuscular slurp," the woman said.

Hannah's eyes widened. "You speak Muffin?"

"Grenadine magnetism," the man confirmed.

"If you know so much about me, then you know I'm telling the truth."

"We just need some help filling in the blanks," the woman said. "But let's back up. Why don't you tell us a little bit about yourself, Hannah?"

The man chirped angrily at his partner, who ignored him. Frustrated, he stood up from his cement seat. Hannah forced herself to peer beyond the wormy brightness of his tattoo. She expected to see the grim, unsmiling face of a man who enjoyed asking the same question over and over, but it was like staring into the sun. She closed her eyes.

"If I talk to you, will you take me to my mother?" she asked.

"Think of it like this," the man said, leaning in close. His presence was like humid air making its way through a swamp. "If you don't tell us what we want to know, you'll never see your mother again. Porcelain?"

Hannah swallowed. "Porcelain," she said weakly.

The woman began to emit a sound like Styrofoam being rubbed together. Hannah's skin erupted into goose bumps. With her forehead pressed against her knees, she shivered, focusing on the fading smell of home. The laundry room at Cliff House vented out into the side yard. Hannah tried to put herself there among the waist-high flowers and clouds of fragrant steam. The voices of the Watchers blended into dissonant music, a symphony of fingernails on chalkboards.

"What are the banished ones going to do?" the man asked, his new question coming through loud and clear. He was somehow able to argue with his partner and interrogate Hannah at the same time. "What are they planning?"

Sunflowers, Hannah thought. *Laundry steam.* But it was no use — she was wreathed in the dank heat of the Watcher's breath. She clamped her palms over her ears and began to shriek. It felt terrific. When she stopped, out of breath, the cell was deathly quiet. She opened her eyes. The man was sitting on his cement seat, silent and still, hands folded in his lap. The woman was leaning against the sink. It was as if they had hit rewind and arrived at the beginning of the session.

"Would you like a drink?" the woman asked.

Hannah still couldn't tell if she was thirsty or not.

"I guess."

The lady tapped the faucet with one of her bejeweled fingers, and the forked tongue slithered across the cell. Hovering in front of Hannah's face, the tongue moved inquisitively, as if it were trying to sniff her. She moved along the cot, sliding as far away from it as she could.

"Never mind," Hannah said quickly. "I'm okay."

The Watcher leaned over and whispered into the basin. The tongue retracted.

"Why don't we let you collect your thoughts," the woman said, straightening up. "I think we could all use a break. How would you feel about that, Hannah?"

Hannah didn't know how she was supposed to feel about any of this. Why was the Watcher suddenly acting like Hannah had a choice in the matter? She couldn't help but feel slightly grateful to the woman for getting the man to stop with his questions. Maybe the key to finding her mother was to tell them what they wanted to hear. But what was that? She decided that collecting her thoughts would be a good idea.

"Okay," she said.

Without another word, the Watchers left the cell. Keeping a wary eye on the faucet, Hannah waited for Nancy, Belinda, and Albert to reappear. But they did not, and she was back to passing the time alone. When she closed her eyes she could see the Watchers' disguises wriggling against a dark backdrop, bursting like fireworks, receding. To distract herself, she chose a moment from her past and tried to lose herself in it.

On the fourth floor at Cliff House, up a short staircase that curved to make Hannah feel like she was turning her back on the sea, was a bedroom that faced the woods. The closet at the back of the room smelled like cedar. Once upon a time she would have been able to pull a string for light, but nobody had bothered to change the bulb in years.

The first thing Hannah saw when she clicked on her flashlight was a shoebox. It was full of guitar picks, each one labeled FENDER MEDIUM. In her mother's photo albums, Hannah had seen pictures of her father strumming a beat-up acoustic guitar, wearing a necklace made from a yellow guitar pick threaded onto a string.

Nestled among the picks was a Slinky. How strange to think of the man she'd never met prodding the wiry toy down the stairs. She didn't know if stores even sold Slinkys anymore — there had been a Toy Palace in Carbine Pass, but her mother had stopped taking her when it turned into a GameStop. That was okay: Hannah was nine years old, hadn't yet punched a single key on the library computer, and Cliff House was full of ways to pass the time.

It was a Saturday morning, and her mother was out in the garden. No lessons today — Hannah could stay in her pajamas until dinner. Crouched at the top of the Tree Room landing, she sighted down the Slinky as if it were a telescope. Satisfied that it was lined up in the exact center of the staircase, she gave it a nudge. The Slinky moved end over end in an arcing tumble. Hannah urged it on silently, counting the steps. Halfway down, the Slinky was swept aside, as if by a gust of wind, and tossed unceremoniously against the railing where it stopped — bent, twisted, and useless. Or at least, half of it did. The other half bounced down the stairs like any old piece of junk. The Slinky's grace had been taken from it so quickly, and in such a strange way, that Hannah had been stunned.

Way to go, dummy.

Hannah's lower lip trembled. She had been having self-critical bursts of thought lately, and they were getting louder.

"It wasn't my fault," she whispered.

Tap your feet twice on the seventh step or you'll be sliced in half, too.

"What?"

Trust me, just do it.

She made her way down the stairs, stopping at the sixth step. This was really stupid. And yet — her skin was prickling, sensing a big, looming presence nearby. The air smelled like rust. She placed her toe against the next step and obeyed the voice: *tap-tap.*

Then she pulled half the Slinky from the railing. Down in the Tree Room, she found the other half.

The Slinky would never work again, even after she glued it together. Forever unbalanced, it would be returned to the closet. And Hannah would always remember to tap her foot twice on the seventh step.

Chapter Ten

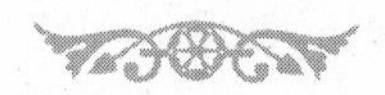

What do you call a moment you remember vividly when you're half-asleep? *Not a dream,* Hannah thought. *Not quite a memory, either.* She could feel the Slinky in her hands, trace its severed edge with her thumb, and then it was gone. The cell's overhead light made it impossible to close her eyes for very long. She stood up, stretched — and froze.

There was a Watcher sitting on the concrete bench. Colors stolen from peacock feathers flitted in and out of the storm that hid her face. One hand held a sequined clutch. The woman's stillness had the unsettling effect of making Hannah feel both ignored and scrutinized at the same time.

"Is the other guy coming?" Hannah asked.

"No. This is just between you and me." The Watcher's voice was soothing and low. "I'm sorry for how you've been treated."

Great, Hannah thought. *But I'm still locked up.*

When the Watcher saw that Hannah wasn't talking, she tried again. "My partner was out of line. There was no reason for him to be so unkind."

"So you're going to help me," Hannah said. "Because Guardians and Watchers work together." She wondered if there was a human face behind the woman's disguise. For all Hannah knew, she could be talking to a grinning skull, or a giant ferret head.

"I can try to answer some of your questions," the Watcher said carefully.

"How long have I been here?"

The Watcher emitted a low hiss that might have been a sigh. "Even if I could tell you, it wouldn't make any sense."

"Please let me out."

"That's not a question, Hannah."

"You don't have to keep saying my name." Hannah played with a piece of fuzz stuck to her sleeve. "I've been telling you the truth, okay? I didn't mean to mess anything up or break the rules. I don't care what the banished ones are doing. I just want to get my mother and go home."

"I'm afraid it's not that simple."

Hannah thought of a phrase that her mother sometimes used to get what she wanted. "Is there a supervisor I can speak to?"

"Any soul above my rank would not be so accommodating."

The Watcher opened her clutch and produced a thin rectangular device. It looked like the kind of phone used by everyone in Carbine Pass except for Hannah and Leanna Silver. The woman plugged the forked tongue of the faucet into the back of the phone. Then she clicked a glossy fingernail against the faucet and it snaked across the cell to hover in front of Hannah's face.

"Stay where you are," the Watcher commanded before Hannah could squirm away. The phone's screen displayed static, as if it were picking up a dead channel from an old television.

"There's nothing on it," Hannah said.

The Watcher gave the faucet a few insistent taps. "How's that?"

The static resolved into a grainy close-up of a familiar face.

"Patrick!" Hannah said, speaking to the screen. "Tell them I didn't do anything wrong. Can you come get me out of here? Can you —"

"He can't hear you," the Watcher said. "This isn't a two-way conversation. It's a video."

"From where? The other side of the door? Carbine Pass?"

"Watch."

Patrick's forehead, ears, and neck were hidden beneath ragged bandages. His face was pale and sweaty, and there were rust-colored rings around his eyes — a far cry from the gentleman she'd met at Cliff House.

"This message is my official resignation. I have only my own complacency to blame." Patrick's voice was cracked and weary. "I forfeit my citizenship according to the precepts set forth in . . ."

Offscreen, papers rustled and someone whispered.

Patrick continued, "City Watch ordinance 948, sub-section B, earthly Watcher bylaws, termination clause 6 point 095, eighteenth revision." He cleared his throat. "My job was to identify human candidates to expand our network on earth, much like the

Guardian program. It wasn't necessary for several centuries, but once the banished souls arrived, it came time for me to put it into practice. One of my apprentices — my most promising, I might add — was a boy named Kyle. He often accompanied me on business, and in this way had a hand in shaping the project. That was my biggest mistake, giving him that kind of access. . . ." Patrick shook his head. "All this time, I thought I had recruited him, when he was the one who had recruited me. I have been an old fool of the worst sort. I ought to have known better. He displayed certain aptitudes. . . ."

Hannah flashed back to the feel of Kyle's hand in hers, their fingers interlocked, as he delivered her safely away from her waking nightmares. It was as if they had glided forward through time, leaving the bad moments behind.

Patrick's face looked like it was trapped in a snow globe. His voice became garbled. ". . . changed his appearance . . . infiltrated my network . . ."

"What?" Hannah said, talking to the screen again.

". . . able to identify the door . . ."

"I'm afraid that's all for now," the Watcher said, reaching for the phone. Patrick was entirely eclipsed by static. She heard his voice come through one last time: ". . . crossed over . . ."

The Watcher unplugged the phone and the faucet retracted.

"So, Kyle is one of the people you kicked out," Hannah said. "One of the banished."

But that meant . . . Hannah closed her eyes. She went back to the moment she'd discovered her mother crumpled beneath the lighthouse. In her mind, her mother was rising slowly through the storm, falling in reverse. Then she was alive again, picking her way along the railing that encircled the glass bell of the lamp room. What was she doing up there? Her mother must have seen him — Kyle — sneaking into the lighthouse, and done the Guardian's job. She had confronted him. And since Leanna Silver was the only person standing in his way . . .

"He killed her," Hannah said, opening her eyes.

"Yes." The Watcher dropped the phone into her clutch and snapped it shut. "Or else he ordered one of his group to do it. We don't know how many came back with him."

Hannah imagined a procession of shadowy figures lining up beneath the lighthouse, climbing the ladder and passing single file through the door. She saw Kyle's hand — the hand she had touched — pushing her mother out into the darkness of the storm.

"Where is she?" Hannah asked, her voice pitching sharply. She jumped up from the cot. "You have to take me to her. Please. I know you know where she is."

The Watcher seemed to be regarding Hannah with pity. But who could tell? Hannah thought she caught a glimpse of the woman's auburn hair through the heat-shimmer of her disguise.

"Give me something I can use, Hannah. Is it true that you personally showed Kyle the doorway?"

"I took him to the lighthouse, but" — Hannah shook her head — "one time, that was all. I didn't know who he was. Or what the door was."

"When he crossed over, where was he planning to go?"

Hannah wanted to scream. She took a deep breath. "I. Don't. Know."

The Watcher seemed to hesitate. Then she brushed past Hannah — a whiff of burning plastic, a stale breeze — and went to the door, where she stopped.

"Your mother is making a fine life for herself in the city. And you'll be free to join her as soon as you cooperate."

Hannah was speechless. She couldn't give the Watchers what they wanted. Was she supposed to live in this concrete sphere forever?

"Wait," Hannah said, but the Watcher was gone.

Chapter Eleven

Whenever Hannah got sick, her mother would knead her temples and gently compress the bridge of her nose. Then she'd dab peppermint lotion on the back of Hannah's neck and behind her ears. Hannah would drift off to sleep and wake to find her head in her mother's lap, eyes watering, nose running — *that's the sickness coming out* — and fall asleep again to her hair being slowly caressed.

Lying on her cot, facing the concrete wall, Hannah could almost feel the phantom massage.

There was a song, lilting and sweet, that her mother liked to hum in these moments, but Hannah couldn't recall the melody. Frustrated, she pressed her knuckles into the cot's thin cushion. How could she have forgotten a song she'd heard a thousand times?

Then, softly, the tune came floating through the cell.

"That's it," Hannah said, turning over and sitting up. Nancy was slouching against the door, humming. "Cork on the Ocean," Hannah remembered. Over on the bench, Belinda began to whistle. Sitting cross-legged on the floor, Albert sang the wrong words, off-key.

"Little baby, I can't stand your stupid face. . . ."

"Cut the comedian act, Albert," Belinda said sharply. Nancy stopped humming. Albert shut his mouth and let out a long, irritated breath through his nose. The foamy, churning sound of waves crashing against rocks echoed inside the cell. Hannah felt a hint of cold Atlantic spray on her face.

"Is 'comedian' a vocab word in Muffin?" Nancy asked. "I'm starting to wish we wrote some of this stuff down."

"Maybe the Watchers will give us some paper," Hannah said. "Where did you go, anyway?"

"Nowhere," Nancy said, poking around the faucet. "We're in a prison cell, in case you haven't noticed. Bet you wish you ate that cushion now."

Hannah reached over the side of the cot and squeezed Albert's bony shoulder through his black long-sleeved shirt. He shrugged her off and spat out, "May I help you?"

"You're real, too. But you disappeared."

"Um. Yeah."

"And you can't just, like, float through the walls?"

"Um. No."

Albert's breath smelled a little bit like saltwater fish. Hannah tried to get her nose out of range without being obvious about it. "I'm just trying to figure out how this all works."

Belinda smoothed her wrinkle-free pants. "We know exactly as much as you do, dear."

"But you knew about the traps back home way before I did," Hannah said to Nancy. "I definitely remember that." She turned to Belinda, thinking of that distracted morning in the classroom. "And I'm pretty sure you know words that I don't know."

"Surely you must have read them somewhere," Belinda said. She pointed to Hannah's head. "There's so much information, stewing about, lost in the mire. I just know where to look. I spend more time up there than you do, after all."

"Totally," Nancy said. "If you didn't already know about the traps, there's no way I could have."

Hannah shook her head. "I swear I didn't. You warned me first."

Belinda scoffed. "Have you ever actually *seen* one of these so-called traps with your eyes?"

"Yes!" Hannah and Nancy said in unison.

"Could you all please quiet down for one second?" Albert said. Hannah waited for him to continue — it sounded like he had something important to add — but he just hugged his knees even tighter and rested his forehead on them, muttering to himself. The temperature in the cell seemed to drop; Hannah wished for a sweater instead of her light flannel.

"Can you make some warmer clothes appear?" she asked.

Nancy laughed. "Sure, and maybe a lobster and a steak and some mashed potatoes and gravy."

"Well, can you try to take me with you the next time you disappear?"

"I doubt it."

"Then what *can* you do?" She looked at Nancy, Belinda, and Albert in turn. "What are you?"

Nancy's body, so tense and springy, seemed to deflate a bit. Lost in thought, she spoke to herself in a near whisper, shaking her head. "That's so weird. . . ."

Hannah suddenly felt guilty, as if she had just pointed out a honking zit Nancy had taken great pains to conceal. "Sorry."

Nancy ran her fingers through her spiky hair, nervously scratched at her scalp. "No, it's just that I don't *feel* like anything at all. I don't *want* anything like you do, Hannah. I sort of don't care if I get out of here or not."

"Nonsense," Belinda said. "Of course you do. We all want to get out of here," she assured Hannah.

"That's not what I mean," Nancy said. "I want to escape — but that's because Hannah wants to. I want exactly what Hannah wants." She ran a finger along the concrete wall. "I just don't know what *I* want. It's not any different. It's not anything at all."

Albert lifted his head. "Yeah." His voice, for once, was full of dazed wonder rather than bored irritation. "I never thought about it before. Until I could see you all, I mean." Albert examined his own hand with newfound curiosity. He sniffed his armpit. Then he stood up. His combat boots were scuffed at the toes.

Albert walked over to Belinda. "Move."

To Hannah's surprise, Belinda vacated the bench without a word and stood next to Nancy. Albert placed his palms against the cement wall and took a deep breath. When he let it out, Hannah tasted salt.

"I'm alive in this place," Albert said.

Belinda frowned. "Maybe you should lower your voice."

"Maybe you should leave me alone," Albert said. He turned and began poking the faucet, his polished black fingernails making metallic pings. Then he jabbed at his Adam's apple, pinched the skin around his collarbone, pressed on his stomach. His eyes widened with each little prod and poke, as if his nerve endings had just begun to work.

"I'm getting us out of here," he announced. "Right now."

"Whatever you're planning," Belinda said, "I don't think it's a good idea."

"Too late," Albert said. "Storm's coming."

Chapter Twelve

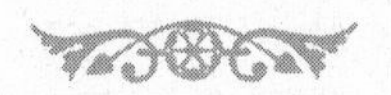

A steep drop-off separated the Silvers' lighthouse from the sea, but one path offered a gradual descent past boulders the size of cars. This was the Widow's Watch. Hannah's favorite spot was about a third of the way down, where the cliffs on either side formed a huge natural amplifier. She had read about a special place inside New York City's Grand Central Terminal, where if you stood on one side of a great archway, you could hear the whispers — *whispers*, think of that! — of people all the way on the other side. This is how she came to imagine the Widow's Watch: a natural telephone service bringing her sounds from across the Atlantic.

Storm's coming.

Albert's words had taken Hannah back there, and she could feel his presence all around her in the rocks, the sea, the vastness of the gull-streaked sky. She breathed deep, tasted the brine in the back of her throat.

Suddenly, Albert began pulling away with great force, taking with him chunks of memory: afternoon along the cliffs, the horizon fading in the dusk; the mad scramble home for dinner, careful not to wedge an ankle between the rocks. A great clap of thunder nearly made her slip off her perch. Raindrops puckered the waves. Hannah placed a palm flat against the rock at her side.

It felt like the concrete wall of her cell.

"You might want to duck under that cot," Albert suggested. "The wind's gonna kick up in a second."

Hannah obeyed.

Back at the Widow's Watch, the skies were overcast. She'd never seen a nor'easter roll in this fast. Lightning flashed and it seemed so close, even though she knew it must be miles out.

"See you around, Hannah," Albert said. Hailstones began to sting her skin; she pressed herself against the wall. Tiny chips of ice began to pile up on the floor of the cell. At the same time, the wind howling through the Widow's Watch was funneled into her ears. She curled up and shivered. The floor of her cell trembled, bouncing her up and down in the tiny space.

The Widow's Watch began to fade away. Hannah struggled to hold on to it. *A boulder the size of a jeep,* she thought. *Seagull poop. Slippery patches of moss.* After a while, she could remember gazing across the sea, listening for the sounds of faraway beaches, but she could no longer see herself there.

She rode out the storm beneath her cot. It wasn't long before there was a hush so complete that she could hear the settling of dust. She crawled out. Albert had vanished, along with Nancy and Belinda. The concrete sphere had been ripped apart by the wind — the cot and part of the wall behind it were intact, but the sink, faucet, and bench were gone. Rubble was strewn about the floor. Chunks of concrete lay in smoldering piles. The cell was open to the sky, where dark clouds were rolling away at an impossible speed.

Hannah climbed over the edge of her ruined cell and dropped down onto a neighboring rooftop. She was alone. There was nothing else to do but run.

Chapter Thirteen

Hannah picked her way across a checkerboard of rooftops that stretched for miles in every direction. Twisted antennae poked up like antlers. Steam leaked out of vents and pipes. The gabled mansions and forlorn chimneys she'd spied from the attic window were nowhere to be found. Buildings in this neighborhood were the color of mustard, their walls stained with a peculiar fungus. In the distance, steeples rose like spears tipped with copper and weather-beaten stone.

Hannah leapt across a narrow alley and landed on a roof that felt like hard rubber beneath her sneakers. She threaded her way past a gathering of empty folding chairs huddled around a low table, through a forest of dials stuck to tall metal poles. They reminded Hannah of the water and electric meters alongside Cliff House: clear plastic bubbles over little round clocks.

The dials displayed symbols like hieroglyphs: dots and scythes and curlicues. They should have been a jumble of nonsense, but Hannah found that she could read them. Astonished, she focused on the stenciled printing on one of the meters until it resolved itself into a word: FOUNDATION.

Hannah kept moving. New gauges loomed, tall and boxy. She darted around a blind corner and crashed into the soft belly of a man in denim overalls. He dropped his clipboard. On the meter next to his head, a row of numbers flipped like a stadium scoreboard.

"Sorry," she said, relieved to see that the man's face wasn't swimming with light and shadow, but frowning beneath an oversized caterpillar of a mustache.

"That's okay," he grumbled, stooping to pick up his clipboard. "Can't make this job any worse than it already is." He watched the numbers change and made a few marks on his clipboard with a pencil. "You see that storm? Now that was a heck of a thing."

The man looked up and Hannah followed his gaze. The dark clouds were gone, but there was still something ominous about the sky. It was too low, or the color wasn't right. Hannah thought it seemed depressed.

"I need a place to hide," she said. For some reason, the man's ridiculous mustache made him seem harmless.

The man tapped the clipboard against his meaty thigh. "You in some kind of trouble?"

"I didn't do anything wrong," she said. "The Watchers just think I did, so now they're —"

"Okay!" The man held up his clipboard like a shield, as if Hannah were lunging at him with a knife rather than asking for help. "You'll be just fine." He backed away from her slowly. "The Watchers are your friends. They're everybody's friends." Without another word he disappeared into the thicket of meters.

Hannah chose a long row of elegant dials housed in brass fixtures and ran until she stumbled out onto a pink rooftop. The surface was oddly layered, as if several small houses had been plopped down and allowed to sink in. Lopsided peaks and valleys gave way to windows and doors cut into unlikely shapes. In a few places the roof crested and swirled and dripped like an overfrosted cake. Hannah slipped into a narrow ditch lined with tiny rectangular windows. The glass had been painted black. She turned and looked back the way she had come, tracing her escape route. Beyond the bristling spines of the meters, she could see a plume of smoke rising from some hidden building. She supposed that was her cell. She hadn't traveled very far.

Staying low, she jogged along the ditch until she came to an alcove that had once held a sort of roof garden. The window was dirty. The tile deck was crumbling. A single earthenware pot was full of brackish water, upon which floated a brittle canoe made from dry, flaking leaves.

From this hiding spot, Hannah could hear voices. She peeked around the side of the alcove. There was a shallow crater where the roof sloped toward a round, stained-glass skylight. Suspended over the skylight was what appeared to be a cauldron. Neon wires connected a panel in the side of the cauldron to a bulky laptop computer perched on a table at the edge of the crater. An old, white-bearded man and an equally old woman were taking turns looking at the computer, studying the sky, and typing on the keyboard. At a different table, a man in a porkpie hat was reading from a monstrous book.

"I'm telling you," said the man in the hat, "the prophecy refers to a snowstorm. At least I think it does. Tell me what this line means to you: *a white-blotched sky*. White-blotched. That's gotta be snow, right?"

"Would you close the book and get over here, Remy?" said the woman. "Your section of the code is all we need."

Remy went to the computer, where he punched a few keys. "If this is a miserable failure, it's not my fault," he said. "Let the record show."

"Noted," said the bearded man. "Now I suggest we stand back."

The cauldron overturned, spilling a river of molten glass onto the skylight. It sizzled as it pooled. Hannah knew she should be putting more distance between herself and the wreckage of her cell, but she was entranced. She craned her neck as far as she dared. The old woman was sitting at the computer now, while the men watched the glass.

"Anything?" she asked, typing furiously.

"Of course not," Remy scoffed.

"There!" yelled the bearded man, pointing. The glass was condensing, rivers of color piling up into an ecstatic swirl. It reminded Hannah of soft-serve ice cream.

"It's ideal," said the woman.

At the far edge of the roof, several figures approached. They were still very small, but Hannah could tell there was something wrong with their faces. *Watchers.* The woman at the computer saw them, too. She jumped up, pointing at the Watchers and shouting at her companions.

"Run," Hannah whispered.

Instead, the two men began to hug and pat each other on the back as if they'd just won the lottery. The old woman couldn't stop grinning.

Four Watchers were distinguishable now, their faces overcast, painted with the lonely sky.

The woman called out to them. "We humbly submit our glasswork and await your verdict."

The fresh glass bubbling onto the skylight had transformed into a pastoral scene: patches of lush greenery and waterfalls sprouting along the craggy sides of a glass mountain. It was beautiful, but Hannah couldn't linger. She ducked back into the alcove in time to see three Watchers emerge from the row of brass gauges at the edge of the meter forest. They seemed to be in no hurry, just out for a pleasant stroll in pursuit of their fugitive. Their faces looked like ticking clocks. The sky swept in around them, slid along the rooftop and seeped like smoke into her alcove.

Hannah made herself as small as possible behind the earthenware pot. The Watchers weren't coming for the glassmakers; they were coming for her. And she was trapped. Without thinking too hard about what she was doing, Hannah tipped over the pot.

Fetid water pooled at her feet. The leaf canoe beached itself against a tile. Hannah bear-hugged the pot, stood up, and hurled it at the window.

She braced herself for broken glass. Instead, the window threw itself open with a frantic unshuttering, and the big pot sailed through the empty air to thunk against something inside. With a hand on the sill, Hannah vaulted in after it.

Chapter Fourteen

As soon as Hannah's feet hit the floor, the window slammed shut and latched itself, settling back into place with a grumpy shifting of its panes. Cheerful smiley-face curtains were tied back on either side. A thin appendage — a smooth glass cord — dangled like a tail from beneath the curtains. Her eyes followed it down along the wall, where it entered a fuse box.

The long shadow of a Watcher crept into the alcove outside. Hannah closed the curtains and backed away from the window.

"Nancy," she whispered.

She waited a moment. Nothing happened.

"Albert. Belinda."

When they failed to appear, Hannah wondered if she'd accidentally left them behind. Why weren't they speaking to her? Had she done something wrong?

She dismissed that thought and turned her back on the window. It was time to keep moving. The room in which she'd landed was full of shelves and workbenches and tables. Shapeless trinkets and unfinished sculptures were crammed into every inch of space.

Gossamer webs of glass connected the artwork (if that was what this stuff was supposed to be) to electrical outlets that lined the walls. She threaded her way carefully, stepping over the pot from the roof garden. Vines of sparkling emerald had already begun to claim it.

Hannah moved as quickly as she dared, surrounded by such delicate clutter. It was like being in the Wayback Machine, the antique store down the block from the Carbine Pass library. You checked your backpack in at the desk and crept around the vases and candy dishes, holding your breath while old Mrs. What's-her-face glared.

Mrs. *Shipley*? Was that right?

Hannah didn't think so, but she couldn't quite remember. How odd — she had been a regular visitor to the store. For once, Belinda didn't chime in with the correct name.

The path to the room's only door took her past a workbench lined with computer monitors. Textured screen savers rippled across them. Underneath the bench, a nest of power cords glittered with fluttery reflections — hints of moths perched upside down where she couldn't see them.

Her heart quickened at the sight of a keyboard. If this place had some kind of network, maybe she could get a map of the city.

The keyboard was completely unlabeled and contained about a hundred buttons. She selected one in the shape of a spiral and pressed it. The screen saver didn't budge. Was the keyboard even plugged in? She tried a triangle-shaped button.

Suddenly, the window unlatched itself. The fuse box sparked and crackled. A hand parted the curtains and reached into the room. Nearly tripping over a stray bundle of crystalline wires, Hannah ran to the door and threw it open. She stepped out into the hallway and slammed the door shut with such force that it rattled the wall.

"Hey! You wanna fight that door, take it outside."

A boy was giving her a look of irritation. He was about her age. His oversized army jacket was unzipped and spattered with paint. Underneath was a striped sweater that hugged his scrawny chest like a bandage. His baggy chef's pants were decorated with brightly colored tropical birds.

It was not a very reassuring outfit. Without a word, Hannah took off down the hall.

"Outside's actually the other way!" the boy called after her.

Hannah sprinted around a corner and into an abrupt tangle of limbs.

"Lemme go!" She lashed out, flailing against the strong hands that gripped her arms, holding her fast. A terrible hissing surrounded her, the unearthly harmony of a dozen voices at once. She bit down hard on a hairy-knuckled hand. The hissing grew more intense. She was trapped in a furious crush.

"Shhh yourself, you cruddy ancient soul." The boy was pushing her captors out of the way. He shoved a doughy arm aside in disgust. "Let her up, let her up, I got her."

The arms and legs didn't belong to Watchers, they belonged

to regular people — *regular dead people,* Hannah supposed. And they weren't hissing, they were just shushing her. The boy pulled Hannah to her feet alongside the crowd, which was jostling for space against a railing.

"You're not one for special moments, I take it," the boy said, gesturing to a little sliver of empty space.

"I really have to . . ." Hannah's eyes followed the boy's hand to the scene beyond the railing. They were standing on a balcony that jutted out over the hollow interior of a four-story building. The ceiling was the underside of the crater she'd seen on the roof. Molten glass was bleeding down through the skylight, flowing to fill the center of the building, crystallizing into rocks and moss and trees and caves and waterfalls. Hannah could see that the interior was ringed with balconies, all crowded with spectators hungry for a glimpse of the remarkable work in progress. ". . . go."

Right before her eyes, a cliffside forest came to life with a crackle, like tinfoil being uncrumpled. Light from the rooftop trickled down into crevices between the rocks, where rivers brought shades of sky crashing down to the floor below. Hannah was overwhelmed by the strange beauty of it all.

Then she saw the shadowy blurs gliding along a second-story balcony.

"Watchers," she said.

The boy sighed. "I know." He was absently flicking the bristles of a paintbrush sticking out of his pocket. "The glassworkers are going to be so proud of themselves for this, and we'll have to hear about it for the next thousand darkdays or so."

Hannah didn't stick around to ask the boy to explain what he'd just said. By the time he'd reached the word *darkdays*, she'd already put the crowd behind her. A few more steps and the balcony became a hallway with rows of doors on either side.

The boy caught up to her. "Slippery, slippery!"

"Leave me alone," she said without slowing down.

"How are things on the other side these days?"

He knows who I am, she thought. Flustered, she turned to face him. "What are you talking about? Who are you?"

"Hey, relax." He put up his hands. "It's pretty easy to tell that you just died. That's all."

"I'm not dead!"

The boy's sly smile disappeared. "Right." He took a deep breath, let it out. "I'm sorry to have to be the one to tell you this, but . . ."

"Is there a back way out of here?"

He shook his head gently. "Once you're in the city, this is it."

"No, *here* here. I mean the building."

"Here here the building," he said. "Are you sure you don't want to stay for the Watchers' verdict?"

She picked up the pace, leaving him behind.

"Okay, new girl!" he called after her. "Yes, there's a way. If you come back, I'll show you."

Hannah paused. The last boy she'd been friends with might have pushed her mother off the top of the lighthouse. But she decided that since this was an emergency, she would let this boy show her the way, then immediately head off on her own.

"Fine," she said, walking briskly back and putting her hands on her hips to show that she wasn't going to be too friendly.

He stepped in front of an unmarked door and held it open for her. When she didn't move, he eyed her curiously. "Are you okay?"

"Yeah" — she swallowed a sudden lump in her throat — "but I'm not too good with stairs."

Poised at the top of the winding staircase, she gripped the railing and steadied her wobbly legs. *Just push off,* she demanded of herself. *Do it!* But it was no use — her limbs would not obey. She peeked over the side of the railing, where a little rectangle of empty space gave her a line of sight all the way down to the bottom.

It was just a plain old empty back staircase.

The boy seemed wary of getting too close to her. "Do you need help?"

"No," she said. "I don't need anything else. You can go back to whatever you were doing."

He didn't budge.

Hannah told herself that things were different in this place. Whatever rules governed her life on the other side of the door no longer applied. She rested a tentative toe on the next step, then planted her foot. An inferno failed to claim her — not even a spark. The temperature remained the same. Relieved, she brought her other foot down. Barely conscious of the boy beside her, matching her step for step, Hannah descended.

When they burst out onto the street, Hannah couldn't stop herself from grinning in triumph. The boy regarded her curiously. There was a chill in the air. Pedestrians rushed past without giving Hannah a second look. They wore long coats with triangular lapels flipped up to cover their necks.

Up and down the street, iron lamps flanked arched doorways, casting muted light that somehow added to the gloom. Apartment buildings seemed to lean forward, as if they'd been planted firmly into the ground at odd angles. Covered walkways painted with elaborate scrollwork connected upper stories. Squat two-seater cars crept past, their windows tinted, drivers and passengers mere hints of shadow.

The boy turned up his own collar and zipped his army jacket. A patch on his sleeve displayed two paintbrushes crossed like the bones on a pirate flag. He spread out his arms.

"Welcome to rush hour in Nusle Kruselskaya." He produced a black knit hat from his pocket. "Here. You might want this."

"No, thanks," Hannah said. She was mesmerized by the traffic. She watched the men and women shuffle along the cobblestone sidewalk. *These people are all dead,* she told herself. It didn't seem possible. There they were, walking and talking — alone, in pairs, in huddled little groups. Here, a man carried a newspaper under his arm. There, a woman stopped, leaned against a wall, and examined the bottom of her shoe. Little hands threw open a window across the street, and a child's face appeared. Where were the skeletons, zombies, ghosts, angels? Nothing Hannah had ever read at the library or seen on the Internet had prepared her for the sight of everyday citizens going about their business.

"They're dead," she whispered. "Dead, dead, dead."

She scanned dozens of faces, her eyes darting all over the place. What were the odds that her mother was somewhere in this neighborhood? She tried not to think about it. There would be time enough later to figure out how to find her mother. For now, her priority was to melt into the crowd and disappear. She picked a direction and started walking.

"You sure you want to go that way?" the boy asked.

"Yes," Hannah said, as if she'd visited this part of town a million times and was headed for her favorite sandwich place. The boy clomped after her.

"So are you going to tell me your name?" he asked.

Hannah tried to pick up the pace, but the foot traffic was surging against her. She was on the wrong sidewalk. Across the street, people were going her way. She tried to find a gap between the cars, or a crosswalk.

"I'm Stefan," he said.

Hannah ignored him. She could still remember that warm, comfortable feeling when she'd allowed Kyle into her life. It had been so easy to let him be her friend. That was the last time she would make that particular mistake.

One of the covered walkways was just overhead. The shade of the underpass held a nighttime chill. Hannah snapped the top button of her flannel. She made a show of looking at the cars, trying to appear deep in thought, hoping Stefan would take the hint.

"I know the Watchers are hard to get used to at first," he said.

Hannah emerged from the shade. Hypnotic music like nothing she'd ever heard drifted from a window, a chorus of wordless chanting, grim and insistent, with a single voice belting a clear soprano melody that weaved in and out. Up ahead, the sidewalk dipped, and the light of a gas lamp mingled with the face of a man coming over the hill. He tapped a cane against the cobblestones. The crowd parted to let him through, shrinking away from his face as it stole the lamplight.

A Watcher.

"There's nothing for you to be afraid of," Stefan said. "I promise."

On the roof the Watchers had trapped her so easily with a simple two-pronged attack. If she turned around, would there be another Watcher ambling toward her from the other direction?

"You don't understand," she told the boy.

She must have sounded genuinely scared — or at least desperate — because without another word Stefan walked into the street and darted between cars, dropping low and sweeping his paintbrush along the ground in one smooth motion as he crossed to the other side. Acrid smoke billowed up from the cement as if he'd opened a thermal fissure. Hannah tasted ash on her tongue and coughed. In seconds, she was alone inside a cloud. A hand appeared, then the sleeve of an army jacket. The hand snapped its fingers, then beckoned to her.

Hannah refused to touch Stefan's outstretched hand.

"Just in case you can't see," he said, "this humble artist is offering to guide you. Better hurry."

The smoke began to clear; figures emerged, heads bent, mouths covered. The cars had stopped in a single-file traffic jam.

"I can see fine," she said, and Stefan whisked his hand away.

"Then come on, new girl."

As the smoke thinned out, dark stains appeared on the walls of the buildings to either side of the street. It was as if the stucco and stone had soaked up the ash like a sponge. Hannah followed Stefan down a deserted alley. The walls were rotten with the same creeping fungus she'd seen on the roof. She watched Stefan's oversized jacket bounce as he jogged a few steps ahead of her. Somewhere stashed away in one of those pockets was the brush that had made smoke erupt from a single line on the ground. In one of the buildings behind her, people were using computers to jump-start a great mountain of glass. Back across the rooftops, a character she'd made up as a little girl had called forth a storm to break her out of prison.

Finding her mother in such a confounding place was going to be difficult. Reluctantly, she admitted that it was a good thing she'd run into Stefan — how was she supposed to navigate this city without help?

Hannah allowed herself this moment of relief before letting it curdle into doubt. Hadn't the same exact thing happened with Kyle? She had let him get his friendly, confident hooks into her so quickly that even now, after what he had done, it was still easy to remember him helping with the dishes, that effortlessly perfect hair shuffling in and out of place above his eyes.

Hannah didn't know if she could trust the boy in the paint-spattered army jacket. But as long as she ditched him as soon as they exited the alley — if she made it impossible for him to help her — then she also made it impossible for him to hurt her.

Hannah resolved to go it alone. Then the alley spit them out and her courage became a fleeting thing, darting away like a quick little fish.

The town square in Nusle Kruselskaya was a garden of statues planted in a field of cobblestones. The ground was choppy and treacherous — it reminded Hannah of a stormy sea, frozen and paved. Snub-nosed trains rode the stony waves, shuttling passengers across the square beneath the statues' outstretched hands, from which clusters of lanterns dangled.

The crowd that passed in front of Hannah was made up of long-haired hippies in bell-bottoms, dapper businessmen in three-piece suits, pilgrims in bonnets and checked gingham dresses. There were furtive children in soiled rags, gaunt old women with walkers, and men in robes and turbans. Boys in cutoff shorts flirted with girls in skinny jeans; boys in trousers courted girls in demure dresses; boys who belonged to some colonial militia walked alongside girls in hoop skirts. Squat men wearing furry animal skins glared at tall men with painted faces. Camouflaged soldiers posed for a group of excited tourists with cameras and fanny packs. Hannah saw brides and grooms, waiters and waitresses, mechanics stained with grease. Knights clanked about in full armor, samurai strutted with flags on their backs, skateboarders ollied and collapsed.

Overwhelmed, Hannah focused on the nearest statue, a man carved from a giant piece of wood. One hand gripped a bundle of hanging lanterns, each as big as the lighthouse keeper's cottage. The other stretched out to clasp the hand of a neighboring statue, hundreds of feet away. In the shadow of this connected limb was a marketplace teeming with booths and tents. A train stopped and Hannah sorted the passengers by hairstyle as they shuffled out: buzz cuts, ponytails, Afros, Mohawks, cornrows, flattops, French braids, beehives.

Hannah sat on the uneven ground. The town square was giving her speck-of-dust anxiety, like when she looked up at the stars and thought about how big the universe must be. Stefan's pant legs were right in front of her face. They tapered at the ankles, where an elastic band held them tight against his skin. Hannah studied the parakeet pattern. Each bird had a great big yellow bill.

"You don't want to sit there," Stefan said. "Who knows what's crawling between the stones."

She jumped up and brushed herself off. "Is something on me?"

"Nah," he said. "But you gotta watch out for failure bugs around here. Clingy little things."

"What's a failure bug?"

"Ah," he said. They walked along the edge of the square. Here, the ground was torn up because the statues' gnarled roots had forced the cobblestones apart and reshaped the pathways. "Now that we're on what I think might be speaking terms, would you mind telling me your name?"

Hannah remembered her mother's words on their final night together: *The city of the dead has no beginning and no end.* Beyond the square, the city just kept sprawling. *Billions of souls. No center and no edges.*

There was no way she could do this alone.

"It's Hannah," she said.

"Not possible."

"Well, it is."

He scrunched up his face, lost in thought. "I'm never wrong," he said. "At least I haven't been in a long time. You have to be a Cynthia."

"Does your magic brush help you guess people's names, too?"

"Whoa, stop right there." He crossed his arms, straightened his posture. "First of all, I do not have a 'magic brush.' There's no such thing as magic, so you might as well put that word out of your mind."

"But —"

"Second of all, I don't *guess names* like a carnival worker. And since I'm pretty sure I used to be a gypsy, I'm offended. Twice."

"You're not sure what you used to be?"

A small army of bald-headed monks streamed past them, singing and keeping time with toy drums. Stefan rolled his eyes. Hannah couldn't tell if he was annoyed by the monks or by her question. "I'll explain it when we get there. This place is making my head hurt."

A giggling young couple in flashy snowsuits brought up the rear of the procession, imitating the monks' song.

"Get where?" Hannah asked.

"You know what they say, Cynthia. Home is where the art is."

Chapter Fifteen

Hannah had always thought of castles as drab monstrosities. Pictures she'd seen online were visions of decay: crumbling battlements, towers with their tops sheared off by wind and rain, high-ceilinged halls where knights kicked off their metal boots and put their feet up by the giant fireplace.

Stefan's home wasn't that kind of castle.

Instead of lording over a hill in the countryside, it was plopped down in the middle of a parking lot in Nusle Kruselskaya. The lot was full of the little two-seaters that seemed to be the trendiest car in the neighborhood. The castle, on the other hand, was massive: a mountain range of gables and domes and towers connected by a head-spinning collection of rooftops.

Hannah followed Stefan between parked cars. They encountered other people coming and going, some of whom seemed to know him. He nodded at a girl wearing two different knee socks — one striped, one plaid — pulled up over her jeans. The girl's orange cap-sleeved shirt said KRUMLOY STREET CAFÉ.

A vehicle pulled up next to them. Hannah jumped — she hadn't heard it approach. These cars ran completely silent. A man in a tunic that looked like it was made from a potato sack leaned out the window and raised a dyed blond eyebrow.

"The boss is looking for you."

He handed Stefan a piece of paper and sped away noiselessly (the tires didn't even screech). Hannah was beginning to think everyone's mismatched outfit was some kind of uniform. Stefan muttered something under his breath and shoved the crumpled paper into his pocket.

Hannah glanced at the oppressive sky above — the same color it had been since her prison escape — and wondered how anybody could tell what time it was when afternoon seemed to last for days. Stefan had tried to answer her questions, but their journey from the town square to the castle had involved evasive action: sprinting down alleys, making last-minute loops in cul-de-sacs, retracing their steps, doubling back, bouncing around the city streets like a couple of rogue pinballs. She struggled just to keep up, much less carry on a conversation. And yet, after all that, Hannah still didn't think she was thirsty.

"Behold," Stefan announced. "The cramped hut of the Painters Guild."

He gestured toward the castle's facade. Domes like painted onions looked especially bright against the dull sky — creamy pastels, candy stripes, solid gold to cap the highest tower. Intricate designs crawled across the bricks, disappearing beneath archways and into windows. As Hannah approached, the artwork seemed to burst out to cover the walls and towers like a seamless tapestry. If she let her eyes go slack and stopped trying to grasp it all at once, it resolved into a painting of a castle on top of a castle. It was as if two buildings were occupying the same space.

"It's beautiful," Hannah said. Twin fountains flanked the arch of the main entrance, each one burbling with cheerful primary colors. For the first time since she'd arrived in the city, Hannah felt a sense of peace. She didn't know if she was doing the right thing by letting Stefan take her here. She stopped questioning herself. She just wanted to dip a finger into one of the fountains and swirl the colors.

"You think so?" Stefan squinted up at the domes. "It always looks kind of silly to me. The tourists seem to like it, though."

He tugged on her sleeve to steer her away from the fountains. She shrugged him off. He put his hands up in mock surrender. "Sorry, no touching, I get it. This way."

Hannah let him walk on without her. High in one of the towers, the window was false — part of the painting — and yet inside, a girl very clearly walked past. Hannah gazed intently at the painted-on window, trying to make it flip to the background, to see if it coexisted with a genuine window. After crossing her eyes with effort, she gave up and hurried after Stefan.

They walked along a curb where the castle met the edge of the parking lot, putting the entrance behind them. The domes became less frequent, then disappeared, replaced by tarnished copper spires. Families of stone gargoyles camped along ledges. This section was closer in spirit to the buildings of Nusle Kruselskaya, lonely things that seemed to draw inspiration from the flat, unhappy sky.

Hannah and Stefan walked in the shadow of the outer wall for what felt like several miles. At times Hannah was convinced it was actually a canvas painted to look perfectly three-dimensional. Then she would blink and it would *be* a brick-and-mortar wall.

Finally, she couldn't take it anymore. "Is this a real castle or not?"

"Of course it's real. I live inside."

"So what is it, then, if it's not magic?"

"It's part of the Guild's journey to Ascension. You saw what the glassworkers are doing. There are other kinds of artists in Nusle Kruselskaya, too. But the Guild's thing is paint."

"You have to paint your way to Ascension?"

"We hope. Didn't you get a handbook?"

"No."

"Well, did you go to orientation?"

"No."

"How did you manage to skip that? They explain all this stuff to the new souls. Anyway, it's your lucky noonday, because I have some extra stuff you can look at." He thrust his hands into his pockets. "If you give it time, things'll make sense. You'll be a professional dead girl by the next lightday." He placed a hand over his heart. "Painter's honor."

"I'm not dead," she reminded him.

"Ah, right," he said, checking off invisible boxes. "Cynthia, female, not dead."

"It's Hannah. What's a lightday?"

Stefan pointed at the sky. "We're in the middle of noonday. Next we'll have darkday, then lightday. That's the cycle."

"How long does noonday last?"

He laughed. "As long as it wants. Look" — he sounded apologetic — "this is me, here."

The gatehouse in this part of the castle blended into the wall so naturally that Hannah almost missed it. But there it was: a plain old wooden door with iron hinges.

Stefan rummaged in his pocket and produced a silver key. He jiggled it in the lock, stopped, and leaned his ear against the door, listening. Then he sighed.

"Get ready," he said.

"For what?"

He pushed open the door. "My stupid afterlife."

The hallway was aflutter with moths. Hannah had seen them before, reflected underneath the workbench in the glassworkers' room. There, the moths had been perched out of sight, hanging upside down like miniature bats at rest. Here, they flapped around in a frenzy, sending tiny puffs of air across Hannah's face. They were all around her, hundreds of them, and yet she had only the vaguest impressions of their forms. Her natural instinct was to swat.

"Chalkdust," she said, failing to hit anything no matter how wildly she swung. "They're everywhere."

"Yeah." Stefan sounded dejected. He plucked one out of the air, pinched its wing between his thumb and forefinger, studied it a moment, and let it go. "They sure are."

An irate voice came screaming down the corridor. "That had better be Stefan Weisz, and he'd better have an explanation for this mess!"

Stefan winced. "I'm sorry in advance for what's about to happen," he said to Hannah in a low voice.

An older boy turned the corner, carrying a briefcase and bearing down on them with a smirk. He was dressed in a cheap gorilla costume, except he wasn't wearing the mask. His human head looked shrunken compared to the burly, leathery muscles of the suit. He marched straight up to Stefan and folded his meaty ape-arms over his chest. The briefcase swung awkwardly from his hairy paw.

"You'd better have about seventeen different but equally good explanations for all the things you left undone before you went out for half a noonday."

The gorilla turned to a shelf and cleared a space by sweeping a few books onto the floor with his paw. Hannah jumped out of the way just before a heavy volume crashed down on her toes.

This is Stefan's boss?

The boy slammed the briefcase down onto the shelf and

popped the locks with his big rubbery fingers. Inside the briefcase was a single piece of paper, which the boy held up and looked over before turning to Stefan with a look of malevolent glee. Then he cleared his throat and began to read aloud.

"Paintbrushes unrenewed, ninety-six. Paint formulas unmixed, one-hundred seventy-eight. Beds unmade, fifty-one. Floors unswept, nineteen. Shelves unorganized, thirty-eight. Leftovers uncaught, including but not limited to failure moths" — he gestured at the air around their heads — "chameleon slugs, memory shards, grekks . . . here!" The boy thrust the paper into Stefan's hands. "A terrible mess. See for yourself."

Stefan frowned at the paper. "Yes, sir. Sorry. I'll clean everything up."

With a huge clawed foot, the boy nudged the encyclopedia-sized volumes he'd thrown to the floor. "Also add to the list four books, unshelved. Somebody could trip over those." He looked Hannah up and down for the first time. "Get your new girlfriend to help you."

"She's not —"

"I'm not —"

But the gorilla just closed the briefcase and walked away, swatting at moths. Stefan crumpled the paper and shoved it into his pocket. "Well," he said, producing a brush and holding it out for Hannah to take. "The sooner we get started, the sooner we'll be done."

Hannah didn't move. "Is that why you brought me here?" She could feel her confusion boiling over into anger. "To help with your chores? And be your new girlfriend? That's . . ."

She searched for the proper word.

"*Gross,* that you think I would just . . ." She shook her head. *"Eww."*

Hannah wished she could go back to the town square for a do-over. She'd melt into the crowd, all alone.

"No, Hannah, wait a minute." Stefan's eyes darted back and forth, like he'd rather be anywhere else and was searching for an escape hatch. A moth fluttered across the bridge of his nose and was gone. He put the brush back into his pocket.

"It's not like that at all. I don't even have an *old* girlfriend, I swear." He thrust his head forward an inch or two, inviting her to examine his face. "I mean, look at me."

Hannah simply turned her back, shooing moths from her hair, and stalked off.

For once, Stefan didn't try to follow. Hannah fought the urge to look back at him. She imagined him standing there, palms up, watching her go, silently pleading to the back of her head. It didn't make her feel very good.

She turned the corner. The hallway was identical: bookshelves, floor-to-ceiling. At the end she took a left, then a right, and finally came to the door.

She pushed it open, preparing herself for the dreary shock of the noonday sky — and discovered a large supply closet. Puzzled, she looked behind her. Had she taken a wrong turn? All the hallways looked the same. Well, she needed a moment to think.

She stepped inside.

"They really ought to do something about the fungus in this horrible city," Belinda said as soon as Hannah found the switch and turned on the overhead light. The old woman was eyeing a wet-looking blob that had spread like a map along the back wall of the closet.

"Come on." Nancy stepped out from behind a cabinet stocked with bundles of paintbrushes sorted by size. "It's not so bad."

"It's thoroughly disgusting." Belinda shuddered. "I don't know what's worse: having to look at it, or turning my back to it. I believe I'll stand in the center of the room."

"Where have you been?" Hannah looked from Nancy to Belinda, incredulous. "I really could've used some help back there. And where's Albert?"

Nancy sat down on a paint can and scratched the skin of her knee through the hole in her jeans. "You wanna take this one, Belinda?"

"Mm," Belinda said, tapping her foot, examining the floor. When she looked up, she was trying to smile. "Hannah, dear, why don't you sit down?"

Hannah looked around. The closet was as big as her bedroom at Cliff House, and it was stuffed with antique dressers full of tiny drawers with dainty handles, like the dusty old card catalog at the library. There were no chairs.

"Too good for a paint can?" Nancy asked.

Hannah remained standing. Belinda looked like she didn't know what to do with her hands, clasping and unclasping them.

"I suppose I'll just get to the point," Belinda said. "No use beating around the bush. Albert is gone."

Hannah didn't want to understand. "You come and go all the time," she pointed out.

She thought back to when Albert had raised the storm, how she'd somehow traveled with him back to the Widow's Watch without ever leaving her cell. For that brief moment, they had existed in both worlds. And Albert had taken a storm from the North Atlantic and dragged it into the city of the dead. It must have been exhausting.

"He's probably just resting," Hannah said.

Belinda shook her head sadly. "If only that were the case."

"You're not getting it," Nancy said to Hannah. "Pretend the closet we're in right now is your head, okay?" She jumped up and slid the paint can onto the floor between them. It was labeled UPHOLSTERY. "Pretend this is me."

Nancy placed a can labeled WALLPAPER alongside it. "This is Belinda."

She slid a third can — CHANDELIER — just behind the first two. "And this is Albert. Now, after the storm, it's like *this* inside your head."

She removed the Albert can, leaving only the Belinda can and the Nancy can.

Hannah prodded the back of her head and the top of her skull. "So there's a hole in there now?"

"Sort of. It's more like . . ." Nancy looked at Belinda for help.

"An *absence*," Belinda said. "An Albert-sized missing piece."

Hannah wondered how she was supposed to feel. Should Albert be mourned, as if he were his own person?

"Albert disappeared and you two decided to hide."

"It's a bit more complicated than that," Belinda said. "We had some things to work out on our own. And we felt that it wasn't in anyone's best interests for us to act too hasty, given the circumstances. You see?"

"No," Hannah said.

"Translation," Nancy said. "We were scared."

Belinda looked at the dressers, the wall, the floor — anywhere except into Hannah's eyes. The old woman was angry with herself, Hannah realized, or else ashamed. Just like a real person would be.

"I was scared, too," Hannah said quietly.

"Ah, but think about how fortunate we are to have arrived here!" Belinda said, clearly happy to be changing the subject. "There has to be an authority figure in the Painters Guild, someone with real power who can help us with our search."

Hannah wondered how long it had been since she'd seen her mother. Trying to figure it out was maddening. Time was elastic, the day just stretching on and on like the city itself, no beginning and no end. She called on events from her past at random (how her mother hated that word!) just to make sure her memories hadn't been ripped away like Albert.

There was the hush of Cliff House on a Sunday morning broken only by humming in the garden. "Cork on the Ocean." Afterward there would be pancakes, her mother drizzling the batter into blobby letters, *H* and *L*, together on a plate with a square pat of butter. Syrup — the good kind from the farmers' market, not the sugary stuff you could buy at the Save Mate, where they seldom shopped. *Slave Mate*, her mother sometimes called it, when she was feeling derisive about the offerings of Carbine Pass, wine sloshing in her big-girl goblet. Or *Shave Mate*, which always made Hannah think of her father's beard in the photographs.

Nancy's blood-curdling shriek pulled Hannah from her reverie. The twin hurled herself across the floor to grab Hannah's arm, huddling close.

"There!" she said, pointing to the back of the closet, where the fungus blanketed the wall.

"Oh, I don't like this one bit," Belinda said. "You can never trust mold like that."

Chapter Sixteen

Hannah braced herself for some new horror. At first there was nothing. She wriggled her arm free from Nancy's grip.

"What's wrong with you?"

"Keep looking," Nancy said, "I swear I saw something. There! See?"

Hannah stopped trying to look directly at the fungus. As before, when she'd seen the facade as a painting on top of a real castle (or perhaps the other way around), the antique dressers and paint cans flipped inside-out without really moving at all, so that Hannah was now seeing the closet as a detailed portrait of itself.

Then it was Hannah's turn to grab Nancy's arm. Something emerged from behind the very last shelf: a smear of excess paint in the shape of a roly-poly lizard with a plump body and a long coiled tail. The lizard waddled toward them on its stubby legs. Paint slopped in its wake as it shed the colors of the room.

"Oh my," Belinda said. "Perhaps we ought to throw something at it?"

The lizard opened an impossibly wide chasm of a mouth, dripping with a vibrant rainbow of drool.

Hannah picked up the nearest paint can and prepared to heave it at the creature.

The door flew open and Stefan burst in. Moths flapped into the room as if they'd been waiting outside the door for their chance.

"I heard a scream," he said, stopping in his tracks, looking beyond Hannah to the lizard, whose saliva had pooled in a shimmering puddle.

"Nice work!" He grinned at Hannah. "I've been looking all over for him. He's quite the little sneak."

Stefan crouched next to the lizard and gave his spiny back a few gentle swipes with his paintbrush. "There you go, buddy." The lizard bopped his head affectionately against Stefan's arm. He left a spot of yellow on the sleeve of Stefan's jacket.

"Sorry if he scared you," Stefan said. "Hannah, this is Charlemagne. Charlemagne, Hannah." He narrowed his eyes. "Why are you holding that paint can?"

Hannah set it down. "What is that thing?"

"Hey, he's got a name."

Hannah swatted at a moth. "Weren't you supposed to be catching these?"

"Weren't you supposed to be storming out?"

"I got lost in your stupid castle."

Stefan leaned down and whispered something to Charlemagne. The creature splatted himself down beneath a dense cloud of moths and puddled into a blob of melted spines and multicolored scales. His mouth swirled open, a rainbow whirlpool that became a black hole. Tongues began to unfurl, one after another, snapping up to slurp a moth and drag it down into the gaping maw. In seconds, the lizard had reduced the moth cloud to thin air.

Charlemagne closed his mouth and unpuddled himself. Stefan gave him a few more swipes with the brush to nudge his spines into wholeness. "That's a good boy."

Hannah wanted desperately to be gone from this place. "Will you show me the way out of here?"

Stefan looked up from his pet.

"Now, wait just a second," Belinda said, stepping forward. "Let's not act with undue haste." She turned to Stefan. "We request an audience with your king or guardian or parent. Or your most knowledgeable archivist. Perhaps a librarian."

"Translation," Nancy said. "Take us to your leader."

Stefan blinked. His head swiveled from Belinda to Nancy. "Who are you?"

Hannah smacked his shoulder, forgetting her no-touching rule. "You can see them?"

Charlemagne perked up, his attention snagged by something out in the hallway. Faster than Hannah thought possible, he took off, tiny legs scrabbling and leaking paint.

Stefan ran out the door after the lizard.

"Wait just a moment!" Belinda said, following him. "Excuse me! Young man?"

"Belinda!" Hannah called out, but the old woman was gone. A single moth alighted on Nancy's shoulder. Hannah brushed it off. At least her twin was still here.

"'Moth-chaser,'" Nancy said. "'A boy who can see us.'"

"No more Muffin vocab! This is serious, Nancy — what should we do?"

"You can do whatever you want. Personally, I think the old lady's right."

Hannah never thought she would miss the days when Nancy and Belinda were just irritating voices echoing inside her brain. They had bossed her around, but Hannah always had the upper hand — they were trapped inside *her* head, after all.

"I can't believe you two," Hannah said. "Just because Stefan can see you doesn't mean we should stick around and help him with his chores."

"You know what?" Nancy ran her fingers through her hair, giving it a spiky flounce. "It feels kind of nice to be seen."

Hannah and Nancy caught up with Belinda in a solarium down the hall, where Stefan was stalking a stray band of moths swarming beneath the glass roof.

"They think it's a way out," Stefan said, looking up. "They're not that smart."

The room was circular and the ceiling flat, giving Hannah the feeling of being inside a giant hockey puck. The sky seeped in through the glass, its dullness of spirit infecting the furniture. Couches sagged despondently.

"Hurry up and get rid of them!" cried a shrill voice from the far end of the room, where students stood behind wooden easels, paintbrushes at rest in their trays. The students' eyes followed a man with horn-rimmed glasses and a long button-down smock, as he pointed to a Gothic arrangement of candles in the wall.

"There! You see? The little blighters have taken roost in the sconce, and now you'll never get them out. I've already wasted an entire class period. This simply won't do."

"Sorry, Professor," Stefan said. "I'm doing the best I can."

Charlemagne puddled himself in the center of the floor.

The professor shot Stefan an icy glare, then turned to his students. "Right then, brushes down!"

When the professor realized that brushes were already down, he dismissed the class with a shooing wave of his hand. The students scurried out of the room, and their teacher followed, slamming the door in Belinda's face before she could introduce herself. Nancy began to pester Stefan, who was trying to coax the moths down within range of Charlemagne's tongues.

Hannah closed her eyes and commanded her brain to pull Nancy and Belinda back in. When she opened her eyes, the old woman and Hannah's twin were both talking, and Stefan was doing his best to ignore them. Hannah would just have to wait while they made up their own minds.

She distracted herself with a series of paintings that hung around the room in heavy, gilded frames. In the first one, she recognized the huddled apartments and cobbled alleys of Nusle

Kruselskaya. There, on a rooftop, among a thicket of dials and gauges, was the meter man, writing on his clipboard.

I know that guy, she thought.

Farther along the wall she found a neighborhood of gabled mansions like the ones she'd seen from the attic. This was a pleasant, hilly district; a country garden stuffed with rambling houses. Next, Hannah strolled past glittering skylines of glass-walled towers and villages of sloppy mud huts.

"Look, I'm already in a lot of trouble," Stefan was saying as he crossed to the middle of the floor, brush dripping with orange paint, Nancy and Belinda in tow. "I can't help you."

"There, you see?" Hannah went over to meet them. "Now can we go?"

"Hannah," Nancy complained, "he won't listen to us."

"I don't even know who you are," Stefan said, "or how you got in here." He held his brush out straight and began jabbing at some invisible canvas. "This whole thing is way too weird for me."

Hannah noticed that Nancy couldn't stop running her hands through her hair, smoothing her eyebrows, pinching her cheek. It made Hannah's skin tingle. She wanted to look in a mirror and examine her own face.

"Well then, allow me to show you what it looks like," Stefan said.

Hannah blushed. "Did I say that out loud?"

"It's time you stopped doing that, dear," Belinda said.

"It's your fault I do it in the first place!"

Hannah watched as a crude face began to take shape in the air, following the swirls of Stefan's brush — circle eyes, triangle nose, smiley mouth.

"That's not how I look," Hannah said. Her hands went to her face. "Is that how I look?"

"Relax," Stefan said. "I'm making it crappy on purpose. Artists have doubts and make bad choices and mess up their work all the time. That's what the failure moths are attracted to. They don't hurt anybody, but nobody wants them around. I mean" — he dabbed pupils into the eyes — "would you want to paint with these little guys buzzing around your head?"

"Wow," Hannah said, studying the sloppy face. It looked like the finger painting of a two-year-old. "That's really bad."

"Thank you," Stefan said, swiping in a few awkward strands of hair and stepping back. "My masterpiece is complete!"

Moths began to descend, swooping and circling the face. Beneath the cloud of tiny blurred wings, Charlemagne came to life. His puddle rippled. Sticky prehensile colors shot up into the air.

"Good boy," Stefan said just as the moths that had sheltered behind the candles burst forth. Charlemagne unpuddled, leaping up onto a clawfoot sofa with the lithe quickness of a cat. His stubby feet left blotches of paint on the floral upholstery.

"Go get 'em!" Stefan yelled happily. Hannah had the feeling that Charlemagne was Stefan's best friend. His messy footprints ended on the arm of the sofa, as if he'd splotched himself into the pattern. Nancy dragged a finger through one of the footprints and sniffed it curiously.

Stefan kicked the leg of the sofa. “Not a good time to hide, Charlemagne.”

“Is there a way to get out of this neighborhood without the Watchers seeing us?” Hannah asked.

Stefan was staring at the ceiling, giving the stray moths a fierce glare. Hannah waved her hand in front of his face. He brought his attention back down and stared at her for a moment. Finally, he seemed to remember what she was talking about. “You’re still playing this game?” He laughed. “You’re so paranoid. I told you, you don’t have to be afraid of the Watchers. Besides, they already know you’re here.”

Hannah felt a surge of dread. “How do you know?”

“Because of that.” He pointed to the doorway. For a moment she didn’t understand, and then she saw it. Peering down at them from a stone hollow above the door was a single glass eye.

Chapter Seventeen

"I can't believe I'm doing this," Stefan said.

His room was much smaller than the supply closet. Paint-stained rags were piled high in one corner, neatly folded sweaters and pants in another. His furniture consisted of an absurdly small desk like a kindergartner's, a dresser with three drawers, and a swan-necked floor lamp.

There were no glass eyes in here. Stefan explained that the eyes were only in the castle's public spaces — studios, classrooms, and exhibit halls. Like most of the artists of Nusle Kruselskaya, the Painters Guild had voluntarily installed the Watchers' spy equipment. When the Guild created artwork perfect enough to gain entry to Ascension, they wanted the Watchers to see.

Hannah found it hard to imagine — the thought of glass eyes following her every move made her skin feel prickly — but Stefan assured her that it worked this way all across the city. Nobody knew exactly how to get to Ascension. The rules weren't entirely clear. Souls banded together into groups to work out their own beliefs. Eventually, if they were lucky, the Watchers would approve of their methods and escort them out of the city.

Hannah thought of the meter man. *Watchers are your friends. They're everybody's friends.*

Stefan pulled an oddly shaped leather bundle from his top drawer, slapped it down on top of the dresser, and unrolled it into a long strip. Paintbrushes of all shapes and sizes were tucked into little belt loops.

"How do you sleep in here without a bed?" Nancy asked. She was leaning against the dresser, arms folded. Belinda was giving the rag pile a look of distaste. They were all four squished together. A sudden movement could result in a tangle of limbs.

"I don't sleep."

He selected a thin brush, which reminded Hannah of her mother's little-used mascara. *She wore it when Patrick and Kyle came over.*

Belinda tut-tutted. "Kids your age, staying up till all hours. Being well rested is an important part of life."

"Yeah, but, this isn't really life." Stefan unfolded a flimsy stool and placed it in front of Hannah. "You might want to sit down."

Hannah sat. "You never sleep at all?"

"Have you been tired since you got here?" He began removing tubes of paint from the drawer. "Or hungry, or thirsty?"

"I don't think so."

"She hasn't had to go to the bathroom, either," Nancy volunteered.

Hannah glared at her.

"I really can't believe I'm doing this." Stefan looked from Nancy to Hannah. "Tell me again how you got here."

"I walked through a door," Hannah said. She had explained her situation on the way to his room, but it was obvious that Stefan still thought of her as a delusional girl who could not accept her own death.

"Because a bunch of banished souls killed your mother," he said.

Hannah nodded. "I came to get her back. But the Watchers think I know something about the banished, so they put me in jail."

"Which you escaped from with the help of your imaginary friend."

"Albert."

"Uh-huh."

Hannah turned to Nancy and Belinda. "Show him."

She didn't know what it looked like when they retreated into her head. She hoped, for the purposes of this demonstration, that it was deeply disturbing.

Judging by the look of pure shock on Stefan's face, it exceeded her wildest expectations. The problem was, it felt like someone had pressed a finger squarely against her forehead, cracked the bone, and squelched into the gray matter of her brain.

Winter at Cliff House began in November. The last remnants of grimy snow at the edge of the driveway didn't melt until April.

Her mother hoarded cans of food in the pantry and pickled acres of vegetables. She froze meat, though Hannah was always in favor of salting it, as if they were on an eighteenth-century ocean voyage.

She and her mother would be trapped in the house for weeks.

Thanksgiving was a last supper of sorts — good-bye to the Carbine Pass library, to the antique store, to the homeless hippie guy whose tie-dyed flag stuck up from the back of his bicycle. Good-bye to the Carbine Pass Savings Bank digital clock. Good-bye to the soccer fields, where the setting sun blasted the tin siding of the concession stand.

At Cliff House, ice hung from the eaves in thick slabs. Two winters ago Hannah had won fourteen Monopoly games in a row, then her mother had won the next eleven. Moods ebbed and flowed, the two of them circling each other like wolves, not talking at all or talking nonstop. Habits formed and were forgotten. Last year her mother would not stop chewing spearmint gum. Hannah tiptoed around the traps, whispering to Nancy and rolling her eyes at Belinda.

The fireplace in the Camp Room got so hot that her mother would put on her bathing suit and read, as if she were on some tropical beach rather than cooped up in a snowbound house on a cliff. Hannah would pig out on homemade ice cream. She was always so much hungrier in the winter. Scarfing mint chocolate chip too fast gave her a dull ache just above her eyelids. It happened every time. She never learned her lesson. Never heeded Belinda's warning to slow down.

Hannah blinked Stefan's room back into place. Her temples throbbed with pain like an ice cream headache with the volume turned up. Belinda and Nancy were gone. Stefan was peering intently at her forehead. Behind him, Charlemagne skulked past the dresser with a woodsy shimmer.

"Do you believe me now?" she asked.

"I've never seen anything like that," Stefan said. "They just sort of . . ." He moved his hands to demonstrate, his thin paint-brush darting about. It looked as if he were conducting an orchestra. "No, scratch that," he said. "It was more like this." He mimed gathering things together and crumpling them up like an invisible piece of paper, which he flicked at the center of Hannah's forehead.

"Ow!" She could feel Nancy and Belinda scurrying about like mice in her brain. It had never been like this before. If she hadn't felt so achy, it would have been funny — Stefan was watching her with a newfound wariness. She tilted her head at the brush in his hand. "You wanna get to it, then?"

He jolted to life. "Right, yeah." He took off his army jacket, which seemed to whisk itself from his skinny frame, and hung it on the doorknob. Then he produced a palette from the drawer and began dolloping paint from the plastic tubes onto its oval surface. "I'll leave your mouth for last so we can talk." He began attacking the palette with his brush, deftly mixing a range of flesh tones. "Now hold still, unless you really do want to look like the face I made in the solarium."

Hannah thought of the moth-nibbled smiley and held herself as still as a mannequin. The first brushstrokes felt cool against her skin, with an after-tingle like the mentholated stuff her mother rubbed on her chest when she had a cough. "Feels weird," she said.

"Just wait until it comes off." He was gripping his brush down close to the bristles as he worked on her eyelids. "Hold *reeeeaaaaal* still." Satisfied, he moved on to the skin around her cheekbones.

"You know," he said after working silently for a bit, "you're lucky. You have automatic friends that are always with you. I wouldn't mind that."

"But I never actually saw them before I came to the city. Have you ever heard of that happening?"

"Imaginary friends bursting into life? No, but that doesn't mean anything. In the handbook they say to think of the city as a beach, and each neighborhood like Nusle Kruselskaya is a grain of sand. Things are so different in other places. Like, you wouldn't even believe it's the same city. But if you're really not dead, maybe the rules are different for you."

He began working on her nose, outlining it first in sketchy downward strokes, then switching to an even smaller brush when he got to her nostrils. "Want some nose hair?"

"Don't even think about it."

"There's a bunch of handbooks on my desk, if you want one. They have illustration contests for the new editions, so I've been collecting old ones for research."

"Have you won any contests?"

"Not yet."

Hannah's headache flared. Belinda and Nancy were arguing, but all Hannah could hear was a distant mumbling. It was a maddening sensation, an itch inside her mind she couldn't scratch. Stefan shaded in the contours of her jaw.

"Keep your mouth closed."

The brush tickled her lips. He was moving quickly now, switching to a fat, stumpy brush to shade in her neck, all the way down to the collar of her flannel. Then he stepped back and regarded his work. After squinting at her for a while, he set the brushes on the palette and turned to the dresser. Hannah caught a glimpse of Charlemagne sliding through the bright cone of light beneath the lamp, but then he was gone.

"I don't see any moths," she said. "That's good, right?"

"Of course. They have a saying around here: When Stefan Weisz is painting . . ."

While he tried to make up the saying they had around here, Hannah practiced moving the muscles in her face. She cycled through smiles and frowns, testing different expressions. The drying paint didn't feel like heavy, caked-on makeup. There was a lightness to it, as if the paint *wanted* to be skin, and Stefan had simply granted its wish.

Meanwhile, Stefan had assembled a small machine on top of the dresser. It looked like the old-fashioned pencil sharpener at the Carbine Pass library, the kind that you worked by turning a crank. A long tube dangled off the edge of the dresser to end about a foot above the floor.

He whistled. "Here, boy!"

Charlemagne bounded out from beneath the rag pile like an eager puppy, shedding gobs of paint. He puddled himself beneath the tube and burbled happily as Stefan inserted his brushes into the machine, one at a time. There was a faint hum. When he removed each brush, it was clean and dry. Excess paint crept down through the tube like a thick milk shake, bathing Charlemagne in peach-colored slop.

"Can I see my face?" Hannah asked.

Stefan knelt down and opened the bottom drawer just a crack, taking care not to disrupt the flow of the paint from the tube, and came up with a round hand mirror.

Hannah took it, but didn't look right away. For some reason, the image of a dolled-up pageant queen popped into her head. She prepared herself for rosy cheeks, pouty lips, pale blue eye shadow. She told herself it was a necessary disguise. The less she looked like Hannah Silver, the better. She held the mirror up to her face and gasped. Stefan had done a remarkable job.

He had turned her into a boy.

"You like it?" Stefan asked.

Hannah was speechless. It was as if he had taken the features from a dozen average boys and combined them into an instantly forgettable whole. She opened her mouth to answer him, but was cut off by scuttling feet just outside the door. Castle-dwellers hurried past, chattering excitedly. Hannah couldn't make sense of their voices until she picked out one word that kept repeating, over and over again in a breathless refrain.

Watchers!

She jumped up from the stool and tossed the mirror on the desk. "We have to get out of this castle."

"We?" He cocked his head. "I live in this castle. And anyway, how do you know they're here for you?"

"You still don't believe me. You think they're about to take everybody to heaven."

"Ascension." His eye twitched. "What if they are? This could be it."

"Well, good luck." She turned to the door. "Thank you for the new face."

"Wait!" He took a step, which nearly brought him all the way across the room. "There's a subway. It'll take you far away from here, fast, if that's what you want. Follow the signs to the exhibition hall. Go through the glass doors and out to the concourse. That's where the station is."

"Exhibition hall to the concourse to the station," she said. "Got it."

"After I leave, count to a hundred before you open the door." Stefan was trembling with excitement. "You should wear something different. . . . I guess you can help yourself to my clothes. Don't talk to anybody. It was nice to meet you, Hannah. Good luck. It'll get easier, I promise. Do I look okay?" He shifted his weight nervously. "Never mind. See you around."

With that, Stefan joined the crowd in the hallway. His army jacket fell from the knob as the door slammed behind him.

Chapter Eighteen

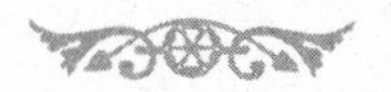

Welcome to the first stop on your journey through the afterlife! It is our goal to make your stay in the city a pleasant and productive one. While you wait to be assigned an orientation leader, please enjoy this complimentary handbook. (If you belong to one of the occupational group classifications listed in Appendix XIV, please skip this introduction and turn to section 765.98A, which in the omnibus edition begins on page 398, and in the abridged children's edition begins just after the illustration of the bear with his hand in the jar of honey.) It might seem like a lot of information, but don't despair! We are dedicated to easing the transition for every soul and have provided you, the newly deceased, with a number of useful resources and helpful hints.

Hannah held one of Stefan's handbooks open to the first page and watched as it revised itself. Words appeared and disappeared before her eyes. Snarky notes popped up in the margins. Before she was even done with the first paragraph, the words *IRRELEVANT* and *AWKWARD* scrawled themselves in red between the lines. This comment vanished, only to reappear as a footnote at the bottom of the page. It was as if the handbook were arguing with itself. She flipped to a glossary page near the back and found the entry for FAUCET, which had dozens of sub-entries. She skimmed a finger down the tiny print: FAUCET, ALBATROSS. FAUCET, BREAKFAST. FAUCET, CRYPTO-. This was impossible. The entry for Albatross Faucet, for example, crossed itself out as she read it.

~~DISPENSER OF LESS-THAN-DELIGHTFUL BEVERAGE. WEIGHTY, LEADEN. DISCONTINUED.~~

She slammed the tattered paperback shut and stuffed it into Stefan's army jacket, which was far too big but completed her disguise (red shorts pulled over her jeans and a single yellow leg warmer that sagged beneath her left knee — the mismatched style of the Painters Guild). She'd cleared out the pocket, keeping only the handbook, a tube of paint, and a single paintbrush.

Hannah closed her eyes against the swelling ache in her head. She wondered what it was like for Nancy and Belinda in there. Had they built a kingdom of her memories, some twisting echo of

Cliff House? Or was it simply a dark void? She implored them to stay calm and hidden away until she reached the subway. Then she opened her eyes and stepped out into the hall.

The stampede of castle-dwellers was orderly: urgent, but not hysterical. The whirlwind of dreadful outfits assaulted her senses. Orange tracksuits were paired with flowery sashes, kilts with striped tank tops. There were purple cardigans and neon skirts, flip-flops and formal gowns. She recognized the Guild's insignia sewn into everything, paintbrushes crossed like bones.

It was a heartening scene. Hannah could slip into the crowd and let it carry her down the hall, one more anonymous student among thousands. Dressed in her own disastrous outfit, she felt an odd twinge of belonging. She hunched her shoulders, disappearing as best she could into the folds of the army jacket, and darted behind a group of older girls with galaxies painted on their shaved heads.

"Do you think this is it? Do you think we're really going?"

The voice belonged to a middle-aged woman whose shirt had one long sleeve and one short. Her bare arm rattled with loose, jangly bracelets. It took Hannah a moment to realize the woman was talking to her, specifically.

She tried to respond, but gritted her teeth instead. There was a jackhammer inside her brain. She was seriously going to kill Nancy and Belinda. Why were they doing this to her? Didn't they understand the danger she was in? She concentrated on staying upright, putting one foot in front of the other.

"It's okay to be nervous," the woman said. "I'd be lying if I said I wasn't."

The pressure was unbearable. Hannah thought she heard herself make a strange noise. Now the woman was giving her a puzzled sidelong glance.

"You know, you don't look so good. . . ."

Hannah reached for her face and had to force herself not to touch it. Was her deception crude and obvious? What had seemed foolproof in the privacy of Stefan's room now struck her as a terrible mistake. She willed herself to ignore the pounding in her head and smiled as best she could.

"I'm just excited," Hannah said. "I feel like I've been waiting forever."

The ceiling of the exhibition hall was the pale blue of a midsummer day, blotched at the edges by wisps of clouds that swirled inward toward the vaulted center. Beyond the clouds, millions of glass eyes formed a glittering mosaic.

Castle-dwellers streamed past her into the hall, chattering excitedly, a procession of tube socks and argyle cardigans. Hannah wondered how long the Painters Guild had existed, in earth time. Hundreds of years? Thousands? She couldn't help but feel a little guilty that the Watchers were coming to take her back to prison, not to escort these people to Ascension. *False alarm. Sorry about that!*

The pounding in her head became more acute, as if Nancy

and Belinda were equipped with an actual jackhammer, and using it to blast through layers of brain and skull. *Stop,* Hannah thought, over and over again. *Please stop.* She didn't know how much more she could take.

Ahead of her, a wide dirt road formed a sort of Main Street, sloping gently down the center of the hall to a horizon line of glass doors in the distance. She had entered through the back entrance, along with the painters. The glass doors at the far end of the street were for the tourists spilling in from the concourse. According to Stefan, the subway station was out there.

Main Street was lined on either side by mud huts and prehistoric shelters made of tanned hides and sticks. Watchers dotted the landscape like blemishes, their faces churning with beastly fur. Humidity settled over the hall like a sweaty blanket. Hannah kept her eyes down and picked up the pace, walking past a row of slightly more elaborate houses. As she suspected, they were gorgeously detailed paintings, three-dimensional and perfectly lifelike. Soon the dirt became gravel, the gravel turned to pavement, and she passed a country cottage with a shingled roof and banana-colored siding. Azaleas and peonies sprouted next to the porch.

She slowed long enough to stare into the depths of the exhibit. In a moment the dual images appeared: a painted house and a real house, jockeying for position. Her ears began to pick up the voices of the surrounding crowd as snippets of conversation rather than a dull murmur.

— *waited so long* —

— I've always heard we'll be able to sleep again —

— don't even remember what sleep is like —

— Uncle Charles and Aunt Sue and Mom and Dad and Ursula —

— can't believe it's happening —

Hannah began to perceive a third layer of the exhibit, an inner clockwork, as if the cottage were teaching her how to see it as it really was.

— I'll look for you up there, Benny —

— gonna miss this place —

— You're nuts —

This innermost layer of paint was like the strands of DNA she'd learned about in her mother's biology class. Except the DNA of the cottage was much more beautiful. Splashes of primary colors wove and unwove themselves. There was a rhythm to the churning. She had the feeling that if it were to stop, the whole illusion of the cottage — and, perhaps, the castle itself — would simply collapse.

— I love you —

The pain in her head expanded to her stomach. She closed her eyes to fight a wave of nausea. When she opened them, the third layer was gone. The cottage was its charming, innocent, solid self — but the flowers had begun to wilt in the rank humidity. Her temples throbbed in time with the sickness in her belly.

"Stop it," she muttered, moving along, wondering what would happen if she puked in this place. "We're almost there."

She hurried past a low-slung apartment block that seemed to be made entirely of archways and iron lamps — one of the buildings of Nusle Kruselskaya.

They've painted the city, she realized. This vast exhibit — the Guild's masterpiece — was made from samples of each neighborhood, rendered in great detail.

She picked her way beneath a treehouse of many rooms, catching the haze of a Watcher in one of the bark-lined windows. The hall was crawling with them. She had the distinct impression that they could see right through her disguise, and were simply toying with her. Who knew what they were thinking?

Main Street became a cement thoroughfare. Her vision swam. She clutched her stomach. She was definitely about to puke. She couldn't help it. Screaming at Belinda and Nancy to calm down, she began to run. Past a ranch house, a temple, the outside of a shopping mall, the road stopped at the glass doors. She was almost there when she felt herself stumble.

The pressure in her head was enormous. Her knees hit the cement. Her hands pushed on her face and the back of her head, trying to hold her skull together. It was going to crack open. The pain intensified so quickly, all she could do was give up.

The exhibition hall went dark. The jackhammer ceased. There was nothing but merciful silence and the absence of hurt.

She opened her eyes. Sprawled on the ground across from her, looking dazed and sick, were Nancy and Belinda.

Chapter Nineteen

Uneasy Guild members edged away from the scene, while others looked on in shock from the benches in front of the mall painting. For Hannah, any hope that she might still be able to blend in to the crowd died with the look of horror on Nancy's face.

"Bad, bad, *bad*!" Nancy exclaimed, scrambling up and helping Belinda creak to her feet. "This is really bad."

Hannah pushed herself up off the ground and risked a look over her shoulder. A small army of Watchers was gliding up the path; several more had emerged from the mall. The air was a sauna. Hannah got the fleeting impression that paint was beginning to drip. Three boys leapt from a bench that had gone soft and runny. Their boots sloshed in the soupy muck of the sidewalk.

The exhibit was coming undone.

The heat shimmer was making Hannah woozy, but she could still make out the figure at the head of the pack. The Watcher's face stole its tattooed glimmer from a neon sign in one of the mall's windows, and the hot-pink glow bled down into the sequins of her evening gown.

It was the interrogator from the prison. The woman raised an arm and pointed straight at Hannah, Nancy, and Belinda.

"Concourse!" Hannah said, urging Nancy and Belinda forward. She clutched at her face. Had the mask slipped? Melted in the heat? She supposed it didn't matter: Her disguise was useless as long as Nancy was at her side, looking just like her.

Some cruel, selfish part of her wanted to take off in a different direction, hide among the exhibits and sneak out through the castle while the Watchers chased Nancy and Belinda into the subway. How long before they realized their mistake?

Ashamed of herself, Hannah shoved the thought aside.

"Let's all remember not to look them in the eyes," Belinda said.

They were past the mall now, into the final exhibit: some kind of futuristic hotel, a honeycomb of sleek, capsule-shaped pods. Ahead, just beyond the glass doors, Hannah glimpsed the concourse. Tourists slid smoothly along a moving walkway that swept them past a wall mural, a map of the castle.

A pair of Watchers hopped off the walkway and strolled toward the doors.

"Oh my," Belinda said.

"We are so done," Nancy said, averting her eyes. Hannah covered her face and peeked out from between her fingers. The Watchers took positions on the other side of the doors, content to wait for their prey. Their faces made streaks like northern lights on the glass. Hannah nearly broke down. All this running, and her mother was just as far — just as *gone* — as she'd ever been.

"Perhaps not," Belinda said. Through her fingers, Hannah chanced a look. The concourse had erupted with roiling black smoke, blossoming along the floor. Tentacles of grime crawled up the mural and snaked toward the exhibition hall, enveloping the Watchers. Soot stained the glass.

"I know this trick," Hannah said, taking Nancy and Belinda by their hands and wrenching them forward. She felt a fingertip brush the back of her head, could swear the furnace heat of a Watcher's breath had come within inches of her ear. Behind her, cameras flashed, one after another. *Not cameras,* she thought. *Eyes.*

They stumbled through the door and into the choking aftermath of Stefan's painted smoke bomb. The Watchers could be two steps away, and Hannah, Nancy, and Belinda would never know unless they bumped into them.

Nancy yelped.

"Hush!" Belinda scolded.

"Sorry, but I think somebody just touched my arm."

"Hannah?" It was Stefan's voice.

"We're all here," Hannah said.

"Where?"

"Here."

Something moved nearby.

"There's a blue light that marks the subway station," Stefan said. "Take the stairs. I'll meet you down there."

Stairs, she thought. *No problem.* This was the dead city, where stairs were just stairs — it was glass eyes and faucets that caused her problems. A faint glow of Easter egg–blue appeared in the fog. It turned out to be a glass orb, perched on a lamppost: the entrance to the station. In a row, they descended stairs that felt awfully spongy, almost as if they were carpeted. A clatter sounded from the depths, followed by a subterranean breeze that chased the lingering smoke from the staircase.

Belinda recoiled in disgust. "How perfectly awful."

"It's better than a jail cell," Hannah said, trying to sound brave. But as she pulled her hand away from the railing, she wasn't so sure.

The staircase was covered in fungus.

Stefan was waiting for them in the station.

"It's empty," he said.

Unless you count fungus, Hannah thought. Then its population probably numbered in the billions. The mossy parasite didn't just grow in the station; it *was* the station. The staircase had been impressively full of the stuff, but down here it had put down roots. Hannah felt like she was intruding upon a secret society. There was a faint buzzing in the air, as if the moldy sprouts were whispering.

There was nothing to indicate the station had ever been anything but a fungal cave. No ticket booth, no turnstile, and the platform that led to the tracks was just another soft bed of spores, with cauliflower-shaped growths popping up here and there like stunted trees.

Belinda closed her eyes and hummed softly to herself, a look of serene panic on her face. Nancy mashed the toe of her shoe into a sludgy growth.

Commotion from the concourse drifted down the stairs.

"They're gonna find us any second," Hannah said. Stefan was already moving across the platform, toward the tracks. A sound like the slurping kisses of an affectionate dog echoed out of the darkness.

"Train's coming," he said. "Help me get this out, quick!" He began tugging at one of the cauliflower growths, pulling it free except for a few stubborn roots. Without his jacket, Stefan's chest had a caved-in look. His sweater was at least a size too small. Nancy and Hannah grabbed hold of the stalk, which felt just like a fresh vegetable but smelled like rotting garbage.

"Ugh, what is this thing?" Hannah asked, leaning back on her heels and pulling with all her strength. It popped free and she staggered back. Neighboring spores cried out in a piercing whine.

Stefan beckoned and she gladly handed it over. "Our ticket," he said.

"Ha!" Nancy clapped with glee. "'Rotten cauliflower' means 'subway ticket'!"

Stefan looked questioningly at Hannah, who shrugged. "Muffin Language."

"Never, ever, *ever* trust a fungus," Belinda said weakly. She was leaning over the edge of the platform, staring into the depths of the tunnel, hugging herself as if she were cold. The tunnel was vaguely tube-shaped all the way around, and the mold that lined it had been rubbed smooth and shiny.

Hannah rushed to pull the old woman back before she could tumble onto the tracks. "I refuse," Belinda muttered. "I simply refuse."

The slurping had gotten louder. It was accompanied by a second noise, the clacking of a machine in motion. Hannah wanted to think of it as the sound of a train, but it was so muffled and unsure of itself. Weren't subway trains supposed to roar fiercely into stations? This was more like a shuffling. A gust of stale wind blew strands of hair from her ponytail.

"You wanna do the honors?" Stefan asked, handing the cauliflower back to Hannah.

She wrinkled her nose.

"If you're gonna be on the run, you'll have to get used to stuff like this," he said. "Now hold it out over the tracks."

Hannah took it gingerly by the stalk. There were footsteps behind them, coming down the stairs.

"Better hurry!" Stefan's eyes shone with reckless abandon as he urged her on, almost as if this were a dare.

"No," Belinda said. "No, no, no. There is simply no way I'm boarding this thing."

The platform began to tremble. The bed of fungus that coated the station became an echo chamber for the slurping of the train. Every spore and patch of mold seemed to be amplifying the sound and sending it straight into Hannah's ears.

She faltered.

"Steady as she goes," Stefan said. The train was a vaguely snub-nosed blur, like one of those high-speed monorails she'd seen online. It passed so close that it scraped the edge of the cauliflower, sending tiny pods scattering like dandelion seeds. Belinda took Nancy into her arms, and they huddled together as it screeched to a heaving, desperate halt.

Flakes of rust settled about the platform like snow.

The train was armored with a patchwork of rusted panels welded together and fastened with blackened nails. Here and there, leather straps crisscrossed at tarnished buckles, holding together a rickety system of pipes. Torn and shredded bits of fabric were stuck to the sides. There were no windows.

Beneath the armor, pinkish flesh squelched. A lump of jelly-like skin slithered out from beneath a lopsided panel and surrounded the cauliflower, drawing it in with a frantic gibbering. Hannah let go and the train ate the ticket in a flurry of ecstatic slurps.

In front of them, a curtain of dangling beads parted to reveal a white-washed door, stuck to the train at an odd angle. The door swung open and Hannah jumped aboard, followed by Stefan and Nancy.

"I'm sorry," Belinda said from the platform. "I can't."

Behind the old woman, a Watcher's face swarmed with fungal patterns as she crossed the platform. Hannah caught a glimpse of a sequined gown. Then the doorway beads came together around her arm, blocking her view.

"I can't do this without you," Hannah said.

She felt the papery skin of Belinda's hand and pulled the old woman in, just ahead of the closing door.

The train car was empty. The walls were lined with travel posters and advertisements that overlapped to keep excess flesh from burbling into the interior. Copper poles and triangular handholds descended from the ceiling. Pages of an abandoned newspaper, the *Dead City Herald*, were scattered along the floor.

The train picked up speed, clattering and slurping its way out of the station. Hannah and Stefan collapsed onto a stainless steel bench. Across the aisle, Belinda and Nancy parked themselves on a wooden seat with wrought-iron legs. Hannah's breath came in ragged gulps. It was some time before she was able to speak.

"I thought my head was about to explode back there," she said to Nancy. "Why couldn't you just sit still?"

"It's not like it used to be," Nancy said. "We don't exactly fit anymore." She shuddered. "It's a nightmare, actually."

Above Nancy's head, a poster implored passengers to VISIT SU-ANKYO — DISCOVER EXCLUSIVE DARKDAY SPECIALS. The words floated atop a glittering skyline of steel and glass towers. Hannah wondered how many different neighborhoods the train was hurtling beneath, how many billions of souls. She looked away from the advertisement. Wherever her mother was, she was just another face in a window, another pair of legs crossing a street.

"We did the best we could, Hannah," Belinda said. "But we couldn't stay hidden a second longer or we'd be . . . how can I explain this to you? *Strained.*"

"Yeah, strained," Nancy said. "You should say you're sorry for almost straining us to death."

"I'm not sorry — it was the only way we could escape."

"Then you know what? From now on, *Hannah* is Muffin for —"

"Girls, honestly," Belinda said wearily. She seemed to have recovered from her near collapse on the platform. Except for her lips, Hannah noticed, which were drawn and bloodless.

"I want to tell you a story," Belinda said. "Listen closely. Once upon a time there were two sisters. One good and one wicked." She thought for a moment. "They were *step*sisters, I believe. There was also a prince, and a faraway land, and some . . . adventures. And at the end, a lesson. The wicked sister learns to be less wicked and more like the good sister, or perhaps the good sister wasn't so good after all. Either way, the moral is universal, even though it's meant for one of the sisters in the story. It doesn't matter which one. The point is, you shouldn't be arguing, because I can't hear myself think. Okay." She slapped her palms against her thighs. "Storytime's over." She turned to Stefan. "When is the next stop, dear?"

He sighed. "Does it even matter?" His body seemed to crumple into itself. When he spoke, his eyes focused on something far away. "I really thought that was it. I thought the Guild had done it." He laughed bitterly and twirled a finger in the air. "Ascension, here we come. Instead, I went backward."

"I'm sorry," Hannah said quietly. "And thank you. For doing what you did. You don't have to come with us if you don't want to."

He turned to look at Hannah with cold eyes. "But I can't go home, can I? You were right — that wasn't our ticket to Ascension back there. They really *were* coming for you. And eventually the Guild will figure out that I'm the one who took you into the castle. I brought the Watchers down on us in a bad way and wrecked it for everybody."

Hannah didn't know what to say.

He continued, "I admit I spent most of my time hunting failure moths and keeping the upper class dorms clean and saying 'yes, sir; no, sir' to a meathead who likes to dress in a gorilla suit. But I'm a good painter — I know I am. It was only a matter of time before some professor or dean or art critic noticed. And the Guild was getting close, everybody said so. Glass and sculpture had nothing on us. We were gonna be first out of Nusle Kruselskaya and into Ascension. Now I'll have to start over someplace else." He closed his eyes and tilted his head back against the wall. "Maybe art's not the way. I don't know."

"I'm sorry," Hannah said again. She tried to imagine what it must feel like to have your personal goal dangled in front of your face and then snatched away. Stefan seemed more delicate and birdlike than ever, as if the slightest touch would shatter him. She let him be and turned her attention to the newspaper on the floor. The page beneath her feet said LORMAYR WOMAN ATTEMPTS KRESH RIVER SOLO SWIM.

Underneath the headline was a black-and-white picture of a woman in a swimsuit and goggles, snorkel clasped between her teeth. A harpoon gun was slung across her back, a fearsome knife strapped to her thigh. She held a pistol in her hand. Hannah wondered what sorts of things swam beneath the surface of the Kresh River. She reached down for a closer look, began gathering up some of the stray sections — and froze.

Kyle was staring up at her from the front page.

Chapter Twenty

The next thing Hannah knew, Stefan was gripping one of her arms and Nancy was holding the other. A pile of torn newsprint decorated her lap, and she was holding crumpled bits of Kyle's photograph in her clenched fists.

"I'm okay," she said, wriggling forcefully to free her hands.

"Take it easy," Stefan said, letting her go. Nancy did the same, and Hannah brushed the shredded bits onto the floor. Nancy removed the halves of the photo from her hands. Across the aisle, Belinda had salvaged a few whole pieces of the newspaper.

"It's *him*," Hannah said to Stefan.

He beckoned for Belinda's section of the paper. She handed it over. It was a full two-page spread beneath the screaming headline TERROR ALERT: FUGITIVE ON THE LOOSE. Blocks of text were broken up by a half-dozen pictures of Kyle. Even the grainy images couldn't hide his TV-star looks.

"I hate him already," Stefan said.

It was as if someone had created a little story out of photographs: Kyle's Trip to the Big City. There he was, crouched in the doorway of a villa, peering out of a window in a high-rise office, getting into a three-wheeled car. In all the photographs, the surroundings were a blur of movement and hustle and bustle. They were action shots, she realized — video stills from different neighborhoods.

The beginnings of a plan nibbled at her brain.

"Stefan," she said, "these are security camera pictures, right?"

"I don't know what you mean."

"I mean if the Watchers are trying to keep track of somebody's movements, they check in with their glass eyes around the city. Like security cameras at a store."

He studied the photographs, then turned to Hannah. "Sure, I guess that's what they've been doing to stay on your trail."

Hannah pictured the Watchers kicking back in front of a giant bank of TV screens, feet up on their desks, shoving popcorn into their scrambled faces. *That* was the side to be on when you were looking for someone.

"We need to see what they see. We could let the Watchers chase us around the city for a million noondays and never get any closer to finding my mother. But if we could figure out a way to hack into their system, then I bet we could narrow down the places she could be."

"*Hack* into their *system*?" Nancy laughed. "We don't know how to do stuff like that. It's probably a little bit harder than using the Internet at the library."

Hannah turned to Stefan, who shook his head.

"The Painters Guild is pretty traditional. We don't use computers. I'm not your guy for this kind of thing. Listen, Hannah, don't take this the wrong way, but it's a crazy idea."

"Crazy ideas are supposed to be *my* specialty," Nancy said.

Hannah scanned the travel posters above Belinda's head. Lormayr seemed like a nice place, full of limestone haciendas nestled among cypress groves. But she wasn't looking for tranquility. "There must be people in the city who know how to do it."

"Well, maybe," Stefan said. "But how are you going to find them? And even if you do, what are you going to say? 'Hello, we'd like you to hack us into the Watcher network'?"

"Being straightforward is often best," Belinda said.

Hannah pointed to the VISIT SU-ANKYO advertisement. "What about there?"

In the picture, monorails sped between glittering towers. The framework of the neighborhood was all right angles and beveled mirrors, adorned with bulbous pods, graceful curves, honeycombs of layered apartments. Hannah thought of New York, Tokyo, Shanghai — cities she'd only ever seen in pictures. Places of luxury, progress, technology.

"Su-Ankyo?" Stefan consulted a map of the subway line that ran all the way across the ceiling of the train car. Hannah watched his eyes travel the length of the map. "Better make yourselves comfortable."

"It does seem quite far," Belinda said. "Is anyone else craving a cup of decaf tea? Or coffee, if you prefer. I don't, personally, but that's neither here nor there."

"You're babbling again," Nancy said. Hannah gave her twin a significant look. Earlier, Belinda's attempt at a fairy tale had been an odd failure, and now she wanted a drink Hannah was sure she'd never tried in the first place. It was like she was doing an imitation of a grandmotherly old woman — as if that's how Belinda thought she should behave, without quite knowing how.

Stefan stretched, cracked his knuckles, and itched his belly. Hannah saw the bony outline of his ribs when he lifted his sweater.

"Are you coming with me?" Hannah asked.

"Nothing else to do," Stefan said. He closed his eyes and settled in. "Nice jacket, by the way."

"You can have it back if you want."

He opened one eye. "It looks better on you."

Huddled in the folds of the paint-spattered coat, Hannah let her gaze rest on a poster of a woman strolling hand in hand with a little girl down an avenue lined with chic storefronts and shop windows. Quickly, Hannah shut her eyes, trying to banish thoughts of mothers and daughters. But memories could be willful, disobedient things.

Weaving Season was Leanna Silver's name for early autumn, when the kids of Carbine Pass went shopping for notebooks and pens and new clothes. For Hannah and her mother, there was a trip of a different sort: a visit to Five Rivers Farm on the northern outskirts of town, where they would stock up on braided cornhusks, dried maize with pebble-hard kernels, and spools of surprisingly tough straw.

"What was I going to be called if I was a boy?" Hannah had asked in the pickup truck during last year's trip.

"Sylvester. Obviously."

"Sylvester Obviously Silver."

"I'm just kidding," her mother said. "You were going to be Boris."

They munched on cider donuts in the little café next to the gift shop. There were zero actual rivers at Five Rivers Farm, but there were plenty of sweets and snacks. The shelves were shaped like hollow trees; a sign said they stocked over a thousand kinds of saltwater taffy.

"More like fifty kinds," her mother always said. "Do they think we can't count?"

After they ate, her mother shopped for pumpkins and apples from the plywood bins outside the café, while Hannah lingered beneath the eaves of the farmhouse, waiting for the witch to come out onto the balcony.

The witch had a broomstick and a cauldron. The cauldron was filled to the brim with Jolly Ranchers and Smarties and hard pink gum that always tasted stale. Every fifteen minutes or so, the witch appeared on the balcony in full costume — pointy hat, black robe, warty mask — to toss handfuls of candy to anyone waiting below. Most kids were allowed one session before their parents snatched them away, but Hannah stayed as long as she wanted. This candy stash had to last her for months; it wasn't like she was allowed to go trick-or-treating in town. Plus, her favorite candy —

(On the subway car, Hannah realized with a start that she'd forgotten the name of the candy. It was a blank spot in her memory.)

— was the rarest. Sometimes you could go three rounds without seeing the famous *(Striped? Gold?)* wrappers cascading down with the rest of the witch's stash.

Eventually, she felt her mother's hand on her shoulder. "Okay, little lady, time to hit the road."

(Her mother didn't talk like that — did she?)

Back home, they performed their own autumn ritual: With mulled cider simmering on the stove, and corn hung on the front door like a holiday wreath, the weaving began.

(Did they work in the garage? No, Cliff House didn't even have a garage. Did it?)

Old craft books open on the table between them, they would start by braiding the straw into thicker, stronger ropes. When they were done, they would . . .

They would . . .

(It was as if a thick fog were rolling through the memory, leaving gaping holes in its wake.)

Hannah and her mother sat at a table. There was a book open

to a blank page. The walls of the room were undecorated. They were supposed to be doing something.

(Her mother's face was distressingly absent.)

They had just been to Carbine Pass. To a farm near the town. Where a witch gave her candy.

(That can't be right.)

They had gone shopping. Hannah and her mother. Shopping for back-to-school clothes.

(But she didn't go to school.)

What year was this memory from?

(Start over.)

The leaves on the trees were changing colors because it was autumn. What did Hannah and her mother always do in autumn?

(Nothing left but a single stray detail.)

A green, cackling face! There was a witch who tossed candy from a balcony above the parking lot of . . .

Of . . .

Five Rivers Farm!

(Hannah let out a breath.)

Her mother had taken her to buy supplies for their autumn ritual. Which was what, exactly?

She had absolutely no idea.

Chapter Twenty-One

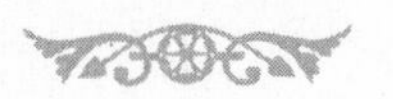

Hannah had grown so accustomed to the train's segmented walls and travel posters, the slats in the wooden bench and the polished swirls in the steel, that it was difficult to imagine her life before she had been a passenger on the dead city subway. The pitch of the train car's slurps, the clatter of its armor, had faded into familiar background noise.

Sometimes it felt as though the train were chugging up a steep hill; other times it tipped forward and hurtled down at freefall speed. Shaken, jostled, bumped, and spun, they rode on beneath the city. Other passengers got on and off, a polite and nondescript group of souls.

Hannah concentrated on holding her fragmenting memory together. She was terrified of slipping into the dull rhythm of the afterlife, like Stefan, who wasn't even sure that he used to be a gypsy. Hannah couldn't let her earthly existence become a forgotten dream. She tried to keep a vision of her mother at the forefront of her thoughts. But this vision was blurry and inconsistent, and only became harder to hold as the train spiraled on and on.

The city wants me to forget, she thought.

In the center of the car, Nancy swung around a copper pole, humming tunelessly. Belinda occupied herself with the newspaper. Hannah noticed a smudge of green paint on the side of her thumb and tried to wipe it away, only to realize that it wasn't paint at all.

It was a hairy patch of fungus, and it had taken root beneath her skin.

"Stefan!"

"Hrm," he grunted, without opening his eyes.

"Is this normal?" she demanded, holding out her thumb.

He winced at her voice, opened his eyes, and held up her hand for inspection. "Huh," he said, vaguely interested. "Does it hurt?"

"I don't think so."

"Does it or doesn't it?"

"I guess it's not painful, but . . . look at it!"

The splotch faded into her thumb and was gone. She recalled the toothpick-sized splinter from the attic in the mansion district. It had just been joined by a patch of Nusle Kruselskaya fungus. She had the disturbing thought that the city was imprinting itself beneath her skin, one neighborhood at a time.

"Huh," Stefan said again, releasing her hand. "Weird."

She massaged her thumb as if she were trying to squeeze the venom from a snakebite. At the same time, Stefan gave her face a quick appraisal.

"Forget your hand," he said. "We really need to touch up your disguise."

"Thank you!" Nancy blurted out with relief. "*Please* do something about that."

"A touch-up would be wonderful," Belinda chimed in. "We weren't going to say anything, Hannah dear, but you do look somewhat . . . worse for wear, at present."

Horrified, Hannah probed her face, which now seemed much less real than it had in the castle, full of cracks and wrinkles.

"How bad is it?" she asked.

"Not quite zombie bad," Nancy said. "But getting there."

"It is a bit grotesque," Belinda admitted.

"The thing is" — Stefan reached into the cargo pocket of his baggy pants and produced a small paintbrush folded in half at a hinge — "I only have this minibrush on me, and I used the last of my paint back at the concourse. And you can't just go into a shop anywhere in the city and buy Guild paint. We make it ourselves, in the castle." He laughed to himself. "Anybody know where I can get a supply of Foundation?"

"The makeup counter," Nancy offered. "Next to the lipstick and blush."

"Not that," Stefan said. "Foundation with a capital *F*. Think of it like . . ." He fished for a word. "Modeling clay. Except back up and imagine the stuff they use to make the clay. The raw material. That's Foundation. Everything in the whole city is made of it — buildings, cars, roads, our paint, the glassworkers' glass" — he rapped his knuckles against the metal bench — "the insides of train cars. It can *be* all sorts of things, if you know how to cook with it and mold it. Honestly, mixing paint from Foundation is a whole other skill that's way beyond me. So even if we could somehow get our hands on some, I wouldn't even know what to do with it. Well . . ." He squinted, thinking to himself. "There are a few things I'd like to try, but . . ."

"How do we get it?" Hannah asked.

"You don't. Watchers deliver shipments to neighborhoods, and then everybody argues about the best way to use it, and somewhere down the line our Guild president gets a cut, and the castle can mix new paint. It's like that in all the districts. And everybody's Foundation use is measured to make sure they aren't making deals on the side and getting more than their share."

"Is that what the meter guy does?" Nancy asked, sliding down the metal bench to sit on the other side of Stefan. "We saw him reading dials on the roof, right after we escaped."

Hannah recalled the alphabet translating itself, forming the word *Foundation*.

"Yeah." Stefan grimaced. "Nobody likes the meter men."

"I think I can help." Hannah reached into her pocket and found the tube of paint and the brush. She showed them to Stefan. "I stole this from your room."

His eyes widened.

Suddenly, the train lurched noisily to a halt. The map indicated it was the second-to-last station stop before the end of the line. The door opened. A tarnished silver fist parted the beads, and an entire suit of armor followed.

Stefan muttered a curse and jabbed Hannah with his elbow. *"Retainers,"* he whispered. "Everybody sit still and be quiet."

She looked at him quizzically. "What about my face?"

"Later." His voice was low and anxious. "Try not to look them in the eyes."

It was nearly impossible not to stare as three medieval warriors shifted their great bulk from the platform to the train. The first knight's face was hidden by a helm shaped like the sweeper on the front of an old-fashioned locomotive. His plumed red crest bristled against the ceiling. A broadsword was slung across his back.

The second knight was a bit more practically dressed, with chain mail peeking out from beneath a leather tunic emblazoned with a yellow cross. His face, shadowed by a half helm, was weathered and crosshatched with scars. A short sword with a ruby hilt was sheathed at his side.

The last man through the door was a massive brute. Islands of coarse hair tufted from his bare arms and shoulders. He rested the spiky iron head of his mace gently on the wooden bench, which creaked in protest.

The three men stood together, shifting their immense weight to avoid falling as the train left the station.

Nancy fidgeted, clearly getting ready to unleash some kind of sarcastic greeting. Stefan leaned forward and shook his head, as if to tell her, *Don't even think about it.* Since he wouldn't explain why he was so scared — the knights hadn't paid them the slightest bit of attention — Hannah consulted the handbook. She flipped to the *R* section and found the entry.

RETAINERS: SOULS WHO CHOOSE TO MAINTAIN A GRIP ON THEIR EARTHLY LIVES INCLUDING, BUT NOT LIMITED TO: FAMILY, TRIBAL STRUCTURES, SOCIETAL CUSTOMS, RELIGIOUS RITUALS, ART, POLITICS, CULTURE, MANNERS OF SPEECH, DRESS, AND BEHAVIOR.

EXTREME RETAINERS ARE CHARACTERIZED BY AN UTTER DEVOTION TO THEIR FORMER LIFESTYLE. THOUSANDS OF SOCIETIES THROUGHOUT THE CITY HAVE PRESERVED THEMSELVES TO A REMARKABLE DEGREE. (SEE APPENDIX 347B FOR A LIST OF KNOWN NEIGHBORHOODS.) EXTREME RETAINERS MAY BE OPENLY HOSTILE TOWARD CITIZENS WHO HAVE OPTED NOT TO RETAIN. SAFETY TIP: WHEN IN DOUBT, AVOID CONTACT WITH EXTREME RETAINERS. WHILE THE TEMPTATION TO ENGAGE WITH LIVING HISTORY MIGHT BE OVERWHELMING, REMEMBER THAT THE CITY OF THE DEAD IS NOT YOUR PERSONAL MUSEUM!

SINCE THE NATURAL ORDER OF THE AFTERLIFE INVOLVES LETTING EARTHLY EXISTENCE FALL AWAY LIKE SO MUCH DEAD SKIN, RETAINERS MUST UNDERGO REGULAR SESSIONS WITH A MEMORY KEEPER (SEE PAGE 546) IN ORDER TO RETAIN THEIR MEMORIES.

WARNING: MANY OF THESE TREATMENTS ARE UNAUTHORIZED AND UNSANCTIONED BY THE DEPARTMENT FOR RETAINER AFFAIRS. WHEN VISITING A MEMORY KEEPER, ALWAYS VERIFY CREDENTIALS BEFORE UNDERGOING ANY PROCEDURE. (FOR AN EXHAUSTIVE LIST OF SIDE EFFECTS, REFER TO HANDBOOK MEDICAL COMPANION PACKET 67.)

While Hannah was reading, the margins were being scrawled in by some unseen hand.

BIASED ARTICLE NEEDS TO BE COMPLETELY REWRITTEN. AUTHOR'S PREJUDICE AGAINST RETAINERS PRACTICALLY DRIPS OFF THE PAGE. RECOMMEND —

"DEMON!"

The angry cry tore her attention from the handbook. The largest of the three men was directing his companions' attention to a spot on the floor at the back of the car. He was pointing so urgently that the veins in his biceps popped up like squiggly blue ropes.

Hannah almost burst out laughing. That hulking warrior was scared of a shadow! The first knight pulled his broadsword from its scabbard. Next to her, she felt Stefan's body tense.

What had been a dark spot beneath a stray flap of paneling unshadowed into Charlemagne.

"That's not a demon, sir," Stefan said, jumping off the bench and holding out his empty palms to show that he was no threat. "That's a friend of mine."

The man in the leather tunic gripped his sword by its hilt and turned to Stefan. Hannah wondered what happened when you got run through by a blade in the afterlife. Stefan was holding his ground, staring down the knight. His hands were trembling.

"He means you no harm," Stefan spoke slowly and deliberately. "Let's all just calm down."

Hannah watched helplessly as the third man began to swing his mace, a deadly pendulum getting faster with each revolution.

Charlemagne launched himself into the air toward the knights. A misty spray of paint landed in an arc across the chest of the man with the mace. His roar of displeasure rattled the posters in their frames. Charlemagne scrambled up the wall before the man could spin his body around.

Nancy and Belinda sprang from the wooden bench as the mace reduced it to splinters. Before she realized what she was doing, Hannah had the cap off the tube of paint.

Charlemagne flashed from the wall in a glimmer of city lights — he had taken refuge in one of the advertisements. The first knight was having trouble with his huge broadsword inside the confines of the train. The man with the short sword had better luck. Knees bent slightly, one arm out for balance, the other brandishing the weapon, he turned slowly, carefully, hunting the paint-lizard. Stefan backed up to join Hannah. Belinda and Nancy were just behind them.

The first knight clanked into the center of the car. He seemed very practiced in standing around menacingly, and did so now, placing Hannah's group under guard while his companions hunted down the demon. Behind him, the two fighters were poking about the train as if they were looking for a particularly fearsome set of lost keys.

"Were you in the Crusades, good sir?" Belinda asked.

"Shut up, Belinda!" Nancy said. "Who cares?"

"I'm appealing to the chivalry of an honorable knight," she replied. Then she raised her voice. "Did you happen to know King Richard personally?"

The great hunk of armor didn't move, as if it were just an empty suit in a display case. Then, all at once, the breastplate and helm began to rattle excitedly. The knight's silver finger pointed at Hannah's legs. She felt Charlemagne squelch between her shoes.

A deafening war cry came from the other end of the car. A ham-sized fist shoved the knight aside. The warrior's arm was a weapon-swinging engine, and in his bloodlust he was going to cleave them all in half.

Hannah squeezed the tube of paint, coating the brush in a huge glob. The mace seemed to slow as her eyes followed it around and around. She could pick out individual spikes. Behind her, Nancy and Belinda were trapped with their backs against the wall.

Charlemagne flung himself into the woodpile where the bench used to be, leaving a blotchy stain on a jagged plank. The warrior shifted his weight, transferring the energy of his spinning weapon into a vicious downward strike. The wood exploded into shrapnel. The mace embedded itself in the floor of the train.

Hannah splatted the paintbrush into the center of an advertisement for indoor pools (MAKE EVERY DAY A LIGHTDAY). The splotch of paint was a bright yellow stain covering a kidney-shaped hot tub. She held the brush aloft and lunged across the car to the opposite wall as if she were closing a long shower curtain. In her mind, the curtain was an impenetrable shield. She hoped that was how it worked: You thought of something you wanted, and just sort of painted it in the air.

"No, that's too much! What are you doing?!" Stefan's voice was hysterical, shrill.

Her line in the air was a vine growing sideways, blossoming with citrus cloudbursts that changed color at incredible speeds, as if there were infinite hues buried within the paint. Distantly, Hannah was aware that the subway train was agitated, its slurps rising in pitch, becoming frantic.

The train car bucked like a mechanical horse and sent her sprawling. She felt an acute stab of pain in her elbow, and then she was upside down, tangled in Stefan's arms, looking up at a lattice of expanding colors and shadows. There was a piercing whine as the train slammed on its brakes.

"Get back!" Stefan dragged her into the narrowest part of the train's nose. The broadsword came slashing through the paint. Nancy moved to cover Belinda as the short sword began to hack toward their heads.

The train came to a stop and began whipping itself from side to side. Metal panels fell to the floor. Nails and bolts rained down; Hannah felt them pelt her back through the army jacket.

"I'm really sorry!" she yelled, hoping the creature would understand. As its armor plating sloughed away, its slurps were amplified. Gelatinous flesh oozed and rippled.

Stefan was on his knees with Hannah's brush in one hand and his miniature travel brush in the other. Lost in a citrusy fog, the knight's weapons appeared here and there, striking out blindly. Using deft strokes, Stefan sketched the color-blossoms into solid shapes. Cement bricks began to appear. The mace lost itself in the almost-wall with a thick splat. The short sword poked through a half-solid brick, its steel awash in paint. Stefan parried with his brush, trapping the blade. The entombed weapons poked out in sculpted protrusions.

With the retainers disarmed, the train calmed down. It began to take one contented, sleepy breath after another. Hannah scrambled to her feet and pulled Nancy and Belinda up with her.

"The paint won't hold these maniacs back for long," Stefan said, turning to Hannah. His sweater was a constellation of tropical colors. Muffled cries came from the other side of the wall. A vaguely melon-shaped brick began to wiggle. Paint flecked off, revealing silver spikes.

Quickly, Hannah parted the beads and opened the door. The train had halted inside a cavern where two tracks ran side by side.

"No more fungus," Hannah said to Belinda, helping her down to the ground.

"No more anything," Nancy said. It was as if they'd gone off the rails in the desolate outskirts of the undercity, where even the fungus had decided it was too dull to live.

Stefan left the door ajar behind him. The light from the train's interior was the only thing helping them see.

"That paint didn't do what I wanted it to do," Hannah said as their footsteps crunched gravel.

"Everybody thinks they can be an artist, like it's *so easy*," Stefan said.

Hannah's fingers felt along her jaw line. How much of the boy-face was left? How much paint had she wasted?

The light from the train faded. They trudged uphill, single file. Hannah echoed Stefan's half-whispered calls for Charlemagne. The darkness closed in. It wasn't until Charlemagne came bolting up from behind them that Hannah realized how close they were to an exit. The paint-lizard skimmed along the rocks, leaving a pink slug-trail, and tumbled out the open air.

Chapter Twenty-Two

Emerging, they traded the darkness of the tunnel for the darkness of the sky.

Belinda sniffled. "Chilly now, isn't it?"

"Darkdays can get cold," Stefan said. "Want my jacket?"

"Thank you, young man. I'll be fine. I'm just delighted to be out of that awful train."

"Do *you* want your jacket?" Hannah asked Stefan. "I feel like I've been wearing it for a month."

"Nah," he said. "Early darkdays are the best. Makes me want to paint a pile of leaves and jump in it."

The mouth of the cave was set into a ridge that overlooked a neighborhood of limestone dwellings. Spotlights shone down from high above the streets. As Hannah's eyes adjusted, the source of the lights came into focus: A flotilla of hornet-like ships infested the sky. Their abdomens were coated in metallic fuzz that glimmered wetly, as if they had been rolled in iron shavings. One ship floated nearby, eerily still. A spotlight blinked on at the end of its long snout. Its undercarriage glowed with the embers of a fiery engine.

Her eyes picked out a light and followed it to the far end of the neighborhood, where a pyramid rose to a point above the hornets. Jutting out from the front of the pyramid was a two-headed beast, stone paws crossed in front. One head was human — the other, a hawk.

"That's a sphinx," Belinda said. "Sort of."

Right, Hannah thought. *Sort of.* She was looking out across *sort-of* ancient Egypt. All the elements were there, but it was as if they had been put into a blender, scrambled up, and spit back out as a strange imitation.

"Cool," Nancy said. "See you later."

Hannah couldn't believe it when Nancy started picking her way down a trail between rocks and low shrubbery.

"You're being difficult," Belinda called after her. "And it's very unpleasant."

Hannah skidded down the trail, caught up with her twin, and grabbed her arm. "Hey, what's wrong with you? We gotta go —"

"What, find your mother?" Nancy pulled away. "Well, guess what? I can barely remember her. I wanna see pyramids and mummies and stuff."

"Listen to me." Hannah lowered her voice. She hesitated — saying the words out loud would make it real. "I'm having a hard time remembering, too, and it's getting worse. Don't let me forget who I am, okay?"

Nancy was taken aback. She leaned against a trailside boulder, thinking, her spiky hair frosty in the glow of an approaching snout-light.

Stefan and Belinda hurried over and crouched alongside the big rock. "Get down!" Stefan hissed. Hannah and Nancy ducked as the cone of light passed over them and swept up the ridge. Charlemagne glopped nervously about the hem of the army jacket. A humid breath descended from the hornet ship, sliding across her forehead, which prickled in a sudden sweat.

Watchers.

All Hannah could do was huddle in the deepening shadow of the boulder and wait for the aircraft to turn its attention back to the neighborhood. Instead, the cone of light widened — it was dropping altitude, coming in for a closer look. The hum of its engine was a low foghorn in stereo. Just as she was about to suggest making a run for it, the snout-light vanished and the foghorn receded. Charlemagne slunk out from the jacket, a slurry of dirt and paint, and curled himself around Stefan's wrist. Hannah rose, cautiously, to look over the top of the boulder.

"Gone," she said. The darkday sky closed in with a cool breeze that swept away the humidity.

Nancy elbowed Stefan's arm. "You didn't tell us about those."

"I've never seen them before," he said. "I'm not usually on the run with the dead city's most wanted."

"That would be Kyle, the banished one," Hannah said.

"*Second*-most wanted, then."

A voice came down from the top of the ridge, a barrage of frustrated curses, startlingly close. Instinctively, they ducked.

"That's no Watcher," Stefan said after a moment. "Come on."

They made their way up the trail, Charlemagne riding on Stefan's shoulders. A pencil-thin beam of light danced just ahead of them and went out.

"Stupid piece of junk!" growled the voice, accompanied by the sound of a fist striking plastic. The light blinked on again, illuminating a thicket of Foundation meters, a night-forest of gauges and dials. The voice belonged to a meter man.

Hannah glanced down at the city below. The houses, the pyramid, even the hornets — Foundation was the core material for everything, a substance that could become steel, cotton, glass, paint. It was hard not to think of it as magic, but perhaps it wasn't much different than back home, where things were composed of atoms and molecules and cells.

The meter man began to sing in a theatrical baritone, drawing out every syllable. One lyric, over and over again: *I hate my job!* His voice faded as he moved away from them, slapping his clipboard against the metal posts. Hannah led Stefan, Belinda, and Nancy through the thicket, past meters that rose at odd angles like abandoned scarecrows. Once they crested the ridge, ancient Egypt seemed like a distant memory.

Spreading out before them was the travel poster on a grand scale.

The towers of Su-Ankyo delivered a million blinking lights straight up into the sky, giving the darkness a creased and folded glow that reminded Hannah of solar systems and dying stars. Glass-sided office buildings reflected a carnival of floating advertisements. First Hannah thought the ads were being cast from blimps, then she noticed they were being projected from shadowy machines that crawled up and down the buildings like leeches. Monorails hummed above traffic-clogged streets. The headlamps of motorbikes and scooters lit the spaces between stalled cars.

Hannah's spirits were lifted by the magnificent skyline, and she practically sprinted down into the jittery glow.

"Hey, zombie face," Nancy said, "you might want to put up your hood."

The army jacket, it turned out, had a thin canvas hood rolled up inside a zippered pouch at the back of the collar.

"I need a touch-up — a hood's not going to work forever."

"Makeup, aisle three," Nancy droned.

"Nothing lasts forever," Stefan said, "no matter how great of an artist I am."

"Maybe the glass eyes can't see as well in the dark," Hannah said hopefully, glancing up and down the alley at the outskirts of Su-Ankyo, where they were huddled around a pile of empty television boxes. Out on the street, savory aromas mingled with pungent odors from steel-sided lunch carts.

"Smells like hot dogs," Nancy said.

In this neighborhood, people seemed to like their food and drink, even though souls in the city of the dead didn't require nourishment. Su-Ankyo thrived on the business of it all. Holographic signs blazed with martini glasses and dinner specials. Greasy fast-food bags swirled in the darkday breeze and collected, fluttering, against hydrants and curbs.

"Frankfurters!" Belinda said. "Of course. I was just trying to figure that out."

Nancy snickered. *"Frankfurters."*

Hannah kept seeing a cat out of the corner of her eye — a cat just made sense in this alley — but it was only Charlemagne, his body flecked with glinting headlights.

Stefan beckoned impatiently toward Hannah's pocket. "Give me all the paint you have left."

She reached into her pocket and handed over the tube.

Car doors slammed at the end of the alley. Lively chatter flooded Hannah with impressions of other lives. *That's why you were such a fabulous dentist,* somebody said.

Hannah thrust her face toward Stefan. "Okay, I'm ready."

"For what?"

She looked down at the top of a box, where Stefan was already putting the finishing touches on a fat mongoose with big friendly eyes and a goofy smile. He turned it over, fully solid in his hands, and painted fur on its whitish underbelly. Next to the mongoose, the tube of paint curled, empty and used-up.

"What a charming little trinket," Belinda said.

"That's what you did with the last of our paint?" Hannah said, astonished.

"*My* paint," Stefan reminded her. "Just keep your hood up, okay? This is more important. Take it."

"More important than my disguise."

"Nothing's free, Hannah. You need a computer; you'll have to pay."

Charlemagne bounded onto the box, puddling eagerly. Stefan squeezed the last of the paint off the end of the brush. Hannah put up her hood, pulling the drawstring tight. Then she snatched the mongoose and headed out into the street.

"Welcome to Jester's Computer Café and So Much More."

The teenage boy behind the desk spoke in a bored monotone. A tri-cornered hat flopped over his face, weighed down by silver bells. His eyes were hidden behind a scraggly curtain of dyed green hair. He licked his chapped lips. "How may I help you today?"

Hannah glanced at the name tag pinned to his frilly tunic.

"Hi, Kevin. I need to use SoulLink."

Hannah had discovered the term in her handbook, which was becoming even more jumbled and confusing in its argument with itself.

Kevin nodded once, bells jingling. Hannah tried to keep her own face hidden in the shadow of the hood, but she knew that Kevin must be able to see part of it. If her appearance freaked him out, he was doing a good job of hiding it.

"I would be happy to assist you with that." His voice cracked. "Have you had a chance to look over some of our additional services?"

He jingled his head to the side to let her see the screen attached to the wall behind him. Text scrolled up like the credits at the end of a movie.

Documents Notarized
Weapons Sharpened
Prophecies Verified
Antiques Appraised
Vision Examined
Essays Critiqued

"I just need a computer," Hannah said.

"If you don't see a special service that interests you, for a small fee we would be happy to find the best local establishment to fulfill your needs. And it's not on the screen yet, but we also sell fine silk vests and cortex implants."

"Just the computer," Hannah said. "And I also have one question."

Kevin looked nervous. "I'm supposed to collect the fee before adding on any special services."

"Answering questions is a special service?"

"I can't answer that until you pay."

She reached into her pocket, hoping Stefan knew what he was

doing. Feeling like an idiot, she plunked down the mongoose. Even in the low light of the orbs that floated about the café, Hannah could tell it was a Guild specialty: a painting of a mongoose hiding a genuine mongoose, or the other way around.

"Dude! No way." Kevin leaned in close, finally brushing a clump of green hair from his eyes. Hesitantly, he reached for the mongoose, barely touching it with a fingertip, as if he were afraid to damage such a priceless artifact. His voice had become an excited stammer. "Did you — I mean — all the way from Nusle Kruselskaya, right? This is — I mean . . ." He shook his head.

Hannah tried her best to pretend like there were more where that came from. "So my question is, are there any glass eyes in this place?"

"Glass eyes, glass eyes" — Kevin bit his lip, thinking — "I don't think we have any in stock at the moment, but I'd be happy to order one for you." He squinted at her face. "Or two, if you need both."

"No," Hannah said. "Like, Watcher eyes. Spying eyes. For people's Ascensions."

His face blanked. Then he grinned. "Oh! I forgot you're not from around here. We got *these* in Su-Ankyo."

He placed his arm on the counter and lifted the sleeve of his tunic. Implanted in the skin of his wrist was a microchip. Tiny LED lights illuminated his veins. His arm throbbed and twitched with electrical impulses.

Hannah grimaced. "I guess I'll just go sit down."

Kevin dropped his sleeve and went back to his examination of the mongoose. "Sure." He waved his hand without looking up. "Anywhere you want."

Most of the terminals were taken, so Hannah had to settle for a machine that wasn't plugged in. A quick survey confirmed that none of the computers even had power cords. And yet, there were dozens of souls here, typing merrily away. She punched a key. The screen brightened to reveal the online SoulLink edition of the *Dead City Herald*.

Kyle was still front-page news. The headline was TERRORISTS OCCUPY JARETSAI STATION. She clicked his picture away. She told herself that Kyle and his banished friends were free to occupy all the dead city stations they wanted, and pick fights with the Watchers from now until the end of time. She was here to get her mother and take her home. After this was over, she'd never see Kyle again, and the Watchers would sort him out. It wasn't her business. Besides, even if she was capable of getting revenge, what could she do to Kyle that the Watchers couldn't do a million times worse? She thought of him stuck in a windowless cell, smiled, and set to work.

At first she sat in front of the search screen, thinking. She had to find a really talented hacker without tipping off the Watchers, in case they were monitoring computer searches. That meant she probably couldn't visit some geeky chat room and talk to anybody directly.

She surfed around in circles, getting frustrated, her fingers jabbing angrily into the keyboard. At the terminals beside her, souls came and went. Kevin's costume jingled. Video games competed to be the café's background noise: monstrous growls and scatter-gun fire and the roar of digital crowds.

It wasn't until Hannah had spent a long time scanning a message board called Hidden Su-Ankyo that she found something interesting: a series of posts by someone calling herself the Lady of the Lake. Hannah was fully absorbed in her reading when she noticed a slight tickle in her thumb.

With a shriek she pulled her hand from the keyboard, but it was too late. The space bar had melted into her thumb. She could see the white plastic beneath her skin, drifting down into her arm. A moment later it was fully absorbed, her flesh stitched together as if nothing had happened. She tried to stay calm, glancing around to see if anyone was watching. Thankfully, most other patrons were leaning close to their screens, slack-jawed and unaware.

Disturbed, Hannah quickly printed the Lady of the Lake's message board posts. She stopped by the desk to collect her pages on the way out and noticed that the screen had a new addition:

Darkday Exclusive
One-of-a-Kind Mongoose Painting
Certified Nusle Kruselskaya Craftsmanship!

Chapter Twenty-Three

It didn't take very long to find the lake. Finding the lady was another matter.

"Read those pages one more time," Stefan said. Hannah shuffled her printouts back to the beginning. In bustling Su-Ankyo, it was bright enough to read during a darkday without even straining your eyes.

They were at the eastern edge of a city park ringed by a monorail, which hummed above their heads at precise intervals. Highways split the park into four sections and met, via bridges, in the center of a perfectly round lake. Thin sheets of water cascaded from the bridges, reflecting the lights of the city in glitchy patterns.

Hannah peered into the water. A digitized version of herself stared back, as if she'd been animated for a video game. Still, she could see that the boy-mask had mostly fallen away.

"This place gives me the creeps," Nancy said.

In a nearby tent, souls huddled over laptops and musical instruments made of jellyfish with helmets. Scratchy beats skittered from speakers arranged along the shore — holographic statues of men and women who opened and closed their mouths to change the sounds.

"Here we go," Hannah said. "The first post from the Lady of the Lake: 'The one true Ascension is borne of neither art nor politics nor special talents.'"

"Old news," Stefan said. "There are different ways to Ascend. There's no one *right* way."

"Post two," Hannah continued. "This is the one that got my attention: 'If those who hold the keys to our Ascension turn their eyes on us, should we not be turning our eyes on them?'"

"Bleep blop," Nancy said, doing a jerky robotic dance as the music abruptly picked up its tempo.

Hannah ignored her. "Post three: 'Our knowledge of the city and its residents must equal those who hold the keys. Only then will we be granted our Ascension.' Post four: 'In images and maps and charts and graphs we will forge our salvation. We will see the city as they see it.' Post five, the last one: 'We welcome all who would join us, but there is a price — give us something precious we have never seen before. Expand our knowledge. Deliver your gift to the edge of the water. If it pleases us, you will know.'"

"Look, Hannah," Stefan said, "this is a dead end. We used up the last of our paint. I can't make anything else until I get more."

Nancy sat down cross-legged in the grass. "Weren't you supposed to be finding somebody to help us?"

Hannah crumpled the pages in her fist and snapped at her. "I'm thinking, okay?"

Low tones from the mouths of the statues rumbled her belly. Car horns and revving engines and shouts of frustrated drivers rattled her brain. The whole neighborhood seemed to teeter on the verge of a complete breakdown, and yet somehow it all kept going while a million lights blinked on and off. Distracted, she didn't even notice Belinda wandering away, down the shore, until she was almost out of sight.

"Hey, where are you going?" Nancy called out.

"I seem to be the only one with any sense!" Belinda said as she disappeared behind the shimmering, half-formed statue of a tall man in a white robe.

"If she gets lost here, we'll never find her," Hannah said.

Nancy scrambled up, and together with Stefan they searched the shoreline until they found Belinda presenting herself to the statue of a woman in a sleek gray business suit. The statue's eyes were closed. Belinda was talking to it.

"I tried to be a wise old woman, but it didn't work. I don't know what I am, or where I come from. But I am surely something that the Lady of the Lake has never seen before." She knelt before the statue. "On behalf of Hannah Silver," Belinda said, "I offer myself to help expand your knowledge."

"How does she know that's the Lady of the Lake?" Nancy asked.

“She always knows things I don’t know,” Hannah said. She tugged on the old woman’s arm. “Belinda, don’t do this.” Hannah was thinking about Albert, and how he disappeared after calling up the storm that freed her from the cell. The memories he had taken with him, the holes in her thoughts.

“Hannah, I want you to promise me something,” the old woman said.

The statue’s eyes snapped open. Solid white eyeballs began scanning Belinda.

“Get away from there!” Hannah pulled harder on Belinda’s arm, but the old woman was rooted to the grass.

As the statue’s eyes moved down Belinda’s face, they turned her skin to pixels. “Hannah,” said the old woman’s digitized mouth. “I want you to promise me that you’ll —”

— Fold your clothes before you throw them in your dresser. Honestly, you’re too old to be so careless.

Hannah sat on her bed, surrounded by piles of clean laundry. Her mother had washed and dried; Hannah’s task was to fold. Instead, she had been tossing her shirts across the room, trying to land them in the middle dresser drawer, which she’d opened all the way so that it tilted slightly downward.

Hannah knew that Belinda was going to badger her relentlessly. She savored the creaking and settling of Cliff House, the smell of clean linen, the rag dolls on the wallpaper doing chores of their own. She picked up a flannel shirt and walked it to her closet, where she hung it on a hanger.

"Please don't leave me," Hannah said. Street noise and throbbing music washed over her. On the edge of the lake, Belinda was half-dissolved by the statue's scanning eyes. Only her legs appeared solid and real. Stefan was hugging Nancy; she'd buried her face in his sweater. Charlemagne oozed in an oily smear where the water met the grass.

"It doesn't hurt," Belinda assured her. "It's actually quite wonderful to be of some use. I'm sorry to have been so fussy all the time, but it really is important for you to —"

— *Match your socks! Unless you want to go rummaging around every morning to find their mates. Seems silly to me.*

Hannah took the rolled-up mess of socks and spread it out on the floor of her room. She matched sporty white socks and thick winter knits. Once, she had hated Belinda for making her do this. It had all seemed like pointless extra work. But now she wanted to cling to her bedpost, claw her nails into the cracks in the floorboards — anything to remain in her bedroom at Cliff House.

On the shore of the lake, Belinda was a mere projection of herself, swarming with digital noise. Hannah's fingers passed through the old woman's transparent arm. With a twitchy expression of contentment, Belinda smiled.

"And for the last time, don't forget to —"

— *Set aside anything that looks especially wrinkled to iron before you put it away.*

With her socks matched and her clothes folded, Hannah was left with a small pile of wrinkly shirts. It was actually nice to have everything neatly put away. As irritating as Belinda could be, she was probably right about folding clothes. Hannah looked around her room, taking inventory, hoarding little images like a squirrel storing nuts for the winter.

The lamp on her dresser with the ceramic merry-go-round at its base.

The beat-up old armchair in the corner, piled high with books.

The alcove with its window looking out onto the lighthouse.

It felt like someone else's life. She took hold of a pair of socks and held them to her face.

The tearing-away was sharp and quick.

Cliff House was gone.

The statue's eyes were closed, its head bowed once again. Belinda had vanished. Nancy's voice was muffled by Stefan's sweater. "Is it over?"

"I think so," he said.

Nancy stood up straight and blinked. She looked at Hannah as if she didn't recognize her. Hannah wondered what she was feeling — when they had arrived in the city, Nancy had been one of three. Now she was one of one.

Stefan was inspecting the grass where Belinda had been. In a movie, Hannah thought, Belinda's shoes would be stuck to the ground, wreathed in smoke. But there was nothing to indicate that Belinda had ever existed at all. For that matter, *had* she existed at all? Even Belinda had seemed unsure. Hannah supposed it would be difficult to suddenly appear when you were already an old woman. She addressed the statue.

"Okay, Lady of the Lake, or whatever you are. Do something."

In her pocket, the argument raging within the handbook grew heated. When she pulled it out, the book tried to shake her off, practically flinging itself to the ground. She gripped the cover tightly and wrenched it open to a page that said, in huge block letters, CLOSE ME!

What a worthless thing, she thought, jamming it down into her pocket, which she buttoned shut.

Hannah glanced at the statue, silent and still. Then she turned to Nancy. "Maybe we should say a few words, or something."

"Go ahead," Nancy said miserably.

"Belinda was . . ." The monorail picked that moment to drown her out with the thrum of its high-speed burn. Cars inched along the highways. Engines belched; horns blared. The city went about its business of being a city. Already, the smell of clean socks, the softness of freshly laundered flannel, were distant, vague things. "She was . . ."

The lake rippled. Hannah took a step back from the waterline. Green phosphorescent bits scattered like frightened minnows as the tip of a fin sluiced through the dark water. The rest of the fin revealed itself as it approached the shore, and Hannah could see hints of something big surfacing. It was headed straight for her. She took another step back and bumped into the supposed Lady of the Lake. Digital fuzz danced around her.

The surfacing creature's bulk glimmered darkly as it thrust itself out of the lake to rest its head on the grass. It was a sleek and polished fish with scales of brushed, blackened steel. Like everything in Su-Ankyo, the fish looked expensive. It even gave off a faint whiff of new-car smell.

"We're all out of cauliflower!" Nancy screamed at it. "Go home!"

Hannah was more frightened of the attention they were attracting than the fish itself. There must have been thousands of bored commuters sitting in traffic, looking out their windows at the remarkable sight at the edge of the lake. The fish opened its jaws. Lips peeled back horribly to reveal a mouth full of glass — flat and vertical, like the wall of ivory that whales had in place of teeth.

There's a special name for that thing, Hannah thought. *Belinda would know.*

"It probably can't follow us on land, right?" Stefan said.

"If you're going to be on the run," Hannah reminded him, "you'll have to get used to stuff like this."

There was a smooth mechanical whirring sound. The glass wall lifted like a garage door. The fish was inviting them into its sparkling interior.

"I think this is our ride," Hannah said, gathering her courage and stepping up onto the fish's spongy lower lip.

"Chalkdust," Nancy said. "Good thing Belinda's not here to see this."

Chapter Twenty-Four

Compared to the subway train, the fish was a five-star hotel. Just inside the glass, a row of plush leather armchairs offered a panoramic underwater view. Lamps built into the richly paneled walls cast a buttery glow, while decorations were sparse but tasteful. There were no advertisements. This was very much a fish intended for selective, private use. The only sound was a low throbbing rhythm, which Hannah figured must be some kind of engine.

"Hey, you gotta come check this out," Nancy said. Hannah was glad to have an excuse to leave her armchair. The endless, sightless void of the lake was creepy. And it seemed to be bottomless — the fish had been diving steadily for some time. She left Stefan to enjoy the murky view with Charlemagne, who blobbed on a footrest.

At the back of the hushed room was a door. Nancy paused. "You ready for this?"

"Open it," Hannah said.

On the other side of the door was a dining-room table placed beneath a crystal chandelier. The table's centerpiece was a pewter tray piled high with pear-shaped fruit. The skin of each one twinkled like a streaky mirror.

"Is that supposed to be for us?" Hannah asked, noting that the engine was louder in here.

"They taste kind of like rye bread."

"You *ate* one?"

Nancy giggled. "Calm down — who else could they be for? There's nobody else here. Try one."

Hannah leaned in for a closer look. She imagined a tiny mirrored seed sprouting stems of glass, growing reflective skins. "It's probably not the best idea to eat random stuff we find."

"It's not *random*," Nancy said. "I wanted to show you because that fruit is officially the first thing I've eaten since I became the way I am now. Out here" — she indicated the room — "instead of in there." She pointed to Hannah's head. "It's the first thing I've ever tasted that wasn't something *you* wanted to eat."

"Oh." Hannah didn't know what to say. Nancy seemed to want some kind of congratulations. "So how was it?"

"Delicious," she said, a little too forcefully.

Hannah sensed that her twin was talking about something other than food. "What do you want to do, Nancy? Do you want to run away and live your life, or whatever it is that you have?" Hannah made a shooing motion with her hands. "I release you. Go."

"Ugghhh!" Nancy clenched her fists at her sides. "Nineteen! Thirty-eight! Four thousand sixty-two!"

"Salamander, what are you doing?"

She stalked past Hannah. "You really have no idea what I'm going through."

"Then tell me!" Hannah said. Nancy stopped in the doorway.

"I don't want to end up like Belinda and Albert," she said. "I've been thinking about it. Where do we go when we vanish like that? I mean, you have Ascension to look forward to, eventually. But what's next for somebody like me? Where are Belinda and Albert right now? Are they just . . . gone?" She looked straight at Hannah. "I want to stay. But I don't want to end up as a great big nothing, helping you find somebody you can't even remember." She turned her back. "No offense." Then she left the room.

Hannah picked up a fruit. It reflected her face like a funhouse mirror, made it look squished. She would have to describe her mother for Nancy, paint a portrait with words. Like Stefan's artwork it would have to be both layered and real. *Better* than real. She had to prove to Nancy — and herself — that she could regain control over her memories. Then Nancy would understand why this was all worth it. Hannah sniffed the fruit, then tossed it back on the tray. Her heart was pounding.

Remember.

Whistling her mother's favorite tune seemed like a nice way to begin — a musical road to the past. But what was that song called? Hannah concentrated hard, tensing her muscles, then tried to relax. Memories should be free and easy things. For a while, she drifted. And drew a blank.

Moving on.

Start with the way she looks.

She closed her eyes. A woman's face appeared in her mind. The edges were hazy, but Hannah felt like she was off to a good start. The face had a warty nose. A pointy hat appeared. Her mother must have dressed as a witch for Halloween. All Hannah had to do was picture her mother without the mask. But the witch just cackled and disappeared, replaced by a lighthouse on a lonely cliff. Hannah thought the lighthouse might belong to her family.

Zoom in.

A storm made it difficult to see. There was something on the ground, a gray lump on the path. She forced herself to zoom in even more. That was her mother, crumpled in her nightgown! This had happened, this was *real.* A sweeping surge of relief cut through her terror. She hadn't forgotten what had happened to her mother, how could she ever forget that? Now there was just the simple matter of putting her mother's face back into her mind so she could transfer that image to Nancy. She reached out and turned her mother over, gently . . .

. . . and screamed. The woman in the nightgown had no face, just a smooth, featureless expanse where the face should be.

Hannah opened her eyes and collapsed into a stiff-backed chair. There she sat, waiting for the face to fill itself in, for the person her mother had been to come back to her. After a while she found herself staring at her reflection in the pile of fruit, multiplied like a bug's eye: two dozen Hannahs, all of them crying.

"Prince of Knuckles!" Stefan said, triumphantly slapping a playing card down on the arm of his chair. They had discovered a standard deck of seventy-three octagons in a drawer, and Stefan was teaching Nancy to play a few dead city games.

Nancy smirked, placing a card to either side of Stefan's. "Pincer attack!"

"The Scabby Twins again? Cheater."

He swept the cards away with mock anger, and they plunked against the glass wall. Hannah was curled silently in her chair, staring into the depths, which hadn't changed much since they'd begun their descent. When the first hints of the shipwreck appeared, they were dreamy shapes that barely registered. But soon there was no mistaking the hull of a freighter, half-buried in lake-sludge, lit by a starry field of lights that flickered like underwater fireflies. Nancy and Stefan abandoned their game. No one spoke as the fish glided over the wreckage. It was as if they were passing through a graveyard.

"There's another one," Hannah whispered, as if a raised voice would somehow wake the ship.

Beyond the freighter, a massive schooner had settled into the bottom of the lake at an angle that left its bow pointing haughtily upward. Layers of wreckage rolled into view as more lights twinkled on. When the entire scene finally came into focus, every corner of the viewing glass was filled with dead ships. There was the flat deck of an aircraft carrier, the rusted tube of a submarine jammed straight down into the lake bed, the skeletal rigging of a once-proud sailboat. Forests of seaweed shivered like prairie grass.

The engine of the fish began throbbing faster.

"Something's coming," Stefan whispered.

Hannah felt the presence before she saw it; a change in the current, a great unseen thing looming — and then a transport fish identical to their own pulled ahead of them, so close she could have touched it if not for the glass. Gracefully, the second fish circled around the nose of a ruined yacht and headed straight for a giant steamship that had come to rest on its side.

"It's going to hit that boat!" Nancy said.

"I don't know," Hannah said. "I think it's going there on purpose."

The fish aimed straight for one of the steamer's massive smokestacks and swam into the opening at the top. Its fishtail wriggled as it forced itself halfway inside, then stopped, plugging the hole.

"I'm really not a lake person," Stefan said as their own fish navigated an alley of boats glued together with sludge and barnacles, angling toward the neighboring smokestack. Here, Hannah caught glimpses of a hidden world behind the portholes and windows of the wreckage. This graveyard had been colonized, and the colony was drawing them in.

The mouth of the smokestack was a black hole, dead ahead. The engine thumped fiercely — it wasn't an engine at all, Hannah realized, but a heartbeat. The fish was excited to be home. Its armored scales scraped against the inside of the smokestack with a piercing shriek, and they were plunged into darkness.

Chapter Twenty-Five

*The fish docked, wedged in tightly. Its heartbeat slowed to a con-*tented pace.

Gradually, the darkness lifted. Hannah stared into a hallway filled from top to bottom with lake water. In front of her, an albino stingray attached itself to the glass with dozens of suckers and began to pulsate. It looked like it wanted to get in. Charlemagne waddled happily up the glass to meet it.

"Look who made a friend," Nancy said, peering over the back of her armchair.

A sudden noise like the grinding of gears gave Hannah a start. Wiry tentacles with crystal tips emerged from the walls of the smokestack and wavered like long pieces of seaweed in the water.

The transport fish's mouth slid open. Hannah braced herself for a torrent of lake water. Instead, the tips of the tentacles flared, and with an electric hum the water surged backward, churning frothily. The crystals flared again and the water behaved as if it had been scolded, carving out a pocket of air that began in front of the fish's mouth and raced down the length of the smokestack.

A final flare-up and the water halted, forming walls that quivered like gelatin. Minnows leapt through the empty air from one side of the hallway to the other.

"I should *not* have eaten that fruit," Nancy said, rubbing her eyes.

"It's okay, I see it, too," Hannah said. She stuck her hand into the space carved out by the retreating water. The air was cool and clammy.

Stefan gave a dismissive snort. "Am I supposed to be impressed? In the Painters Guild there's this old lady, Hilda, who does way crazier things with watercolors."

Hannah stepped out of the transport fish's mouth. The floor beneath her was a flat, condensed surface of water. Her toes sank in, but it held her weight. She turned back to find Nancy and Stefan standing in the mouth, watching her.

She said, "What were you saying about Hilda?"

Nancy took Stefan's hand and together they joined Hannah. Charlemagne made himself into a hockey puck and careened from one side of the hall to the other, shedding globs of paint that misted away.

Stefan took hesitant steps. "Think about all that water above us," he said.

Up ahead was a round steel door with a wheel for a handle, like a bank vault. Hannah wondered if it was locked. What would happen if the walls suddenly collapsed on them? When they were near the end of the hall, the wheel spun and the door opened.

A man and a woman stepped forward to meet them, smiling cheerfully.

The man wore a uniform the same color as Stefan's army jacket. On his head was a helmet in the shape of a bowler hat with a very thin brim. His face was acne-scarred, with the scratchy hint of a mustache. Next to him was a tall woman in a radiant sari and beaded leather sandals. A single jewel was set into the middle of her forehead. They were both wearing wristwatches with square faces the size of credit cards.

"Throckmorton's my name," said the man. "This wondrous dewdrop to my left is Urvashi."

The woman gave a slight bow. "I am perfectly capable of introducing myself, delightful sunflower."

"Apologies, tea cake."

"All is forgiven."

"Now, then!" Throckmorton said, looking from Hannah to Nancy to Stefan. "Which one of you is responsible for this marvelous gift?" He tapped his wristwatch and a grainy projection of Belinda appeared right in front of Hannah.

Startled, Nancy jumped. Hannah waved her hand in front of the projection's face. Belinda stood completely still. There was nothing behind her eyes. It was just a lifeless hologram.

"What did you do to her?" Hannah asked, voice cracking with the sudden hope that Belinda might not be completely gone. "Where is she?"

Throckmorton looked puzzled. "We had assumed she would be with you, after you sent us down that little preview." He glanced at Urvashi. "Didn't we, melon ball?"

Urvashi nodded. "We did indeed, my finely aged cheddar."

"So you don't have her," Hannah said, dejected.

"It appears that none of us do," Urvashi said. "Unfortunately, the price of your admission was that peculiar gift. So before we send you back to the surface, may I ask what, exactly, she was? Our scans had not detected a soul like her before, someone who appeared to never have been human at all." She raised an eyebrow at Throckmorton. "Please correct me if I have any of this wrong, sugarplum."

"You are, as always, very much on the mark, turtledove."

"Please," Hannah said. "We've come a long way. I have these" — she pulled the Hidden Su-Ankyo message board postings from her pocket — "from the Lady of the Lake. I need your help to see what the Watchers see, like the Lady says. It's important."

"I am truly sorry, dear," Urvashi said. "But we simply cannot allow it."

"Rules are rules," Throckmorton said. "The way is shut to those who cannot pay the entrance fee."

Nancy splashed her foot into the floor. "We rode all the way down here in your stupid fish and now you won't even let us in?" Her voice had a hysterical edge. "Here's what I think of the Lady of the Lake!" She kicked water in Throckmorton's direction.

There was a blur of movement from behind Urvashi and a third person appeared in their midst, a few steps in front of Nancy: a girl with long black hair wearing a collarless one-piece tunic. Poised perfectly still in a low stance, she brandished a sword with both hands on the grip, elbow out to the side. With an expressionless gaze she shifted her eyes from Nancy to Hannah.

"Eri," Throckmorton said. "It's all right. Please stand down. You are no doubt frightening our visitors."

"They are not our visitors until you invite them across the threshold, Sergeant Throckmorton," Eri pointed out in a quiet, reasonable voice.

Urvashi sighed. "That is true, Eri, and we appreciate your vigilance. But I think this conversation will be easier for everyone if your sword is put away."

In one graceful motion Eri straightened her posture and slid her sword into a scabbard on her back — *SHNK!* — so that the hilt poked up over her shoulder. Then she took a position beside the door.

"What is it with you people?" Stefan said. "The Guild doesn't treat people like this."

"I am truly sorry we couldn't do business," Throckmorton said with a regretful smile. "You will of course be transported back up to the surface in the same manner." He bowed crisply. "Good darkday to you all." He took Urvashi's elbow. "Shall we, rice pudding?"

She turned to the door. "Lead on, my tangy vinaigrette."

"Wait!" Nancy said. "I have something to say. I'm just like the old woman. I mean, we come from the same place."

With a look of interest, Throckmorton waited for an explanation.

"Nancy!" Hannah said sharply. "Stop." She gave the soldier an apologetic shrug and said, "She doesn't know what she's talking about."

Nancy continued, undaunted. "You can study me, or whatever it is you want to do. But on one condition."

Throckmorton raised an eyebrow. "I'm listening."

"It's time to go." Hannah reached for her twin, but Nancy sidestepped.

"Like Hannah said, we need to see what the Watchers see. We're looking for somebody."

Throckmorton consulted Urvashi. "Opinion on this matter, sunset?"

"I say we give them a chance, meadow lark."

"You two are gross," Stefan said.

"Nancy," Hannah whispered. "You don't have to do this. What if you —"

"I can do what I want," Nancy said firmly. "And this is it."

Hannah sighed. "Then I have a condition, too, Mr. Throckmorton. You don't get to keep her stashed away in some lab. We all stick together."

Urvashi smiled. "Of course, love."

"It's actually okay if me and Hannah aren't together all the time," Nancy added quickly. "Whatever works best for you."

"In that case, welcome to the Dead City Surveillance Institute!" Throckmorton beckoned for everyone to follow him through the vault door. Hannah heard the *SHNK* of Eri's sword being unsheathed, and glanced at the girl just in time to see her thrust the blade through the wall of water and pull it back in one impossibly fast strike.

On the tip of the sword was a sightless fish, speared and wriggling.

Chapter Twenty-Six

The Institute was unlike anything Hannah could have imagined when she first saw the skyline of Su-Ankyo in the subway poster — which seemed like a lifetime ago. How strange that each new neighborhood felt like the shedding of an old skin in favor of a new one. Maybe that's why souls like Stefan (and billions of others) were content to let the past slip away. Why bother holding on to an old life when the city offered a new beginning every couple of blocks?

"A worthy question, Hannah Silver," Eri said. Hannah winced.

Nancy had been led away for tests. Throckmorton had assigned Eri to show Hannah and Stefan the facility, or at least the parts they would be allowed to use. The girl was clearly a retainer of the strangest sort: knowledgeable about all kinds of bizarre Institute technology, but also formal in speech and traditional in manner. She had an unsettling way of staring right through Hannah, as if she were contemplating both her face and the back of her head simultaneously.

Hannah wondered if Eri had actually been a warrior in her time on earth, or if it was something she'd picked up in the afterlife. Did they used to give weapons training to teenage girls in feudal Japan? She pondered this as she followed Eri through corridors lined with thick bundles of multicolored wires. Crystals sparkled, embedded among the bundles. Souls bustled about, vaguely irritated, carrying armfuls of crystal-tipped tentacles or jars full of mush that sparked and fizzed. It was a bit like moving through a honeycomb of stressed-out bees.

She gave Stefan a nudge. "What do you think of this place?"

He just grunted, keeping his eyes down. Being around the hums and buzzes of circuitry made him skittish.

"Are you taking us to the computers?" Hannah asked.

"We do not use computers," Eri said.

"Are you telling me that we came all this way for nothing?" Stefan asked angrily. Charlemagne, wrapped around his neck like a scarf, dripped lazily down the front of his sweater, matching the stripes.

"I do not know what you came here for."

"I'm — we're — looking for my mother," Hannah said.

"You may find her. Or you may not."

"Thanks for the vote of confidence," Stefan said. "What do you people even do here?"

Hannah thought she heard a tiny sigh escape Eri's lips. Without warning, the girl stopped at a desk where a man in a safari hat was hunched over a thick book. As if it recognized the presence of a relative, the handbook in Hannah's pocket trembled. She stilled it with a hand.

"I require the use of this desk," Eri informed the man, who looked up from his reading with irritation and lifted the brim of his hat.

"It's occupied," he said.

Eri tapped a quick pattern into the face of her wristwatch. Her head erupted into flames. Hannah and Stefan jumped back. It took Hannah a moment to realize that the flames were actually radiant bursts of light, and at each light's core was a tiny glowing object swooping in a complex orbit. Hannah could make out a sparrow, tree, sword, pony, and teapot. It was like watching a weaponized charm bracelet spring into action.

The man at the desk took a slow, resigned breath and tapped his own wristwatch. Instantly, his hat was alive with bouncy, excited sprites of his own: binoculars, telescope, beetle, lobster, coffee mug.

Eri closed her eyes and her charms attacked, breaking their orbit and homing in on the man's hat like tiny guided missiles. Each item found a target: Her pony kicked his telescope, while his lobster snapped its claws at her tree. The sprites flitted and spun and battled. All at once there was a sound like shattered glass, and the man cried out in frustration as his telescope vanished, followed by his coffee mug. Eri's victorious items did a quick synchronized victory dance, then blinked away.

"I was just getting up anyway," grumbled the man, taking his book and stomping down the hall.

"Can I get a watch like that?" Hannah asked.

Eri ignored her and slapped the sightless fish she'd caught down on the desk. With a stubby knife that appeared in her hand, she sliced open the fish with a single assured stroke. Its marbly, goopy innards spilled out.

"Oh, come on," Stefan said, turning away.

"This is how the members of the Institute will Ascend," Eri explained.

"By slicing open a fish?" Hannah asked.

"The fish is the city in this demonstration." Eri began flaying it with expert strokes, flicking her knife under the scales. "Our work is to lay the city bare. To expose its every part. To look, to listen, to record, until we have examined each block and street and house and skyscraper and castle and citizen down to every . . ." She lopped off the fish's head. "Last . . ." Carved out the eyes. "Raw . . ." Separated its fins. "Nerve."

Hannah was convinced she could see a precise logic in the destruction of the fish, as if its guts were highways and rivers.

Eri continued, "Some seek to make the city beautiful through art, or perform gymnastics between its high-rises, or simply exist as they always have." With a *swish,* she used the flat of the blade to sweep the gutted fish into a wastebasket alongside the desk. "But the Institute seeks the purest truth. That is the key to Ascension: a map of the entire city, just as it is."

Hannah expected Stefan to mutter something like, *It doesn't take much talent to make a map.* But he was looking away from the greasy smear on the desk, staring at a squiggly cable that ran along the ceiling.

"A place like this must need a whole lot of Foundation to keep things running," he said.

"More than some," Eri answered. The knife vanished up her sleeve. "Less than others."

She moved noiselessly on down the hall. Hannah shot Stefan a look to ask, *What was that about?* He shrugged, tight-lipped. Behind them, the wastebasket rattled, vaporizing the fish guts in a puff of smoke.

The cavernous map room was full of echoes: machinery clanking into place, technicians chatting, the faint whine of the ever-changing 3-D display. The chamber was ringed by a perimeter of user pods shaped like clamshells. Hannah's pod was outfitted with all manner of lenses, gadgets, speakers, and dashboards that jutted out all over, swallowing her up in a crooked mouth of titanium and plastic. Chalkboards and notepads hung about her head, scribbled with mathematical formulas. Every time she shifted her weight, trying to get comfortable, a new piece of equipment poked her in the spine or bashed against her elbow. The speakers emitted a low but constant chatter, as Institute mapmakers gave and received orders.

— Klonjutsk neighborhood is edging into the upper garden district of Frydz, propose resurveying.

— Anybody scoping the Kresh River, over by Duquoj? That lady's doing the backstroke!

Hannah poked around for a dial to turn down the disembodied voices.

"Do not touch anything," Eri said from the clamshell to her right, without even looking at Hannah. She was typing on her wristwatch while her sprites were scrambling about the clamshell, busying themselves with buttons and knobs. Eventually, five crystal-tipped tendrils dropped from the ceiling of the shell. Eri's tree settled upon one, infusing it with a cheery glow. The other sprites followed, and in a few seconds all five of Eri's crystals were pulsating with the energy of the tiny charms.

"When do we get those?" Hannah asked.

Puddled at the edge of the map, Charlemagne swirled like a tie-dyed shirt, trying to lap up bits of information as it flooded past, his tongues getting zapped and scrambled for his trouble. Hannah could barely watch — the map was incomprehensible, gibberish code, a behind-the-scenes glimpse into an arrangement of letters and numbers and symbols flinging themselves about the room with wild, dizzying abandon. How this was supposed to represent the dead city, Hannah wasn't sure.

"Your demon will behave," Eri said to Stefan, who was seated in the clamshell to her right. "Or I will remove it."

"Why does everybody think poor old Charlemagne is a demon? All the little guy wants to do is eat."

Hannah watched as the paint-lizard successfully slurped a string of code. His fluid skin crackled as he buzzed with newfound energy.

“This is the map room,” Eri said. “There are rules.”

“Okay, okay. Here, boy!” Stefan called, and Charlemagne launched himself up into Stefan’s clamshell.

Dozens of new and excited voices came bursting through Hannah’s speaker. Next to her, Eri joined the chorus: “Acknowledged. I’m pulling it up right now. Yes. Jaretsai Station. Over.”

Hannah tried to remember where she’d heard that name before. Her heart began to race, and she had the sudden destructive urge to kick one of the lenses free of the clamshell, just to hear it shatter.

“I have to scope something,” Eri said as her sprites began to dance in their crystals. “Institute business. I will take you with me as your orientation to the map. I suggest you hold on.”

“To what?” Stefan said.

Handlebars rose from the sides of Hannah’s seat. As if she were at the eye doctor’s office, lenses dropped in front of her face. She gripped the bars and braced herself for a plunge.

The pods didn’t move, but the map did.

At the sound of a single chime, the voices in her speaker fell silent. Bits of information changed course, flowing across her clamshell like water over smooth stones. Sleek and aerodynamic, the pod accepted the flood of data. Hannah found herself surrounded by threads of letters and numbers that smeared together into a backlit fog. A soothing, programmed voice came through her speaker, announcing a destination: "Druftilliger Crossing."

Elegantly, like swans gliding atop water and coming in for a landing, the blur surrounding the clamshell condensed into shapes. Fuzzy lines and blocks of color sharpened, and a neighborhood materialized. Druftilliger Crossing was a district of neat brownstones and motor carriages that sputtered along, belching smoke. Eri piloted smoothly around a corner, beneath the branches of a stately elm. Hannah heard giddy laughter, and a moment later realized that *she* was the one laughing. It had been a while. Zooming around the map made her feel light and free. She had completely forgotten that life — and the afterlife — was sprinkled with moments of pure, effortless joy. She waved at a man in a top hat and a monocle as he stepped out of a carriage.

"They cannot see you," Eri said. "We do not exist for them."

"It's like we're Watchers," Stefan said, his voice hushed and awestruck. Hannah would never mention this to Stefan, but in its own way, the Institute's map was just as beautiful as the artwork of the Painters Guild.

The map had to draw and redraw itself constantly. This effort produced a sound like a mosquito flying into Hannah's ear. Eri steered beneath a concrete overpass, where they stopped short with a halting *thump* that rattled the map to its core. For a split second, the gibberish code reappeared, and streets and buildings were reduced to skeletons of data. Hannah blinked and the city came rushing back.

They cruised alongside the mighty Kresh River, through a swampy tree-house district, past miles of huts on stilts. Foundation meters were buried in the marsh, their dials rising above the surface like lazy crocodiles. Meter men waded along, clipboards wrapped in plastic bags.

The voice of the map identified the neighborhood: "Hud-Faroja."

Hannah was exhilarated. She felt like she had closed the distance between herself and her mother just by gaining access to the Institute.

The scene glitched. Eri rocketed them down a deep dark well, and there was a sickening shudder as the map redrew itself.

Stefan moaned. "I think I'm gonna puke."

They threaded a logjam of glass walkways that connected minarets with an aerial garden, where a young couple was strolling hand in hand. The man stooped to pick a sunflower and then vanished as Eri took a hard left and halted abruptly in the shadow of what had once been a magnificent transit hub.

The speaker crackled. "Jaretsai Station."

Hannah gasped. *Watchers!*

Snout-lights from hornet aircraft played along the building's facade; it looked as if the entire armada from the Egyptian neighborhood had surrounded the station. Hannah knew that she was safe in the map room, completely hidden from the hornets, but even their virtual presence made her blood run cold.

"Zooming in," Eri said. They shot past stalled traffic that choked the roads around Jaretsai. Above the cars and carriages and bikes, locomotives sat motionless on elevated tracks. Passengers peeked out from their cabins, craning their necks to witness the spectacle.

As Eri took them in for a closer look, Hannah realized what all the commotion was about: The station was decaying before her eyes. It was like witnessing the decomposition of a great stone beast. In the light from the hornet ships, every little crack was visible. Hannah watched as the cracks widened, sending avalanches of brick dust crumbling down. Iron windowpanes rusted, showing a century of water damage in a few seconds. The proud arches of the main entrance sagged, as if the pillars were getting tired.

"What's happening to this place?" Hannah asked. A few of the hornets had landed. Watchers streamed out, their faces made grim and shadowy by the darkday sky.

"The Watchers are at war with a group of rebels." Eri's voice was flat and neutral, as if she were explaining the rules of a boring game.

Something about the word *rebels* made Hannah's mind begin to churn. "So this is a battle?"

"You are witnessing the aftermath," Eri said. "The rebels have fashioned weapons of rot and wither. Soon they will make their escape from the station, the Watchers will hunt them, and it will happen all over again. We have been tracking their movements — they are skilled at evading capture."

Eri's words nibbled at her brain. Hannah could sense an important connection buried in her past, but it eluded her. She struggled with the logic of it. How could she possibly be involved in the destruction of Jaretsai Station?

Eri kept zooming in. Hannah watched as weather-beaten gargoyles curled their wings about their bodies and went to sleep. A sense of resignation hung in the air, as if the station had simply given up on being useful and was now quite content to be a gutted old building.

The word *rebels* reminded Hannah of another word: *banished*. But what did that have to do with her?

"Hannah." Stefan was trying to get her attention. "Hannah!"

"Sorry," she said. "I spaced out. What is it?"

"It's *him*."

Eri had enlarged the map so that they were nearly pressed against the side of the building. A boy peered out of a broken window. His face was familiar — Hannah wondered if she'd seen him in a movie. He was certainly good-looking enough to be an actor. Was he one of the rebels? She felt her hands go numb, and loosened her white-knuckled grip on the handlebars. Why was she suddenly dizzy with rage?

"Do you know him?" Eri asked.

Hannah opened her mouth, but couldn't find the right words. Did she?

"Yeah," Stefan said, incredulously. "She does. His name is Kyle, and he killed her mother."

"At the lighthouse," Hannah blurted out. Impressions came to her, snatches of conversation. *He killed my mother.* She watched Kyle as he turned away from the window to yell at someone. She was fairly sure that she hated him, so it must be true. His face appeared in a different window, where he was joined by a man with a bushy beard. The man wore a necklace, from which dangled a single yellow guitar pick.

I've seen that guy before, too, Hannah thought. *But where?*

"Session paused," Eri said.

Jaretsai Station and the hornets became sketches outlined in strings of raw data. In a moment, the outline reverted to a vague smear. Still, the withering station was burned into Hannah's mind.

Eri turned slightly in her clamshell so that she was facing Hannah. "It would have been helpful to know about your memory gaps before logging in to the map."

"My memory is fine," she lied.

"This boy, Kyle, was responsible for the death of your mother, and yet without Stefan Weisz to remind you, it seems to me that you would not have recognized him."

"Well . . ." Hannah couldn't think of an explanation for this. "I'm here for my mother and that's it. So how do we find her?"

"*Please* tell me we don't have to do any more flying around," Stefan said. Hannah glanced over at him. His hair was a mess; his eyes were bloodshot.

"There are one hundred seventy billion souls in the city," Eri said to Hannah.

"Okay, so thanks for the orientation. What's the first step?"

Eri stared at her for what felt like a very long time. Finally, she asked, "What is your mother's name?"

Hannah shifted uncomfortably. "It's . . . the last name is Silver . . ." She closed her eyes. Names drifted up out of the haze — Diana? Lottie? — but none of them sounded right. "I just . . . I'm having a little trouble, lately. . . ." She took a deep breath. "Can we start with something else?"

But not much else was peeking out of the murk of her past. Nothing was real except for things that had taken place in the city of the dead. Everything before she arrived in the attic was lost in a dense fog.

"Slinky," she said at last. Eri just kept staring at her. The clamshell felt like it was shrinking. Her limbs were tangled in the equipment. *I have to get out of here.* Gingerly, she wriggled free and hopped down to the floor. Stefan joined her. Charlemagne, abuzz with pixels, followed.

"You okay?" Stefan asked.

She nodded and tried to sound casual. "I just need a break."

"A *break*? Hannah, trust me, your past doesn't come back. It just gets further away."

Tears welled up and Hannah gave in. She let her vision blur. Stefan's mouth opened. He reached out to her, hesitantly, before pulling his hand back.

"I've been losing it for a while now," Hannah admitted. "But there was always something to hold on to." She wiped her eyes. "Now I can't remember what she looks like. I can't remember who she is."

"Hey, what'd I miss?"

Hannah turned to find her twin in the octagonal doorway of the map room. Nancy took a huge piece of gum from her mouth, wadded it up, and stuck it on a sign that said PLEASE LOG OUT. "They told me you guys were in here."

"We're just taking a break," Stefan said.

"It's okay," Hannah said. "I already told her about it."

"What, your memories?" Nancy shrugged. "Mine are pretty much gone now, too."

Hannah's heart sank. The thread that bound them together had unraveled. What reason did Nancy or Stefan — or Eri — have to keep helping her now? She thrust her hands into her pockets, felt the pages of the stupid handbook.

Eri joined them near the door. "As I was saying, you should have been honest with me about your problem."

The girl's monotone voice, her unblinking stare, her whole matter-of-factness — all these things got on Hannah's last nerve. Without thinking, she flung the handbook at Eri. The book sailed through the air, pages fluttering.

SHNK.

Neatly sliced, the two halves of the handbook hit the floor, pounced on each other immediately, and rolled away like wrestling dogs in a spray of ink and torn paper.

"Because," Eri said, sheathing her sword, "I know someone who can help you remember."

Chapter Twenty-Seven

Hannah's bare feet splashed in the water that pooled at the base of her chair. She had pulled up her leg warmer and cuffed her jeans so they wouldn't get wet. The water covered the entire floor of the Memory Keeper's office, a spacious room furnished with nothing but a single chair and a small round café table, upon which rested a polished metal bowl. Three of the walls were bare, but the one directly across from Hannah was studded with crystals.

Throckmorton and Urvashi waded about, busying themselves with strange preparations. Urvashi lifted the hem of her sari to keep it dry. Throckmorton sloshed through the water in heavy combat boots.

"Do you guys have a leak somewhere?" Hannah asked. She raised a foot and examined her toenails, trying to remember the last time she'd clipped them. She could not, of course.

Urvashi jabbed a finger into her wristwatch. "Have you heard anything about a leak, garlic knot?"

"All sectors are sealed up tight, fish stick." Throckmorton adjusted one of the wall crystals, polishing it with his sleeve.

Hannah plopped her foot back down. "So why is there water all over the floor?"

"All in good time, Hannah," Throckmorton said. "I *do* hope this experience is as rewarding for you as it is for Eri."

"I recall Eri's first visit," Urvashi said. "There was a moment afterward when I actually caught the hint of a smile on her face. Do you remember that, sunrise?"

"Ha, ha!" Throckmorton's hearty laugh bounced around the room. "I do indeed, owl feather."

All at once, Throckmorton's sprites wiggled out from beneath his helmet, while Urvashi's rose from her shoulders. Hannah watched as a cannon and a lamp found the crystals in the wall. Soon each one was blazing with color.

Throckmorton splashed to the door behind her chair. "See you quite soon, Hannah."

Urvashi patted Hannah's shoulder. "Good luck, dear."

The door opened and closed with a resounding boom, followed by the sound of another bank-vault wheel being turned, locking her in. She wished that Nancy and Stefan were allowed to be here, but Eri had explained that the Memory Keeper only worked with one person at a time — privately.

The crystals slid out of the wall and dropped into the water. Concerned about getting electrocuted, Hannah tried to lift her feet but found them stuck to the floor. She could wiggle her toes, but that was it. The water around her ankles had formed the same kind of gelatinous skin that she'd seen at the entrance to the Institute.

"Hey!" she screamed. "Let me go!"

The water began to burble and sploosh around the crystals, as if someone had just turned on the Jacuzzi jets. Bubbles and froth tickled her legs. A stream of white-capped spray shot up from the floor in a graceful arc and landed in the bowl, which quickly overflowed. Water pooled on the table and ran off the sides.

Hannah squirmed in her chair. "Is this supposed to happen?"

A thin jet of water spurted from the bowl to hit her square in the forehead. She felt a gentle pressure and considered moving out of the way, but something compelled her to stay put.

"If you saw a cat in a tree and a hamster in a mailbox, which would you save first?" asked the bowl of water, with the rude voice of a man in a hurry.

Instead of finding this deeply disturbing, Hannah felt a burning desire to engage in conversation. "Why would there be a hamster in a mailbox?"

"You've recently caught a classmate cheating on a math test. This particular classmate is the son of your father's boss. It was his cat in the tree. Do you tell a teacher what you saw, or keep it to yourself?"

"Why does it matter if it was his cat?"

"The brakes on your mother's car have failed. Up ahead there's a fork in the road. The left path leads to a bridge under construction, the right leads to a mailbox factory. What do you name the hamster once you've rescued it?"

"Petunia J. Cuddles."

"That's a nice name," agreed the bowl of water. "Not as nice as Hannah Silver, but it'll do. Now. I understand we aren't beginning a major campaign of remembrance here, just a little nudge in the right direction."

"It's my mother — I know I'm supposed to be looking for her, but I can't remember anything about her."

The bowl of water sighed. "I've seen this before. The city'll do that. Gimme a second." The Jacuzzi jets gurgled, cranked up, and turned the whole floor into fizzy waves. Hannah felt a second jet of water hit the back of her head at the base of her skull.

"Uh-huh," said the bowl on the table, muttering to itself. "Yep. There we go, a little boost, easy does it. . . ."

Tolliver's Old-Fashioned Cherry Licorice Bites!

Hannah almost cried out when the name of her favorite candy popped into her head. She could picture it, too: The wrapper was yellow and waxy, and the logo was licorice blossoming like a flower. The witch at Five Rivers Farm tossed them down sparingly — even among treats, they were treats — so Hannah's mother would always let her stay to get as many as she wanted.

In her mind, Weaving Season sprang to life. The taste of hot apple cider was on her lips, the deep sweetness of the nutmeg that made her jaw tingle. Homemade autumn decorations — little straw dolls — peeked out from kitchen cabinets and sat on shelves in the Tree Room. All at once she was cocooned in memories of autumn at Cliff House — crunchy leaves that blanketed the driveway, smoke from the woodstove curling up out of the chimney — and she could barely feel the jets of water against her head.

"How's that, kid?" the bowl asked. "Better?"

"Mmm," she mumbled happily, eyes in a half-lidded stupor.

"Try this on for size."

The water misted into a spray that wreathed her entire body. Seasons changed: There was the lopsided snowman she'd made, with its frozen celery nose. Then it was spring cleaning time in the dusty upper rooms, and Hannah was matching sneezes with her mother, flipping her mop upside down to snatch a spiderweb from a corner of the ceiling. Then she was in sandals and a bathing suit, climbing down to the Widow's Watch to let the ocean breeze chase away the summer heat.

"Now we're cookin' with gas, eh?" the bowl yelled triumphantly.

Memories went off like fireworks. It was almost too much, like being stuck inside a candle shop where your sense of smell felt a million times more powerful. (She remembered WickMasters in Carbine Pass, which also sold gourmet mustard at the counter.) The bowl was babbling on excitedly.

With a jolt, she recalled her mother's bleeding hangnail and the smell of fried chicken. Their argument about the Internet, so frustrating at the time, was the most welcome thing Hannah could possibly imagine. She could explore Cliff House now, hear the off-time clicks of the water heater in the basement, pedal the squeaky old exercise bike, organize the books in the Reading Room according to the color of their spines. She could hear the sound of her mother's footsteps, the whistle of the tea kettle, a glass plunking down on the Tree Room table. There had been a rhythm to their lives, two people in orbit, colliding and clashing and moving side by side through the seasons, while the floorboards creaked and the garden grew and the lighthouse kept its watch.

And in an upstairs closet, she remembered with a smile, was a box full of her father's guitar picks — *Fender medium.* She could see the old photographs of him with his beat-up old acoustic, the funny contortion of his mouth when Hannah's mother snapped a picture of him singing. There was his bushy beard, and that yellow guitar pick he always wore as a necklace. . . .

Stunned, Hannah began to cough.

The man at the window of Jaretsai Station.

Was her own father one of the banished? Had he been in the lighthouse that night, when Kyle had —

"Hold up, whoa, wait just a minute here!" the bowl of water said, ripping her back into the waterlogged office, cruelly dismissing her reverie. She felt woozy, as if she'd almost drowned.

"This is not the kind of thing I like to find out when your head's already wet, you hear me?"

"My father," she mumbled. "He's with Kyle." She reached out to grab the edge of the table to steady herself. Her feet kicked freely through the water.

"I ain't talkin' about your father. Never mind him. Listen, kid, this ain't your first trip to the city."

"What?" Bowl of water, chair, table. She tried to keep them all separate in her mind, even though her vision was making them overlap.

"What I'm trying to tell you is, you've been here before!"

Chapter Twenty-Eight

The first thing Hannah saw when she opened her eyes was the grim line of a mouth. She blinked, groggily, and Eri's face came into focus. Hannah was mesmerized by the severe part in the girl's hair, which looked like it had been created with a ruler. She tried to sit up, but a hand pinned her shoulder.

"You are not well," Eri said. "Rest. You are safe here."

From what? Hannah wondered. "How long was I out?"

"You were never 'out.' You were in a between state after your session with the Memory Keeper. Sergeant Throckmorton ordered me to take you to the infirmary, but I brought you to my room instead."

"Thanks," Hannah said. "But I feel fine."

Eri hesitated, then pulled her hand away. Hannah sat up and got her bearings. The girl's room was almost laughably bare. Besides the cot Hannah was on, a squat table held a wristwatch floating in a dish of water, which was connected to an outlet in the wall. A tri-folded screen made one corner of the room into a private dressing area. Two identical robes hung from hooks. A sword was displayed on an ivory rack.

Stefan sat on a stool by the door. Charlemagne was perched like a parrot on his shoulder, proudly sparking and blipping with bits of digital noise.

Hannah rubbed her eyes. "That's a new look for him."

"Welcome back to the land of the dead," Stefan said. "Check this out." He held up his dry paintbrush. One of Charlemagne's tongues shot out, wet the bristles, and retreated.

"Now this is the cool part." Stefan's elegant brushstrokes curled through the air. Hannah felt a rush of warmth — she had missed his painting. After a few seconds, the air sparkled with a miniature dragon that hovered, flapping its wings.

"Soil my carpet at your own peril," Eri warned. Stefan rolled his eyes and Charlemagne slurped the dragon whole, removing it from the air as if it were a failure moth.

"I don't need to get more paint," Stefan explained. "Ever since he ate part of the map, he's like a little recycling machine." Stefan nuzzled the scruff of the paint-lizard's neck. "Aren't you, boy? Aren't you?"

Eri sat down cross-legged on the floor and began cleaning her sword with a white cloth. A rustling came from behind the screen and Nancy's head peeked around the side.

"That is not meant to be a head decoration," Eri said without looking up. One of her robe belts was dangling from Nancy's forehead, tied like a sweatband.

"So, Hannah," Nancy said, "what was the Memory Keeper like?"

"Um . . . wet. You'll never guess what I found out." Right away, Hannah regretted saying this. The details of her session felt highly personal, like secrets she'd learned about herself, and she didn't feel like sharing them — especially not with Eri in the room.

"Oh yeah?" Nancy took off the belt and tossed it, still looped, over the corner of the screen. "Well you'll never guess what *I* found out, either."

"You first," Hannah said.

"The Institute doctors —"

"Technicians," Eri corrected.

"Whatever — these people who dressed like doctors examined me. Wanna know what I am?" Nancy was practically beaming. "Foundation! I'm *made* out of Foundation. Pretty weird, right?"

Hannah's mouth dropped open. She looked from Stefan to Eri, who seemed to be waiting for her reaction. "How?" she managed to say. And then: "Who made you?"

Hannah knew the answer. But Nancy said it out loud, anyway.

"You did, genius."

Hannah shook her head. "But I didn't *mean* to. It just happened."

Nancy joined Hannah on the cot. She nearly said something, then started laughing.

"What's so funny?" Hannah asked, thinking: *If somebody told me I was made of dead city powder, I wouldn't be laughing.*

"Nothing," Nancy said. "Everything. I don't know. It's just nice to finally know what I am, I guess. It doesn't really change anything, when you think about it. I'm still *me,* no matter what. I can still do whatever I want." She slapped Hannah's knee. "So what's *your* big news?"

I saw my father at Jaretsai Station, with Kyle.

Now that it was her turn to share, Hannah couldn't bring herself to say it. She closed her eyes and dismissed the thought. She told herself that she never even knew the man — it was no different than if Kyle had been standing next to a complete stranger. Because that's what her father was to her, anyway. A box of guitar picks, a Slinky, some old photographs.

"Hannah?" Nancy gave her a nudge. "You're spacing out again."

Hannah thought of the Memory Keeper's words. *This ain't your first trip to the city.* What did that mean? She had certainly never been here before. It didn't make any sense. All these distractions, when she finally had the tools to find her mother. She resolved to focus on the task at hand.

"I remember everything," Hannah said finally. She stood up. "I can help program the map, or whatever we need to do. So let's get back to it."

Stefan shifted his weight on the stool. "I might sit this one out, if it's all the same to you. I'm still feeling a little dizzy."

"Porcelain," Nancy said.

Eri pinched the cloth between her thumb and forefinger to clean the edge of the blade. At the same time, she stared at Hannah without blinking.

She knows there's something I'm not saying, Hannah thought.

Eri propelled herself to her feet and sheathed her sword. "I have been instructed to notify Sergeant Throckmorton as soon as you recover."

"That sounds like a bloody awful idea, don't you agree, my little beagle nose?" Nancy batted her eyes at Stefan.

"Ugh," he said.

Hannah's mother loomed so large in her mind now, she couldn't wait to get back to her clamshell. "Eri, would you mind taking me to the map first?"

"To defy orders from my superior is unacceptable," Eri said. "My allegiance is to the Institute."

"Fine." Hannah sighed. "But didn't you already defy orders when you took me here instead of to the infirmary?"

For the first time, Eri's movements betrayed a hint of uncertainty. She ground her toe into the carpet, wiggled her heel. "Perhaps, if you were to stop hiding things from me, I would be more inclined to —"

Nancy snickered. "Unpledge your allegiance?"

Eri's icy glare sent Nancy scurrying off the cot. "Hey, I get it," Nancy said from behind the screen. "We *have* to be more fun to hang out with than Urvashi and the Sarge."

"I do not 'hang out,'" Eri said. Then, to Hannah: "My superiors want to keep you here. Something they have discovered about you intrigues them. They will not let you leave. If you tell me what the Memory Keeper told you, then perhaps I can continue to help you."

"And if I tell you, we can go straight to the map?"

"Yes."

"The Memory Keeper told me I've been to the dead city before. I don't know what that means or how it's possible. Happy?"

Eri nodded. "Yes."

Hannah almost burst out laughing. "So that's it? Now we're friends and I can trust you?"

"Allegiance is not the same thing as honor, Hannah Silver. My sword is my own. These are lessons my father taught me, and I visit the Memory Keeper to remember them."

"Great," Hannah said. "Then let's hang out. Also" — she nodded toward the low table — "can I try on that watch?"

When Hannah turned down the corridor that led to the map room, she nearly smashed into Urvashi. Only the glittering of the woman's jeweled fingers caused her to stop short. Behind Urvashi, several more Institute members — including the man in the safari hat — waited impassively.

"You feeling better, love?" Urvashi said gently, leaning forward so that Hannah was forced to take a step back or risk bumping noses.

"Eri," Hannah said, but the girl was no longer at her side. Throckmorton came out of nowhere to rest a hand on Hannah's shoulder, studying her face, smiling his implacable smile. She ducked away and found herself backed up against the wall.

Urvashi's teeth were blindingly white. "Off to search for your mother, then, dear?"

"Oh yes, my cozy hearth rug," Throckmorton said. "I believe she's looking for her old mum. You remember your old mum better now, do you, Hannah?" Throckmorton's grin stretched into a sick exaggeration of itself. "Eri wasn't taking you to the map room without coming to us first, was she?"

"That she was, feather pillow." Urvashi shook her head. "That she was. Naughty, naughty."

Throckmorton winked. "Sneaky, sneaky. You'll be a good girl from now on, won't you, Hannah? The Institute is *very* interested in you, and I'm going to have to ask you to extend your visit. You wouldn't mind taking a bit of a holiday here, would you?"

"I do hope she'll stay, calamine lotion," Urvashi said. "It would be a shame for such a nice, *interesting* girl to —"

SHNK!

At the familiar sound, Hannah slid down the wall. Crawling between Throckmorton's pressed uniform pants and Urvashi's brightly patterned sari, she found herself face-to-face with the man in the safari hat, who'd knelt to intercept her. His sprites zipped out from his collar and all at once the telescope and the lobster were swarming her face. She fell sideways and clawed madly, trying to pull herself from the forest of legs. A hand locked onto her forearm and she flailed, but a moment later Nancy was dragging her free.

In the center of the hallway, Eri was half-crouched in her fighting stance. Stefan was at her side, paintbrush sparkling with a dab of digitally enhanced skin from Charlemagne, who slunk about the floor with an arched back like a jungle cat poised for battle.

"You are a member in good standing with a high probability of Ascension!" barked Throckmorton, fearlessly confronting Eri's sword. "Cease this *mutiny*, and I will see that your punishment is lenient."

"I am bound by law to Hannah Silver," Eri said calmly. Her sprites blazed from underneath her hair and menaced Urvashi, who swatted at them.

Throckmorton blinked in confusion. "Bound by what law?"

"The law of hanging out," Eri said.

Stefan began to paint and Throckmorton tapped his wristwatch. "I know your tricks, lad." A sprinkler in the ceiling above Stefan doused his brush with water. Instead of splashing to the floor, the water congealed into a tendril, globbed over the paintbrush, and covered Stefan's entire hand in a sticky film.

Urvashi's own sprites — five angry buzzards — blazed up from her sandals to confront Eri's charms. The man in the safari hat brandished a pair of silver revolvers with oversized barrels.

"Come on," hissed Nancy. But Hannah shook her head. She wasn't about to let Eri and Stefan create a diversion while she ran.

They would go together, or not at all. She pulled Eri's extra wristwatch from her pocket and held it so that Throckmorton could see it.

"Eri showed me how to program this," Hannah lied. "Back away or I'll open the floodgates and fill this place with lake water."

Throckmorton frowned. "What floodgates?"

That split-second distraction was just long enough. With a sideswipe, Eri sliced the tendril in half and, with the flat of her blade, flicked the rubbery thing into Throckmorton's face. Charlemagne launched himself in the air just as Stefan freed his hand, and the paint-lizard swiped a generous helping of himself onto the bristles.

With a few deft slashes, Stefan painted them all into the eye of an electrical surge, sparkling and crackling with bursts of heat lightning. It was a cosmic data-storm, a digital cloud shot through with swirls of ash that bloomed into complex snowflakes before dispersing.

"Lemme see that watch," Nancy said, tugging Hannah's sleeve.

"No way!" Hannah shoved it back in her pocket. The four of them began to move down the hallway as one, with Eri calling out directions and striking out from the center of the cloud whenever an Institute member got too close.

"The law of hanging out?" Hannah asked.

Eri's sword flashed. "Floodgates?"

Stefan held out his arm like a falconer for Charlemagne to perch. "Just get us to the smokestack where the giant fish docked."

"That is far too dangerous. It will be locked down. There are other ways out."

Eri tapped her watch and her sprites performed a quick dance around her forehead before vanishing. All around them, the smoke began to clear. Grime-encrusted figures stumbled about as Throckmorton barked orders and Urvashi repeated them.

"I'd rather swim out of here than listen to those two for another second," Stefan said. He was covered in soot, as if he'd just survived a volcanic eruption.

Turning to the wall, Eri spun the lock on a small door. "Let us hope it does not come to that. The lake is very old."

Hannah didn't ask what she meant. When they had all followed Eri through the door, the girl closed it, spun the lock, and ordered them to stand back. With a single downward blow she sliced the wheel-lock from its shaft and nodded to Stefan, who slapped a messy coat of paint over the metal, sealing the door shut.

Eri led them down a narrow passage and into a workshop strewn with rusty scrap metal. A bench shoved against the wall held several empty bins labeled FOUNDATION FOR SUBMERSIBLE REPAIR ONLY. In the center of the room was a vessel propped up on a lift like a car in a mechanic's garage. It was a steel contraption shaped like a two-liter bottle of soda.

There was a muffled explosion down the hall, followed by the resounding crash of metal on metal. Eri and Stefan performed their door-sealing trick on the entrance to the workshop. Hannah discovered a ladder up the middle of the lift and began to climb.

"This thing looks pretty leaky," Nancy said.

Hannah reached the submersible's rust-flecked hatch. "At least it's not a fish."

Chapter Twenty-Nine

The interior of the ship was a cramped mess.

"I think this heap of junk belongs out with the wrecks," Stefan complained, picking up a tarnished pipe that had been severed by what appeared to be blows from a hatchet. There were no seats, just leather straps dangling in loops from the ceiling. In the front, where the cap of the soda bottle would be, was a single porthole. Hannah lit the submersible's only light source, a lantern that sent shadows flickering across a control panel full of surprisingly shiny brass fixtures in the shape of skulls, dice, and guitars. It occurred to her that this old ship might be someone's hobby, and she hoped it actually worked.

"How do we get it in the water?" Stefan asked, peering out the porthole, through the thick glass wall of the workshop, into the murky lake where the ghost ships rotted. Hannah watched Charlemagne chase a cockroach into a pile of magazines.

She thought quickly. "Maybe if you let me have your brush —"

Whatever she was about to say — she wasn't exactly sure, herself — was interrupted by a thunderous *BOOM.* She watched in amazement as the workshop's door went sailing past the porthole, propelled by a fiery explosion, spinning into the glass of the chamber's large window like a hundred-pound Frisbee. The submersible shuddered on its lift. Hannah heard footsteps in the room as the Institute members surrounded the ship. Their voices dragged her spirits down. Maybe she should have allowed Throckmorton and Urvashi to keep her without putting up a fight. Maybe she could have found a way to use the map, then made her escape.

Too late now.

"Look!" Nancy said. Hairline cracks spiderwebbed across the window.

Throckmorton's voice screamed, *"Back down the hallway! Get back, all of you!"*

The cracks gained velocity. Oddly beautiful, they raced outward from the collision point, unfurling like thin ribbons of white against the murk. A jet of water the width of a pin came spitting through the glass and splattered against the submersible.

"Perhaps we should steady ourselves," Eri said, reaching up for a leather strap. Hannah did the same, just as the workshop's window gave way in a maelstrom of jagged glass. The submersible was ripped from its mechanic's lift almost as soon as Hannah's fingers closed around the strap, twisting her shoulder. She gripped with all her might as the lake rushed in with the full force of the deep behind it. The workshop was swamped in seconds, the submersible tossed and spun like clothes in a dryer, and Hannah prepared to be knocked senseless. But before she knew it, the ship was floating gently along. The silence outside was total except for the muffled and distant clanks of the settling wrecks. The workshop had been claimed by the lake.

"Everybody okay?" Hannah took inventory. Eri was standing as if they had barely moved. Nancy had flipped her legs up, wrapped both feet around her strap, and was swinging like a pendulum. Stefan was upright but his eyes were closed. Charlemagne had emerged from behind the magazines, a pair of long feelers waving atop his head.

They all gazed out the front porthole as the submersible drifted out into the lake. Hannah was struck by the size of the Institute's complex. They had been confined to a small section, no bigger than a freighter. How many chambers were hidden down here, how much strange technology? The sub slid lazily past the ruins of a magnificent clipper ship. A faded sign proclaimed HONEYMOON CRUISES.

Eri and Stefan went straight to the control panel. Hannah and Nancy moved to the back of the ship, where the wall was decorated with carefully arranged discs about the size of dinner plates. It took Hannah a moment to realize that they were old vinyl records. Whoever was restoring the submersible was like one of the antique car guys who hung out in the parking lot of the Carbine Pass Diner.

Nancy squinted at one of the labels. "Killian Porterhouse and the Kresh Monsters."

"This one doesn't have a name," Hannah said, reaching for a blank record. It slid aside, revealing a porthole that looked backward at the now-open wall of the workshop. A glint of silver floated between the submersible and its former home: the round door, destined to float aimlessly until it joined some other piece of wreckage.

"What's that?" Nancy pointed above a ruined battleship's conning tower, where the glow from the Institute faded. In that dark place, a blubbery shape rose from the deep. It took a moment to lock onto its target, then jetted across the bow of the battleship, heading straight for them. An undertow, soft at first, swiped the submersible, upsetting its balance. Hannah couldn't tear her gaze from the pursuing horror: lips curling back, jaws opening. Teeth of glass, teeth of steel.

"Big fish," she said, wondering if it would chomp them in half or return them to the Institute in its belly. Then, over her shoulder at Eri and Stefan, who were carefully matching the brass fixtures of the control panel to a scribbled chart they'd discovered tacked on the wall, she screamed, *"Big fish!"*

"It's coming up fast," Nancy said.

"*This* is the auxiliary thruster," Stefan said, wiggling a fixture in the shape of a polished top hat. He tapped the chart. "It says so *right here.*"

With a groan, the submersible began to shake and rattle its way forward.

"I will drive," Eri said, elbowing him out of the way.

Hannah watched out the back. Headlamps buried in the big fish's eye sockets pierced the murk. Wrecked ships moved in and out of inky pools of shadow.

"Acceleration should be the skull," Stefan said to Eri. "The skull!"

Eri calmly eased the skull fixture up on the panel. The ship registered its protest with an irate clatter. A gasket blew beneath the floor and Charlemagne lost himself in a mist of hot steam.

"Do not panic," Eri said. "I will deliver us."

Hannah stared at the back of Eri's head and wondered, *Who is this girl, really?* Eri's behavior — turning her back on the Institute, sacrificing her shot at Ascension for the sake of Hannah's quest — suddenly felt like the cold, calculating moves of a politician rather than a girl who just wanted to hang out.

"My sword is my own."

Hannah flinched — she had been thinking out loud. "Sorry, Eri, I didn't mean —"

Eri shot a fierce look at Hannah over her shoulder. "I did not say anything."

At the same time, Eri's voice chimed in from elsewhere in the ship: *"My sword is my own."*

Stefan was struggling to remove Charlemagne from his shoulder. The paint-lizard hopped down to the control panel and slithered to the floor.

"My sword is my own," Charlemagne said, in a perfect imitation of Eri's voice.

"Wow." Stefan tried to be casual. "I guess he's doing that now."

"The demon mocks me," Eri said.

"He's not a demon!" said Stefan and Hannah in unison.

"Hey!" Nancy slapped her hand against the inside of the hull. A metallic *thud* echoed. "The fish is changing."

Out the rear porthole, the transport fish had backed off slightly, but its face was sprouting long tentacles, catfishy antennae that grew in pursuit of the submersible. The antennae whipped through the water, crystal tips nearly bashing the porthole.

Then the crystals flared. The noise inside the submersible changed abruptly from the creaks and groans of water pressure to an empty silence.

"Air pocket," Hannah said, uselessly, since they were already poised in midair — the tentacles had carved out a hallway around them. The submersible had just enough momentum to carry itself across the air pocket and smash through the wall of rippling water at the other end. If the fish succeeded in making a larger trap, the submersible would find itself stranded on the dry lake bed.

"The honeycomb is our deliverance," Eri announced.

"Nice vocabulary," Nancy said.

Hannah looked down the narrow nose of the submersible and out the front porthole. The headlamps from the big fish illuminated a sheer rock wall looming just ahead. This side of the lake didn't slope gently — it was practically vertical, and full of caves.

"It's not Muffin," Hannah said. "It's a way out."

The mouths of the caves were ringed with carvings that appeared in the light of the headlamps. Names of districts: LORMAYR, FRITH, YEUNKISH. Hannah scanned the honeycomb, thinking quickly.

"Eri, remember how you said the Institute tracked the rebels? The banished?"

"Every last raw nerve."

"Do you know where they went after they left Jaretsai Station?"

"Of course."

"Can you take us there?"

Stefan looked at her in disbelief. "I thought you didn't care about Kyle! You said you were just here for your mother — what happened to all that? What could you possibly hope to gain by getting us involved in —"

"My father is with him!" Hannah said.

Nancy coughed. Stefan just stared.

In a few seconds, Eri would have to steer them into a cave or they'd smash into the rock wall. Instead, she abandoned the controls and spun to face Hannah.

"No more secrets."

"That's my last one."

Eri turned back to the panel. "Hannah Silver, grab hold of that rose and spin it when I say. Stefan Weisz, do the same with the candle, pulling it back with all your strength." Hannah placed her fingers against the pewter fixture. Stefan held the candle-shaped lever to her right.

"Air pocket incoming," Nancy reported from her spot next to the rear porthole. Eri tried to turn a dial shaped like a high-heeled boot and the fixture came off in her hand. She tossed it over her shoulder and tried a key, which slid forward without breaking. The submersible changed course, nosing up along the honeycomb wall.

"Now," she said. Hannah turned the rose. Stefan yanked the candle back. With a surprisingly lithe maneuver, the little sub halted, spun, and darted into a cave marked CAYMIRI.

Chapter Thirty

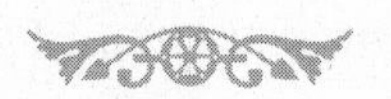

The cave expelled the submersible into a labyrinth of pillars and stilts. Golden rays of light speared the depths, illuminating stone archways and the crumbling steps of an amphitheater. Hannah snuffed the lantern. Eri steered the ship between rusty hinges that flapped in the languid current, past half-disintegrated awnings that clung to long-abandoned shops. The main street of this sunken district dead-ended at a stone wall that was home to a family of parasites shaped like holiday wreaths. They dangled their crimson ornaments toward the sub in greeting, or warning, or threat.

Hannah spotted a massive sluice gate at the base of the wall. "Down there."

"Yes," Eri said. "I mapped this."

"All clear on our tail," Nancy said from the rear porthole. "I don't know if we lost 'em, but we're alone."

"We did not lose them," Eri said.

As soon as they were through the gate the sunlight was all around them, pooling along the flat bottom of what appeared to be a narrow man-made river. Eri nosed the submersible upward and Hannah squinted. Silhouettes like long footballs blocked the light in places. *Boats,* she realized. They broke the surface and the sun brightened every seam and crevice of the sub, bathing her in warmth. She stumbled over to the hatch. It was as if the light were pulling her from a long slumber beneath the city of the dead, guiding her up out of dreams to face the morning.

Not morning, she reminded herself. On solid ground alongside the river, Hannah helped Stefan, Nancy, and Eri climb out.

"Happy lightday," she said.

Stefan shielded his eyes with a hand. "Ugh. Lightdays are the worst."

"Wharf." Nancy giggled. "Jetty. Dock. Quay."

Hannah and her twin had once used a dictionary of nautical terms to add vocabulary to Muffin Language. Her eyes adjusted, and she saw what Nancy was getting at: Caymiri was a maze of canals, a twisting riddle of high-traffic waterways. Gondoliers steered their banana-shaped boats with wooden poles, drifting beneath arched bridges. Along the sidewalks and docks, crowds gathered in bars and cafés, overflowing onto bobbing rafts. Charlemagne flitted about the sidewalk, saturated with bright yellow hues, soaking up the sun. A fine mist hung in the air.

"Hey, Stefan," Hannah said. "Take a big whiff."

He breathed in through his nostrils and looked at her questioningly.

"Briny," she said.

"That's a boy smelling the *ocean*," Nancy corrected. "Not a bunch of little rivers."

"Canals," Hannah said. She spotted a paper tacked to a dock-side hut advertising boat trips and sightseeing jaunts along the famous —

"Floating canals of Caymiri," Stefan said, tilting his head to look up into the sky. The mist hung like sheer drapery from aerial thoroughfares of flowing water that hoisted all manner of yachts and dinghies high above the neighborhood. Gondolas swooped and splashed, sending runoff down to be collected in great copper tanks and pumped back up to feed the canals. Recycling stations hummed with the flutter of enormous bellows, onionskin accordion machines suctioning up and down.

The steering poles of the gondoliers pierced the bottom of the canal, so that looking up, Hannah could see their candy-striped tips poking through and disappearing back up into the water.

"Ow!"

She felt a familiar pinch in the webbing between her thumb and forefinger. Mist from the air was collecting on her hand like poured mercury. The little worm of water clung to the side of her thumb, then slipped painlessly beneath the skin and vanished. Hannah thought of the other invaders: toothpick from the attic in the mansion district, fungus from the Nusle Kruselskaya subway station, space bar from the computer in Su-Ankyo, and now floating canal mist from Caymiri.

The words of the Memory Keeper came back to her, sudden and sharp: *You've been here before.*

Hannah wondered if this was the city's way of welcoming her home.

"My sword is my own," Charlemagne said, nuzzling the sleeve of her jacket. She looked up from her hand. The submersible was becoming a source of amusement for a gang of local children, who had taken to pelting its rusty hull with pebbles, abandoning the puppet theater that rose above the quay like a felt-wrapped vampire's castle.

She looked up and down the docks. "Where's Eri?"

Stefan frowned. "She was just here."

"She went that way." Nancy pointed toward the lobby of an apartment building. A green awning proclaimed DOCKSIDE ARMS.

"You didn't mention it until now?"

Nancy shrugged. "Do I have to do everything?"

Hannah considered Eri's absence. Maybe they were better off just going their separate ways. What was Hannah going to do when she saw Kyle, when she saw *her father*? Demand the location of her mother and expect to skip merrily away? She promised herself that when she got back home — *if* she ever got back home — she would become the kind of person who made detailed plans instead of just throwing herself into crazy situations.

"We have to get out of here," Stefan said. "Now."

On the lower canal, gondoliers steered furiously out of the way as a group of sleek black ships surfaced. The teardrop-shaped subs crowded the canal, water sloughing off their backs, pointy noses poking traffic aside. Hannah counted eight gorgeous little pods of polished black steel. She led Stefan and Nancy through the crowd of pedestrians, dodging workmen in overalls and ladies in comically oversized feathered hats. Suddenly, a hand shot out from behind a barrel, pulling her down with such force that she almost landed flat on her back. Eri's angry face was an inch from hers.

"I thought you were right behind me. Why were you standing on the dock next to our ship waiting to get caught?"

"We were distracted by the famous floating canals of Caymiri," Stefan said.

Hannah pushed herself to a crouch and peeked around the barrel. She saw Urvashi's sari among the crowd and caught the light glinting dully off Throckmorton's helmet.

Hannah pointed at the Dockside Arms. "That's where the banished are hiding, isn't it?" The building was a nondescript ten stories, with a top floor that jutted out to meet the upper canal. There was nothing sinister about the place, but the buildings in her bad dreams always started out vaguely inviting, too. The temperature of the mist in the air seemed to drop, and she shivered.

Eri nodded.

"It looks so peaceful."

"The Watchers have not yet tracked them here. The Institute is always several steps ahead."

They waited behind the barrel as a papier-mâché float made its way along the sidewalk, carrying a smiling, waving woman with a sash across her chest that said LIGHTDAY QUEEN. Hannah wondered briefly, with an absurd flicker of hope, if the woman might toss out a handful of Tolliver's. When the float's cakelike shape blocked the line of sight between the canal and their hiding place, they ran into the lobby of the Dockside Arms.

Waiting for them in the corner was a single glass eye.

Hannah raised her hood and hid her face with her hands.

"This one does not spy for the Watchers," Eri said.

Hannah peeked through her fingers. Eri and Stefan were standing directly under the glass eye, fearlessly peering up at it. Stefan pointed. "She's onto something, see? There's all this electric stuff around it."

Hannah joined them beneath the eye. It was difficult not to flinch. But they were right: This eye had been *captured*. Its lens was imprisoned behind a thin, mesh screen connected to a battery pack, which was Velcro-strapped to the wall. Wires led away from the eye to the pack and disappeared up into a freshly drilled hole.

"The rebels have corrupted it," Eri said.

Charlemagne scampered toward an open elevator door. *"Corrupted,"* he said. *"Corrupted."*

"Guess they know we're coming," Stefan said.

Hannah wondered if Kyle was watching her on a screen at this very moment. She forced her mouth into what she hoped was a fearless scowl and glared unblinking into the eye.

Nancy followed the paint-lizard into the elevator. "Going up?"

"Top floor," Eri said, and they filed inside.

"Gotta press all the buttons," Hannah said as the doors slid shut. "Or the cable will snap and the elevator will fall. Remember that, Nancy?"

Hannah pictured the teachers' elevator at the Carbine Pass Middle School. What day was it back home? Had years passed since she'd entered the city? Or was it more like minutes?

"There is no cable," Eri said, pressing a button marked PRESIDENTIAL SUITE. Hannah felt water pressure beneath the floor of the elevator car, and up it shot like a popped cork.

"So what's your father like?" Stefan asked. "Why is he working with Kyle?"

"I don't know," Hannah admitted.

"Well, is he going to tell you where your mother is?"

"I don't know," she said again, looking helplessly at her companions. "I've never met him before."

Eri jabbed her finger into the EMERGENCY STOP button and the elevator halted.

Hannah put up her hands. "That's not a secret I meant to keep, I swear. I just didn't have a chance to tell you guys the whole story."

"So we are meeting, uninvited, with a murderer and a complete stranger," Eri said.

"Sorry," Hannah said. "You don't have to help me, you know." She narrowed her eyes. "Why *are* you helping me?"

"Because I believe what Stefan Weisz believes."

He raised an eyebrow — *This is news to me.*

Eri hit a button to cancel their Emergency Stop and the elevator resumed its journey. "That Hannah Silver is on her way to Ascension, and we would be foolish not to follow."

Chapter Thirty-One

When the doors slid open, Hannah expected to be staring into the faces of Kyle and her father. The Presidential Suite of the Dockside Arms *was* crowded with souls engaged in strange work, but there was nobody waiting for her. Cautiously, she gave Nancy's hand a squeeze and stepped out of the elevator. The suite was actually a single massive room lined with huge picture windows. In the distance, Hannah recognized minarets bristling like arrows in a quiver.

The room had been designed for lightday living, and the brilliance of the world outside was parceled into shadows by iron sculptures placed against the glass. All along the buffed hardwood floor, spiral patterns twirled and spun, as if the shadows had been brought to life by the wiry artwork. Out one of the open windows, Hannah could see a gondola bobbing on the floating canal. A pair of middle-aged men in soccer jerseys tossed a large canvas bundle inside, and the boat slipped out of sight.

Stefan fidgeted nervously with his paintbrush. "You sure we've got the right rebels?"

Granite countertops and L-shaped desks had been pushed into squares throughout the high-ceilinged suite — it looked, to Hannah, like an office set up in a great hurry. Every surface was being used for some kind of manufacturing. Little piles of gritty powder — she thought it must be raw Foundation — were being sifted from vials to scales by men and women in lab coats, while carpenters hammered wood into interlocking boxes. In one corner, hidden behind a screen like the one in Eri's bedroom, silhouetted figures were welding.

"Those things again," Nancy said, pointing to the far wall. Glass doors opened onto a long roof deck, where hundreds of Foundation meters took their measurements.

Hannah's eyes strayed back inside. The centerpiece of the room was an object about the size and shape of a pickup truck, with a tarp thrown over it. She wondered what it was, and was about to suggest they go take a peek, since nobody seemed to be giving them any trouble.

Then Kyle strolled out from behind it.

Hannah's thoughts were clenched in barbed wire. Her mind, red and angry, launched her body into a dead sprint across the shiny floor, sneakers squeaking. Stefan shouted in alarm — without thinking, Hannah had snatched his paintbrush. There was a tiny bit of Charlemagne on its tip.

"Kyle!" she snarled in a voice that came from some long-buried place. As the name escaped her throat it called forth an image of her mother crumpled beneath the lighthouse, rain-soaked nightgown shrouding her face. And now here was the boy responsible, the boy who had come to her house and scattered his false kindness like poison. She hadn't considered revenge before this moment, but now that Kyle was right in front of her, smiling warmly as she closed the gap, every nerve ending fired with the same message: *Hurt him.*

As if pitching a softball, she windmilled the brush and flung the dollop of paint underhanded, launching it straight at his forehead, where his shaggy bangs flopped so perfectly. Hannah screamed in triumph as the paint found its mark, the digital splatter hitting Kyle directly between the —

No.

Missing him as he sidestepped with impossible quickness. His fluid grace made Eri seem like a clumsy oaf. It wasn't until she heard Nancy's voice beside her, the syllables stretched like a song played at half-speed, that Hannah realized Kyle's ability to give time a little nudge. He'd used the same technique to help her bypass the stairs at school, except this was a nudge in the opposite direction, and everything except Kyle moved in achingly slow motion.

The paint splatter gradually, harmlessly fizzled out. Hannah was aware of her legs pumping ever so slowly. She watched as Kyle's eyes darkened to black pools and leaked ribbons of smoke that curled prettily upward to wind about a chandelier. The shadow sculptures that played along the floor grew like a dreary forest to bind Hannah's arms behind her back. Branches fastened her ankles to the floor.

And then Kyle blinked away a final puff of smoke and time crashed into itself in a dizzying rush.

"— kill you!" said Nancy, the end of her sentence abruptly sped up to normal speed. Hannah glanced over to see that Eri, Stefan, and Nancy were trussed up alongside her. She squirmed against her shadowy restraints, which seemed to emit a low, satisfied hiss, as if they were finally getting a chance to fulfill their purpose. She could feel them tightening, cutting off the circulation in her wrists.

Kyle wiped ash from the corners of his eyes and shrugged. "You can't kill me. I'm already dead."

All around the room, an assortment of weapons clicked and murmured and howled into place. *That's what they've been building,* she thought. Off to her right was a teenage girl brandishing what appeared to be an oscillating fan with plastic blades. It looked far from dangerous, but Hannah remembered the aftermath of Jaretsai Station: aging brick, corroded metal, broken glass.

"Welcome to the revolution," Kyle said with an infuriating smile. "First of all, I'm really sorry about tying you up. It's just for right now, until we all calm down a little bit. Cool? Okay. Let me know if it's too tight or anything."

Hannah struggled against her bindings. Kyle's eyes coughed up a wisp of smoke and the shadows eased off. She was still held fast, but she could move her wrists to recover circulation.

Hannah decided to get straight to the point. "You killed her."

He looked directly into her eyes. She saw herself — an angry, squirming girl — reflected in his pupils.

"I'm so unbelievably sorry about what happened to your mom. Things got out of hand that night, and if I could take it all back and do it another way, I would. Seriously. I know it's going to be hard for you to believe anything I say, but I think if you give yourself a little time, then you'll understand. At least I hope you will. Because you were both so nice to me, it really bums me out that it got so messed up. That was some amazing lasagna, remember? Even though my arm is still a little sore from doing all those dishes." He laughed. "Oh, man."

Furious, Hannah could barely listen to him speak. His words seemed to move in and out of the red mist in her head. And yet he was so beguiling, the way he moved as if sliding between particles of air, the universe clearing a path. She wondered, briefly, what kind of person he'd been when he'd been alive on earth the first time. Then she chased the thought away. The fact that she was wondering about him at all meant that she was once again caught up in his peculiar gravity, and she was ashamed of herself.

"You threw her down and left her to die," Hannah said. "I found her in the mud."

Kyle took a step toward her. He smelled of pine and woodsmoke. She told herself that he stunk, that his lies stunk, but it wasn't true: His scent was comforting. She breathed out as hard as she could, pushing it away. His expression became grim. He nodded gravely and looked down at the floor. Then he raised his eyes back to Hannah.

"This isn't easy for you to hear right now, I know, but she got in the way of something way more important than any single earthly life. The reason we were banished in the first place is because we learned the truth about the city of the dead, and the reason we came back is to share it with everyone."

"You are a fraud," Eri said coldly. Kyle ignored her.

"Yeah, so, listen, I don't know you, or anything," Stefan said, "but you're not exactly proving yourself to be a decent soul by keeping us tied up. Also that thing with your eyes . . ." He shook his head.

Kyle regarded Stefan for the first time. "Painters Guild, right? Maybe you can do a group portrait of us. *Return of the Banished*, or something. It'll be a classic." Behind him, titters swept through the ranks.

"No problem, I'd be happy to."

Hannah caught Eri's glance and rolled her eyes. Stefan was trying to appeal to Kyle as if they were old pals, about to put this whole pesky incident behind them.

"Let us go *now*," Eri said.

"You know, this concerns you" — Kyle nodded to Eri — "and you" — he smiled at Stefan — "as much as it does Hannah. So check it out." He clapped once. "There is no Ascension. It's a total lie. There's no magical place with gardens and fountains and pretty birds and fluffy clouds that souls get whisked away to after they do something really cool that impresses the Watchers. Everyone's been suckered into believing in some grand reward that never existed in the first place." He shook his head sadly. "The truth is — the truth that me and my friends got banished for wanting other souls to know — is that nobody goes anywhere. The city is the beginning of our afterlives and it's also the end. Everybody's just here. That's it. Here." He gestured to the window, where Hannah could see the tip of a single minaret, sharp and focused against the sky. "The city, forever and ever."

"Wrong," Stefan said. "People Ascend all the time. I've seen the Watchers come and —"

"And what?" Kyle put his arms out, palms up. "What have you really seen?" He closed a hand into a fist, pretended to think for a moment, then pointed a finger at Stefan. "But! You bring up a good point. Where *do* souls go when the Watchers come and take them away?" He yelled over his shoulder. "Yo, Benjamin! That's your cue, buddy!"

At her father's name, Hannah felt a cold knot form in her stomach.

"Psst." Nancy strained against the shadows around her shoulders to lean her head a little closer to Hannah. She began to whisper while Hannah craned her neck to see her father, who hadn't yet appeared.

"I want you to know I'm glad to be part of you, sis."

"Why are you telling me this right now?" Hannah whispered back.

"I just wanted to tell you before I said good-bye."

"Ladies!" Kyle turned his attention toward their whispered conversation. "Something you'd like to share with the group?"

"Nancy, don't . . ." Hannah pleaded.

"It's my turn, dummy. I'm going to find out what happened to Belinda and Albert." She stuck out her tongue. "See you around."

Nancy's departure jolted Hannah's body, stretching her bindings, whipping her head back in its shadowy cradle.

The Game Room at Cliff House was full of clocks. Two stately grandfathers with gold-plated faces and pendulums that swung behind little windows. Seven cuckoos mounted on the wall. Eleven unplugged radios gathering dust on an end table, and two that took batteries, flashing 12:00. One masquerading as a dartboard, another in the shape of a parakeet. A square mirror with hands of onyx that ticked as loud as a typewriter. Her father's contribution was a clock in the shape of a grapefruit wearing sunglasses. Sometimes, for no apparent reason — or perhaps because it was broken — two small bulbs lit up behind the sunglasses and a tinny speaker at the navel said, "THAT'S JUICE-A-RIFFIC, BABY!"

The game that Hannah and Nancy made up revolved around the grapefruit, and was the reason this room was called the Game

Room instead of something more fitting, like the Clock Room. Hannah stood with her knees bent in a baseball player's ready stance, waiting for the grapefruit to speak. She had played the game so many times that she could hear the little crackle of the speaker before it even said the word *That's*, and could be well on her way to the largest grandfather clock before the grapefruit finished its sentence.

Nancy screamed inside her head: *Twelve forty-one!*

As soon as the speaker crackled, Hannah pulled open the glass door that protected the face of the grandfather clock and spun the minute hand around and around until it matched the time Nancy had chosen for this round of the game. Then she shut the door and moved on to the cuckoo clocks, nimbly dodging the birds that popped out as she twirled the hands to twelve forty-one.

The game had only one rule: finish setting all the clocks before the grapefruit spoke for a second time. The tricky part was that nobody knew when that was going to be. Sometimes she had three minutes, sometimes thirty. Once an entire hour had gone by, but that was rare. The clock radios gave her the most trouble because they had to be plugged in to the power strip and *then* set. And recently, Nancy had added a new wrinkle: She liked to scream out other times while Hannah was trying to concentrate.

Four fifty-eight!

On this occasion, Hannah didn't tell her twin to shut up. She just ran from clock to clock, savoring the sound of Nancy's voice, wondering if she would ever hear it again.

Nine thirty!

Hannah breathed deeply, inhaling the memories of the Game Room: the smell of cheap plastic mingling with aged wood, the cuckoo clock that spit out a squirrel instead of a bird, the stain on the rug where she had spilled cranberry juice.

Eleven thirteen!

She was spinning the winged hands of the parakeet clock when Nancy laughed hysterically and the hands began moving by themselves. Behind her, the grandfather clocks chimed angrily. Cuckoos exploded from their perches.

Three thirty-nine!

Digital clock radios blinked with smiley faces.

Six fourteen! Eight twenty-three!

Dizzy from the frenzied chimes and the madcap revolutions of the minute hands, Hannah collapsed in the middle of the Game Room. Nancy couldn't stop laughing.

How do you like that, Kyle?

Chapter Thirty-Two

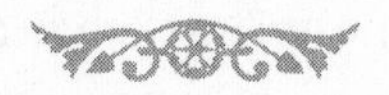

Shadows grasped at thin air in the place Nancy had been. They hissed and sputtered and slunk away, reshaping themselves into patterns on the floor. Kyle investigated the empty space.

"Interesting," he said, kneeling down and tracing his finger along a floorboard. "How'd she do that?"

Hannah could barely hear him over the racket of the Game Room clocks, which resounded in her head. She tried to make the presence of her twin linger, clinging desperately to the little habits that made Nancy real, like the way she picked at the ragged hole in her jeans. There was a brief ecstatic moment when Nancy seemed to pop back into life, full of obnoxious energy.

Then the clocks went silent.

Nancy tore herself away from Hannah so quickly that her sudden absence was a tremendous shock. Hannah's body ached. She pictured the paint cans in the supply closet at the castle, vanishing one by one. A phrase formed in her mind — Nancy's final contribution to Muffin Language.

"'Empty closet,'" Hannah said, "means 'a sister who's gone away.'"

Kyle raised an eyebrow. "I don't get it."

"Excuse me," Stefan chimed in.

"I wouldn't expect a murderer to understand," Hannah said to Kyle.

Kyle stood up. His left eye was obscured by smoke that seeped from his tear duct. "I said I was sorry, Hannah. What more do you want me to do? *This entire world is a lie.* And we're going to expose it. We are on the side of truth, here — you have to see that." He turned to the girl with the oscillating fan. "Can you please find Benjamin Silver and tell him that his daughter wants to see him?"

She nodded briskly and ran off.

"I don't want to see him," Hannah said. "There was only the two of us, me and my mother. Nobody else."

"EXCUSE ME!" Stefan yelled, exasperated. He thrust his chin toward the roof deck, which had also drawn the attention of several banished souls.

Outside the suite, Foundation meters were spinning out of control. Hands moved backward, springs popped, displays blinked 12:00. Hannah could feel a rumbling beneath her feet as the meters went completely haywire. She smiled.

Nancy.

A frantic meter man began rushing from dial to dial, tearing pages from his clipboard and crumpling them up before simply tossing the entire clipboard away. The Presidential Suite was thrown into turmoil.

"Somebody deal with him!" Kyle yelled at nobody and everybody. It was the first time Hannah had ever heard him raise his voice. He seemed to forget all about his captives and took off running toward the deck. Outside, the meter man cupped his hands around his mouth and sent a blood-curdling noise halfway between a bellow and a shriek into the empty sky.

Eri's lips moved, but Hannah couldn't hear anything over the man's terrible cry. She felt her bonds slacken as Kyle got farther away. Eri managed to wriggle her watch free. Her sprites emerged, glowing faintly in the lightday sun, then brighter as they fanned out to fight the shadows. Hannah felt her bindings simmer. Dark branches writhed and hissed. Then Eri's sword glinted and the bonds retreated, slashed and torn, to lick their wounds flat against the hardwood floor. Hannah rubbed circulation back into her arms and legs.

The brain-rattling sound had drawn most of the banished to the roof deck, where there seemed to be some confusion about what to do. When the windows that faced the floating canal shattered inward, spraying the room with a torrent of foul-smelling water, Hannah assumed the wailing of the meter man had vibrated the glass into pieces. But then a banished weapon roared and the withering shot — a spinning top — sailed between two Institute submersibles that tumbled into the Presidential Suite, riding the crest of the canal.

Hannah pulled Stefan down beneath a granite workbench. Water pooled about their knees and ankles. Eri's sprites zipped past in a complex aerial weave, slamming into the first submersible as its hatch raised to reveal Throckmorton and Urvashi. Banished souls came charging back in from the roof deck to head off this unexpected invasion.

Tucked away beneath the workbench, Hannah watched in horror as Stefan's chest began to change its shape. Something was crawling under his sweater. When Charlemagne popped his head up through the collar, Hannah burst out laughing.

If only Nancy were here to see the chaos she'd sparked, Hannah thought. From her hiding spot she could look out upon the canal side, where more Institute subs had begun to arrive, disgorging troops. Throckmorton led one squad, Urvashi another, and the room became a blinding swirl of Institute sprites. The banished did their best to form a skirmish line to protect their tarp-covered treasure. Hannah picked out the girl with the plastic fan weapon. The man next to her wielded two kitchen hand mixers reshaped into pistols. A woman in camouflage fatigues hoisted a shoulder-mounted tube while another loaded it with what appeared to be laundry.

There was a standoff.

Stefan leaned close to Hannah's ear, Charlemagne puddled around his collar like a gaudy necklace. "Maybe we can steal one of those subs?"

She considered this. Where would they go? Back into the depths of the lake, through a different network of tunnels?

Before she could answer, the meter man's shriek came to a sudden end.

"Maybe we can steal," suggested Charlemagne in Stefan's voice. Hannah peeked around the side of the workbench. Beyond the meters, dots had appeared in the sky like tiny holes in a sheet. Her ears picked up a low buzzing sound that she had heard before. With a start, Hannah realized that the meter man's cry had been a summoning.

Then Kyle burst into the suite, screaming a single word.

"WATCHERS!"

Chapter Thirty-Three

Kyle's warning was the green light for several things to happen at once.

A banished soul accidentally discharged his weapon (a plastic PVC pipe strung with Christmas lights and trailing a power cord that plugged into a backpack). Throckmorton ducked as a baseball grazed the top of his helmet and embedded itself in the glossy hull of a submersible.

A wave of humid air blasted through the suite, announcing the arrival of the hornet ships. Hannah's skin broke out into a damp sweat. The entire room fell into a prickly stillness as everyone paused, sick and unsettled.

With a sound like ice cracking on a frozen lake, the submersible that had been struck by the baseball began to rust. The steel alloy frame crumpled, the open hatch sagged and dislodged itself. In seconds, the vessel was a forgotten piece of scrap metal. Hannah thought that decaying was worse than blowing up. At least an explosion wasn't *sad*.

The Institute struck back. At the very edge of the battle lines,

Eri disappeared into the lightning swerves and twirls of a thousand sprites, sword slashing furiously.

"We have to get her out of there," Stefan said as he crawled out from beneath the bench. Hannah pulled him back in, just as a stray shirt from the laundry cannon landed on a swivel chair in front of their hiding spot. Immediately, the shirt spread itself out, fabric suctioning like an octopus. Hannah watched, disgusted, as the shirt's armpits stained themselves yellow. The chair's molded plastic shape became rigid and uptight. Before her eyes, the design of the chair moved back in time through rustic kitchen furniture, then rough-hewn stools, before collapsing in a pile of rotten old wood.

"Thanks," Stefan said shakily. "I could have been babyfied."

Cautiously, she peeked out. Kyle had ducked behind a sofa with an old white-haired nurse and a man in a cowboy hat. They were sprinkling a jar of Foundation inside the barrel of a gun shaped like a weathervane. It was a good spot: Kyle was shielded from the battle with the Institute, and angled so he could ambush the Watchers, whose hornets were just beginning to land on the roof deck — six, seven, eight of them — setting down on twiggy legs beside the meters.

Turning back to Stefan, Hannah suddenly felt as if the city had just opened its arms to her. In her mind she was already flying free, leaving the Dockside Arms far behind.

"You've got a weird look on your face," Stefan said nervously.

"We could steal one of those," she said, to hear how convincing it sounded. Not very. She tried again. "We could definitely steal one of those."

"One of those what?"

"Hornets," she said. "Eri could probably fly it. Right? And then we'd *really* see what the Watchers see. We'd be inside one of their ships! We could fly it straight to my mother's house."

Stefan opened his mouth but no words came out. A little boy scampered past their hiding place, hands clutching a neon squirt gun. She could hear Urvashi's voice calling out commands.

"Let's go," Hannah said. "Before somebody wins."

Stefan was incredulous. "You think we can just waltz onto one of their ships?"

Charlemagne un-necklaced himself and crawled up the side of Stefan's head, curling his tail around Stefan's ear. He stared at Hannah with his eager liquid eyes.

"Not without a disguise," she said. "You know what a Watcher looks like, don't you? The tattoo?" She nuzzled the paint-lizard. His body stole its pattern from the granite of the workbench.

"Of course I do," Stefan said.

"I'm not talking to you." Hannah poked Charlemagne with a tentative finger.

"Oh no," Stefan said. "No way." The paint-lizard glooped down over his face, swimming like a blurry eel.

"Tattoo," said Charlemagne. *"Watcher."*

"See? He gets it!" Hannah said.

Stefan sighed. "I can't believe I'm doing this."

The Watchers arrived cloaked in moist, chewy air, like a midsummer swamp. Even Hannah's eyeballs felt coated in slimy heat.

She left the army jacket hanging on a hook beneath the bench, worried that someone might recognize her in it. Stefan wore her checked flannel over his striped sweater. The mismatch seemed to throw Charlemagne into gleeful overdrive and their faces swam with his plaid energy. They stumbled through ankle-deep water, sloshing past wrecked submersibles and overturned desks. As long as they walked side by side, shoulders pressed together, Charlemagne was stretchy enough to splatter across both of their faces at once.

Just two more Watchers out for a stroll through the battle.

In the center of the room the tarp hiding the mysterious object fluttered. Shadows slithered around it, crisscrossing in the middle, securing it like a ribbon-tied gift. As Hannah and Stefan passed it, a projectile came screaming out of the fray near the canal, heading straight for them.

"Duck!" Hannah pulled Stefan down. A UFO-shaped piece of metal came spinning down the side of the tarp and landed at their feet.

Throckmorton's helmet. The suite erupted with high-pitched battle cries, followed by screams of terror. She thought of the little boy with the squirt gun. What were all these souls doing to each other?

When Hannah tried to pull Stefan up, he wouldn't budge.

"No way," he said. "I'm done."

"You can't be done," she said. "We have to move."

"Why? Ever since I met you, it's been one terrifying ordeal after another. When does it end? When we steal a Watcher's ship and fly it to your mother's house? Then what? What comes after that?"

"You can start painting again." Hannah tugged violently on his arm.

"I can? Because I guarantee they'll be coming after us, unless you think they'll be happy to lend us a ship."

He shook his head fiercely, which looked like the waving of a checkered flag. Hannah felt something give way inside her — it was as if someone cracked an egg in her brain and the yolk was sliding down the base of her spine, spreading out into her fingers and toes.

"You're the first real friend I ever had," Hannah said. "The only one who didn't come from inside my head."

"That says a lot about both of us."

"I'm sorry I took away your Ascension. I hope you find another way to get there. But first you have to get up."

"According to Kyle, there is no Ascension. But according to Eri there *is*, and you're supposed to take me there."

"I'm sure Kyle is lying."

"Yeah," Stefan said. "And what about you?"

Hannah paused. Charlemagne cycled impatiently through his patterns. "I just want you to keep being my friend."

Stefan went very still. Hannah wished she could read his thoughts. Then he held out his hand. "Let's go get Eri and a hornet, in that order."

Relieved, she helped him up, just as the Watchers' eyes began going off like flashbulbs. Both the Institute and the banished broke ranks and scattered.

Hannah and Stefan didn't dare raise their eyes. She watched all manner of shoes — from steel-toed boots to elegant pumps — slosh away in retreat. She wondered if everyone was heading for the elevator. Then splashes came, one after another, as souls fled into the canal.

"Charlemagne," Hannah said, "we can't look up right now. Can you steer us toward Eri?"

"My sword is my own."

With her eyes shut, the chaos of the room was intensified. She tried not to think about bungling into a decay weapon. Or a Watcher.

Quickly, they devised a system: Charlemagne would gurgle in Stefan's ear if they were to move left, and Hannah's if they were to move right. She could feel frantic souls giving them a wide berth. Nobody wanted to get up close and personal with a pair of Watchers.

When she thought she heard the metallic whine of an impossibly sharp sword, she risked a quick glance before snapping her eyes shut again.

"Eri," she said. The girl was jabbing at an errant sprite. "It's Hannah."

"And Stefan. Don't stab us."

"We're stealing a hornet."

"In that case," Eri said, "hurry. Your costume is ridiculous. I will cover your escape."

"Do you think you can figure out how to fly the . . . Eri?" Hannah risked another glimpse. Eri had already sprinted to the tarp. She began cutting shadow bonds with her sword.

"Watcher," Charlemagne warned.

Hannah closed her eyes before she could see the object underneath the tarp. She held on to Stefan's elbow as they waded through the wreckage. The shouts and cries had been all but silenced — the suite was emptying out. The Watchers were taking souls, clearing the room.

She heard Kyle yell, "Now!" and a clean, fiery heat cut a swath through the humidity. Sizzling water lapped at her shins.

"Faster."

They held each other, stumbling, running as best they could.

When the first Watcher screamed in pain, the noise was so grating that Hannah felt it in the nerves of her teeth. Like a dentist's drill, it rattled her to the core. She looked back. She couldn't help it.

Kyle and his companions were firing over the top of the sofa. The white-hot rooster from his weathervane found its mark and lifted an entire squad of Watchers into the air. Cloudbursts of Foundation turned their disguises against them, mutating their masks into fiery squids that licked at their faces as their legs kicked helplessly.

Stefan pulled her along. She kept her eyes open and caught his astonished glance: They could be defeated! The Watchers guarding the roof deck rushed to aid their stricken companions.

Outside, hornets idled on delicate legs. The meters were still spinning out of control. The meter man was a ghost in overalls, haunting his metal forest.

They made for the nearest ship. At rest, its translucent wings were folded back, sparkling in the lightday sun. Clusters of glass eyes were arranged like bouquets on either side of the snout-light, which curved almost all the way down to the deck.

There was a hatch beside one of the wings. Stefan groped for a handle. While he struggled, a dull wave of energy — a blunt sonic *thump* — rippled the roof deck. An eerie calm descended, bringing with it the musty odor of a long-abandoned attic. Dust seemed to settle from nowhere.

"How's that door coming?" Hannah asked as the bright shiny tiles became drab and cracked beneath her feet. She thought of Eri, hacking away at the tarp on Kyle's mysterious object. Had she unleashed a wave of decay?

"Got it!" Stefan gripped the handle and pulled. The door swung upward.

Hannah sucked air between her front teeth. The ship had a passenger: a Watcher in corduroy pants and a T-shirt. His face swam with the blue-tinted controls of the dashboard behind him.

Hannah knew that she had to look away, but it was already too late. The Watcher's eyes were backlit sunspots. She prepared to find herself alone in a tiny cell. Three steps to the sink, three steps to the cot. And yet — the world did not recede.

The Watcher was clutching his face, pawing at his disguise.

Hannah touched her own face and felt bare skin. Next to her, Stefan's mask had also disappeared. Puzzled, she jumped out of the way as the Watcher fell from the hatch and hit the roof deck, writhing, trying to regain control of his mask.

Then she figured it out: *Charlemagne.*

The paint-lizard had leapt from their faces to splatter himself into the Watcher's eyes.

Rays of lightday sun shimmered between Charlemagne's body and the Watcher's mask. All around them, the Dockside Arms was falling into disrepair. Hannah peered into the suite. There were souls moving about, but they were just blurry shapes.

"Come on, Eri," she muttered.

Inside the ship, a buckle clicked as Stefan strapped himself in. "I think I found some kind of steering thing," he announced.

"I don't see Eri," Hannah said. The roof began to sag like a neglected porch. Tiles reverted to cobblestones.

A bright flash lit the suite and Hannah looked away, blinking. When she recovered her sight, two figures had appeared in the ancient stone archway that used to hold glass doors.

"Eri!" Hannah yelled, waving her hand. Eri had rescued a boy in the costume of an angel — her companion's head was wreathed in a spectral glow. But then Eri shoved him roughly to his knees, and Hannah realized it was Kyle. His halo was composed of Eri's sprites, absorbing the smoke that billowed from his eyes. His expression was blank.

Eri presented him, wordlessly, to Hannah. Kyle's body sagged and he bowed his head in the resigned pose of the defeated.

SHNK.

Eri's sword was in her hands, its blade poised just behind Kyle's neck. Hannah's stomach lurched as she understood what kind of scene she was witnessing.

An execution.

Eri cocked her head. With perfect stillness, she questioned Hannah with her eyes. Hannah was too far away to be sure, but she could have sworn that she saw Eri raise an eyebrow, as if the most powerful thing Eri was feeling at this moment was curiosity.

It was up to Hannah to decide Kyle's fate.

Hating him was easy when he had the upper hand, when there was nothing she could do but step aside and let the Watchers handle the situation. But now Eri had delivered the chance for swift, brutal revenge, and Hannah didn't even have to swing the blade. All she had to do was nod her head.

She wondered what would happen to an executed soul. Kyle had claimed he couldn't be killed. Would Eri's blade merely hurt him, or would it somehow *end* him? Hannah didn't know. But Kyle had known exactly what would happen when he pushed Leanna Silver from the lighthouse. He'd known that he was taking Hannah's mother away from her, cleaving the Silvers in two. And what was his excuse? *She got in the way of something way more important than any single earthly life.* As if he didn't have a choice. As if his only option was to leave Hannah to find her mother's broken body.

Hannah shook her head. Kyle was wrong. There was always a choice.

"Don't do it!" she yelled. Kyle's shoulders jerked in surprise. He lifted his head to gaze at her through eyes obscured by smoke.

"I think I found the START button," Stefan said.

Eri sheathed her sword and charged across the deck. Her sprites abandoned their orbit of Kyle's head. Hannah watched him crawl back into the suite. She wondered if he would ever understand why she let him go.

As Eri sprinted past the fallen Watcher, her hand took hold of Charlemagne's spiraling tail. Without breaking her stride, she peeled him away from the Watcher and flung him straight at Hannah, who ducked.

Charlemagne made himself into a water balloon, sailed through the hatch, and splashed all over Stefan.

Now the Watcher was free. Hannah was careful to look away, keeping her eyes on Eri as the girl dove headfirst into the ship. The Watcher's long shadow loomed. Hannah scrambled inside. She reached up and found the latch, but the Watcher's hand slammed against the door, propping it open.

"Hey there, Hannah-bear," he said. "Need a ride?"

Chapter Thirty-Four

The hornet's control panel was a square of touch-sensitive glass. The slightest brush of a fingertip sent the ship plunging down toward the city streets or up into the heart of the sky.

My father's fingertip, Hannah thought as she watched him steer with practiced swipes of his hand across the panel. His fingers were long and slender, the nails well-groomed, with perfect semicircles at the end of each one.

"Mom's nails are so different," Hannah said. She was sitting in the copilot's chair. Behind her, Eri and Stefan were buckled into a two-seater bench, trying to help Charlemagne put himself back together.

"What, bitten down to the quick?" Her father glanced over, then went back to the display. "Hangnail city, right?" Hannah took note of his expert movements as he piloted. She suspected he didn't really need to give his full attention to the controls.

My father, Hannah's mind kept repeating. *This is my father.* It didn't seem true. The word didn't connect to the man. Sure, he had the beard, the guitar pick necklace. But they were just things — *items* — like the Slinky in the shoebox.

"You remember her, then," Hannah said.

"Of course. Watchers get memory-keeping benefits."

My father, the Watcher.

"But how did you know who *I* was, if you —"

"Died before you were born? Sorry about that, by the way." He laughed, a little too heartily. "Not much I could have done about the ice on that bridge. Anyway, you know what an APB is?" He didn't wait for an answer. "All points bulletin. It's what cops send out to other cops if they're hunting for somebody."

He swiped his finger along a round mirror at the end of his armrest, and Hannah's face appeared on the panel. It was a photograph taken in her cell — she was sitting on the cot.

"I didn't even know you were in the city until you'd already escaped," he explained, dismissing the APB. "They say you blew up the wall. How'd you manage that?"

"A friend helped me."

She watched him wipe a streak of orange paint from his forehead.

"Listen, I know how you were treated there. If I had been on the case from the beginning, you and Leanna would both be in the safe house, together. Keeping you locked up was a terrible misunderstanding." He slid his ring finger across the glass and the ship banked hard to the right. "Not that I blame you for leaving when you had the chance, but if you had just stayed locked up a little while longer, I would have had time to file the paperwork to take charge of your case."

"Paperwork?"

"Ooops!" Her father made a circle on the glass as if he were drawing on a steamed-up window. "Hold on a second."

A view screen appeared within the circle, displaying the city. The ship was cruising through a neighborhood of Renaissance towers a hundred stories high — it was as if someone had taken elaborate castles, rolled them into a long cylinders, and stuck them into the ground like fenceposts.

"Wrong turn," her father said, chuckling. "Hold on."

He mashed his thumb into the view screen, leaving a print, then enlarged the whorls of the print and traced a line with his pinky. The hornet nosed toward the ground. The skin of Hannah's face was pummeled by the force of the maneuver.

Behind her, Stefan doubled over, clutching his paint-spattered stomach. "I think I'm gonna be sick."

"If you have to, puke into the disintegrator, please," Hannah's father said. Then, leaning close to Hannah, whispered, "What's his name again?"

"Stefan."

Hannah felt slightly nauseous, too, like she'd eaten pizza at the Carbine Pass Fair before taking a ride on the wooden roller coaster. But it was a distant sensation. Everything seemed unimportant except the city zipping past on the view screen as the hornet brought her closer and closer to her mother. Soon she would be at her mother's house — the safe house, her father had called it. And to think she could have been there long before lightday, if only she'd remained in her cell. Albert, Belinda, and Nancy might still be with her — but what of Stefan? And Eri? If her father had simply plucked her from the Watchers' prison, she never would have met them. Her only friends would still be the ones who had sprung from her lonely mind. She missed the standoffish boy and the fussy old woman. Most of all she missed her twin. But she didn't think she would take it all back, even if she could rewind her journey and stop Albert from calling forth the storm.

The ship righted itself. On the screen, the neighborhood changed to a dizzying network of elevated trains.

"Anyway," her father said. "Yes. Paperwork. We get thousands of those fugitive bulletins a day. By the time yours came down the pipeline to my desk, I had already been assigned to go undercover with the banished."

Eri piped up from the backseat. "You are a spy?"

He shrugged. "Not usually. But for this case they had the perfect cover story for me. I pretended to betray the Watchers, and Kyle couldn't resist having another traitor in his group."

"*Another* traitor?" Eri asked.

"Kyle used to be a Watcher, too," her father explained. "A very long time ago. That's how he knows about Ascension."

Hannah noticed that her father had a habit of rubbing his palm in a circle on his right knee, which he'd worn down to a shiny patch of corduroy.

My father, the stranger.

There was an uncomfortable silence. Finally, Stefan cleared his throat. "Knows what about Ascension, Mr. Silver?"

"Well, for starters, that it doesn't exist."

This time, the silence was more than uncomfortable. Hannah's thoughts went immediately to Stefan — at least when he'd run away from the Guild, Ascension was still his goal. He could always start over somewhere else. But her father had just ripped that goal away for good. And he had done it so casually, as if he were talking about the closing of a restaurant.

Hannah watched her father as he idly checked their location on the screen and made a minor adjustment to their altitude. How could he be so cruel?

She broke the silence. "It's not true. You're lying to us, just like Kyle lied to us."

"Sorry, Hannah-bear, but —"

"Don't call me that!"

This time he met her eyes. "Sorry," he said. "I've had a lot of time to think about what I would say when I finally met you, and . . . I don't know, I've just always imagined calling you that."

"Please don't."

"I refuse to believe what you are saying, Benjamin," Eri said.

Hannah's father raised a pointed eyebrow in her direction.

She glared back. *"Eri."*

"Right. Eri," her father said. "I'm in a position to know more than you about this stuff."

“Do not speak to me like I am a child,” Eri said.

“I know you’re lying,” Stefan said excitedly. “You have to be. Here’s why. If there’s really no Ascension, and it’s this great big myth that the Watchers keep spreading, and Kyle is *so dangerous* for knowing the truth, then why did you just come out and tell us like it was nothing? Aren’t you supposed to be keeping the secret from people like me and Eri? Isn’t that your job?”

“Actually,” her father said, “a lot of people know the truth. And plenty of others don’t believe in Ascension for reasons of their own. Kyle just happens to have certain . . . abilities that make him more dangerous.”

“Wait,” Hannah said. “If a lot of people already know the truth, how come the whole lie doesn’t just fall apart?”

“Stefan,” her father said, “what did you think when Kyle told you there was no Ascension?”

“That he was crazy.”

“And how about when you heard it from me, straight from the Watcher’s mouth, as it were?”

“That you were lying.”

“So how about when somebody comes up to you on the street and starts ranting and raving about how there is no Ascension? What do you think then?”

Silence.

“You see?” her father said. “It sells itself. People *want* to believe it. All we do is give it a nudge in the right direction.”

"I have seen Watchers take people away," Eri said, a slight note of panic entering her voice. "Countless times with my own eyes."

"And what do you think happens to those fortunate souls?" Her father smiled like he was enjoying himself. A wave of nausea made Hannah clench her teeth. "They become Watchers. *That*'s the reward. The city's a big place, and it's getting bigger all the time. We're always going to need more eyes."

"I think I just figured out why you don't care that we know all this," Stefan said glumly.

"Congratulations," her father said. "It's your lucky lightday. Welcome to the City Watch."

Instinctively, Hannah braced herself for the *SHNK* of Eri's sword, for a blob of paint to gum up the glass. When nothing happened, she looked back. Stefan appeared shell-shocked, his mouth hanging slightly open. Eri was staring at the back of the pilot's chair, as if she could see through it.

The fight had gone out of her friends.

"I have no wish to become a Watcher," Eri said finally.

Her father enlarged the viewing circle. The ship had flown into a deep chasm. Far below, a meandering river spun a huge waterwheel attached to a complex of log cabins. The cliffs on either side of the chasm were packed with adobe dwellings and angular modern houses.

"Here we are," her father announced. "Quophosh. Leanna's safe house is just ahead."

"I honestly don't think I'm Watcher material," Stefan said.

Her father flashed a broad, friendly smile. "I'm sure you'll do just fine. Consider this my thanks for all the help you've given Hannah."

"My answer is no," Eri said.

"A lot of souls say that," her father said. "At first."

The Quophosh safe house was perched at the edge of an outcrop near the lip of the chasm. Here, the land had been sculpted into a suburban cul-de-sac. Hannah's father set down on a grassy island in the middle of a horseshoe-shaped street. After they had all climbed out of the ship, he closed the hatch and pressed a button on his keychain. The hornet's glass eyes blinked twice.

The next thing she knew, she was standing on the doorstep. Her father was smoothing his shirt and checking the reflection of his face in a narrow window. He took a deep breath and turned to Hannah.

"Do I have anything stuck in my beard?"

After every improbable thing that had happened to her in the city of the dead, this moment on her mother's doorstep felt the most like a dream. There were nagging thoughts lurking at the edges of her mind, truths about the city she tried to shove away. The only truth that mattered was that her mother was behind this door.

She raised her hand to the bell.

"You know," her father said quickly, before she could press the button, "I haven't actually been to see your mother since she's been in the city. So I guess I'm pretty nervous, too."

Hannah paused. Her father looked down at his feet.

"You knew she was here and you never came? Not even once?"

He glanced back at Eri and Stefan, then studied a bit of peeling paint on the siding. "I got . . . caught up in things."

That's what happens when you become a Watcher, Hannah thought: The city itself gets to be more important than any of the souls who call it home. No beginning and no end. The Watchers, the banished, the Guild, the Institute — all of them were obsessed with a game that had no rules and no winners.

Her father was still explaining himself, but Hannah tuned him out and rang the bell.

The click of a latch, the turn of a knob, the creak of a hinge.

It should not have been possible for Hannah to jump so high without a running start, but she was beyond questioning how certain things were possible. All she knew was that her feet were off the ground and her chin was on her mother's shoulder, arms and legs wrapped around, clinging, unwilling to let go.

"Hannah," her mother was saying, again and again. "My little girl."

When Hannah was finally able to pull herself away, she set her feet down on the doorstep and actually saw the person she'd traveled so far to find. Her mother looked beautiful, but a hint of sadness — that old coastal melancholy, gray as the north Atlantic — crept across her face.

"Oh, Hannah." The corners of her lips played at a weary smile. "I didn't expect to see you here so soon. You were supposed to live a very long life."

"I'm not dead!" Hannah wiggled her fingers as if that confirmed it. "I just came through the door to find you and take you home."

Her mother knelt down to look her in the eyes. "You did *what*?"

Hannah swallowed. Her mother actually seemed angry. "I came to get you, through the lighthouse. What else was I supposed to do?"

"Excuse me, Mrs. Silver?" Stefan piped up timidly. "Is there any chance I could do some laundry while I'm here? I've got . . ." He indicated his sweater, which was covered in bits of Charlemagne.

Hannah's mother blinked at him, stood up, then turned to Hannah's father and put her hand to her heart. "Benjamin," she said, exhaling the word.

"I, too, would be grateful for a wash," Eri said.

Her mother didn't take her eyes from her husband, who seemed to shrink from her gaze.

"Leanna, I'm sorry I haven't been around," he said, scratching a sideburn.

"Can we go home now?" Hannah looked from one parent to the other. "All of us?"

Her mother pushed a strand of hair away from her face. She placed a gentle hand against Hannah's forehead, then her cheek, then her shoulder. "Why don't we go inside and sit down," she said.

Her father shuffled his feet anxiously. "I . . . I actually have to be going."

The look on her mother's face made Hannah want to kick her father in the shins.

"We're right in the middle of an important case," he said. "I have to get back to work."

"Fine," Hannah said. "Then go."

"I'll be back as soon as all this business with the banished is over with — and it will be soon. We've got them on the run — and then we'll have our entire afterlives to catch up." He turned to Eri and Stefan. "You two are coming with me."

"We won't *be* here when you get back," Hannah said. "We'll be at Cliff House." She interlaced fingers with her mother. "Right?"

Her father flashed a quick smile, white teeth appearing within his beard. "I'm afraid it doesn't quite work like that. Once you're in the city, you're in the city for good. You can't go back."

Hannah felt the future she'd constructed in her mind — the Silvers back together at Cliff House — decay and collapse as if it were struck by one of the banished weapons.

"But I'm not dead," she said.

Her father couldn't meet her eye. "I'm sorry. That's just the way it is."

Her mother pulled her close without letting go of her hand. Hannah thought of the first time she'd ever met a Watcher, that night in the Tree Room. "But I've seen people cross over," she protested. "I know it's possible."

Her father considered this. "*Possible,* certainly. But to get that kind of travel permit from the mayor's office is no easy task."

"Good thing you're a Watcher, then," Hannah said.

He frowned. "If I were just applying for *me*, just a solo pass, it would still take a thousand darkdays for the paperwork to go through. And there's all the exams, the vaccinations. . . ."

"Benjamin," her mother said sharply, a tone Hannah knew well. "Our daughter came a very long way. And the Silvers are Guardians. That has to count for something."

He looked at her as if she had just suggested they take a flying leap into the chasm. "You want me to take her to see the mayor? The *mayor*, Leanna?"

"She's our *daughter*, Ben. She traveled through the door to find me."

"I have a *job* here. I can't just —"

"Take a little time out of your eternal afterlife to spend with your family."

"I'm still trying to adjust to *having* a family again!"

"Well then, by all means." Leanna crossed her arms. "Don't let me keep you from your adjustment period."

"You know what? Fine. You want to see the mayor?" he asked Hannah.

"Yes."

"I don't," Stefan said.

Hannah gasped as her father's face began to crackle and distort. The coarse hairs of his beard grew like vines to meet the hair on his head. A swampy halo of humid air covered the porch. She looked deep into the whirlpool of her father's mask. His eyes flashed, and her feet left the doorstep once again, but this time she traveled much farther.

Chapter Thirty-Five

The mayor of the dead city was a hulking mahogany desk the size of a circus tent. Or else it was the green-shaded lamp on top of the desk, which could only be reached by a ladder. Or else it was tucked away somewhere in one of the hundreds of drawers that popped open and closed like an arcade game as attendants rushed between them.

Hannah wasn't sure, and confusion seemed to be rampant among the attendants, too. The arena-sized office that housed the desk was full of crisis and commotion, made even worse by the tour groups that oohed and aahed their way through, cameras flashing.

"The mayor's house is the oldest dwelling in the city," explained a prim tour guide to a class of name tag–wearing students. "And they say the oldest souls still live here."

A boy's hand shot up. "Oooh! Where?"

The tour guide waved her hand dismissively. "Just . . . around."

Hannah, her mother, her father, Eri, and Stefan had arrived in the midst of all this activity and found themselves promptly ignored. Her nerves were frayed. Each time a drawer slid open, there was a sound like shoes squeaking on a gym floor. Each time a drawer slammed shut, a dusty thud echoed off the distant ceiling. The attendants all looked nervous, sweaty, and overworked, with the ghostly pallor of those who spent all their time indoors. Hannah could only guess at their errands.

"What's a guy gotta do to get some service around here!"

Her father was still in his Watcher mask, and his voice was a horrible croak that gave Hannah chills. The tour group scattered at the sound. An attendant came sprinting up.

"Shh! Are you mad?" The man had a patch over his right eye, but his left bulged at the affront. "His Honor doesn't allow Watchers in his personal chamber! How did you even get in here?"

"He doesn't allow" — Hannah winced at the ear-shredding sound of her father's voice — *"Sorry, just a second . . ."* His beard unswirled and his face emerged. His voice returned to its normal state. "He doesn't allow Watchers, but he allows tour groups?"

"Ah!" The attendant said ecstatically, as if he were glad Hannah's father made this point so he could rebut it. He slid a paper from his folder. "That tour group had one of these" — he waggled the paper — "Application Q98 dash 119B. They filed thirteen lightdays ago, giving it adequate time to be routed through the proper channels for signatures, and *then* their permit appeared in my inbox with a full darkday to spare. Efficient, no?" He thrust his face forward, hands on his hips. "Where's *your* application? Hmm? Did you even take the time to file? Do you even know what kind of permit you need? The information is available at any Watcher precinct. Shame on you, sir! Shame on you for taking matters into your own hands and simply showing up! This is not how governments are effectively run, you know!"

The attendant was out of breath.

"I'm here to see the mayor," Hannah said.

The attendant peered down at her, lifting his patch to reveal a perfectly normal eye.

"Aha." The attendant laughed drily. "Aha. The mayor. Of course. You can just walk in here and see the mayor. Oh!" He put his hands up in mock surrender. "By all means, be my guest. The mayor! Why didn't you say so? There's not a waiting list for *that*. No paperwork to be filled out for *that*. Why, you should feel free to — hey!"

Hannah, Eri, and Stefan all had the same idea at the same time. Together, they pressed through the crowd, making their way to the desk. They stood next to a ladder and knocked on one of the drawers.

"Mr. Mayor?" Hannah said.

An attendant wearing the white uniform of a milkman hopped off the ladder to confront them. "What do you think you're doing?"

Hannah knocked again. "My name is Hannah Silver. I'm not dead and I really need to get home."

"Young lady, I must insist you fill this out." The attendant produced a thick binder full of papers.

Eri sliced it in two.

The drawer popped open with a *screech*, just as the first attendant arrived with Hannah's mother and father. He was irate.

"Now you've done it, you . . ." He placed his mouth near the desk. "Your Honor, I am so, *so* sorry. These people just barged in and —"

A silkworm popped up from the drawer on a gilded platform and began to spin a sparkling thread.

"Is that the mayor?" Hannah asked.

But the attendants were focused on the silkworm. They took notes on identical pads.

"Uh-huh." The first attendant nodded in response to the lengthening thread. "Okay. Right. Yessir."

The silkworm's pedestal descended and the drawer slammed shut with a *bang*. The drawer directly above it slid open and an elaborate paper airplane launched itself out. The man with the eye patch chased after it while the milkman addressed Hannah and her parents.

"The mayor says he knows who you people are." The attendant checked his notes. "The *Silvers*. He says you've got a lot of nerve showing your faces in here after what happened with the door in the lighthouse." The milkman cleared his throat. "The mayor wants to know how hard it could possibly be to be a Guardian. He wishes for me to remind you that it consists of exactly one job: not letting people walk through a door."

Hannah grabbed the handle of the silkworm's drawer and pulled it open. The attendant screamed and covered his head as if she'd just tossed a grenade.

"I want to go home!" she yelled into the drawer, but the worm was nowhere to be seen. Frustrated, she slammed it shut and opened another one. Empty. "Where is it?" she asked the attendant, who was cowering on the floor.

"You're not supposed to be able to do that," he said quietly.

Hannah didn't understand what he was talking about. Then Eri tried to pull open the same two drawers. They didn't budge. She even placed her feet against the desk and leaned back, throwing all her weight behind it. Nothing.

"Huh," Hannah's father said, looking at her curiously. "How about that."

She felt her mother's hand on her shoulder.

A drawer popped open and the attendant jumped to his feet, composing himself in time to receive an origami flower. Carefully, he smoothed the paper and began to read aloud.

"The mayor says you have an intriguing bloodline and he apologizes for belittling your contribution to the safety of the city."

"So can we go home now?" Hannah asked. She wasn't even surprised at her ability to open the desk drawers. By now she was pretty sure the Memory Keeper had been telling the truth — one way or another, she *had* been here before. The city itself seemed to recognize her.

"Uh . . ." The attendant scanned the paper. "The mayor says

on one condition. There's a door in the basement. If you can open it, you're free to go."

"A door to Cliff House?" Hannah asked.

"It could be Ascension," Stefan said.

"Why can't the mayor open it himself?" asked Hannah's mother.

The attendant waited patiently for them to quiet down. "Basically — and he didn't say this, but I know him pretty well . . ." He lowered his voice. "The mayor's a very busy old soul and he doesn't really care what happens to you."

The attendant with the eye patch suddenly reappeared, panting. He handed the unfolded paper airplane to Hannah's mother. "Sign at the *X*. This document certifies that you do not hold the city, the office of the mayor, or the mayor himself responsible should you fail to open the door and blink out of existence for all eternity. It's standard boilerplate stuff."

Stefan handed his paintbrush to Hannah, who took the paper before her mother could object and whisked her name onto the line. The attendant frowned at the wet paint and shook the paper in the air to dry it.

He sighed with displeasure. "Right this way, people, I'd like to get off work while it's still lightday. . . ."

The stone staircase led down into the basement of the mayor's house. They stood at the top while the attendant flipped on the light. Halfway down the stairwell a bare bulb flickered.

"This is the oldest known part of the city," he said, bored and in a hurry. "This particular stairway was here long before anything else."

Hannah squinted down into the gloom. At the bottom she could just barely make out a door.

"Good luck," the attendant said. "I'm fairly sure we won't be seeing each other again, so . . . that's that!" He strode briskly away down the hall.

Hannah sneezed. It was very dusty.

"Bless you," her father said. "Listen, Leanna, I've got a funny feeling about this."

"Well, the timing of your feeling is just perfect, Ben," her mother said. "What have you gotten us into?"

"Hey, it was your idea to go see the mayor."

Hannah thought of Albert, Belinda, and Nancy, and what they had sacrificed to bring her to this moment. She wondered if it could have happened any other way. "It's okay, Mom. I can open it."

"Hannah . . . I don't want to lose you again."

The Hannah her mother knew was distracted and unsure of herself, always second-guessed by the voices in her head. But Hannah had left that girl behind, and she wasn't going to stand around arguing. She sidestepped her mother and put her foot down on the second step, skipping the first. She pictured the lighthouse staircase side by side with the stairs down to the Tree Room: two stained-glass memories, lined up, letting in the light.

She brought her other foot down on the step. *Trapdoors to the pit,* she thought.

"Stay behind me, everybody," she said.

One more step down, and the stone walls on either side of the old staircase were gone. There was a vastness to the space down here, as if the mayor's basement sprawled beneath the entire city.

One hundred seventy billion souls.

Fuzzy *click-clacks* came out of the darkness like the crawling of distant limbs. None of the traps back at Cliff House had prepared her for that.

"Did you hear something?" she asked.

"No," her mother said.

"Can you guys still see the walls?"

Her father, after a moment: "Yes, Hannah."

So she was on her own, standing in the middle of *nothing,* until she heard a mad skittering, closer and closer. All at once, metal-tipped spears were launched from beyond the absent walls of the staircase, from the endless dark place only she could see. And with them came a great volley of darts. At the same time, a wooden fence flipped up like a stepped-on rake, trapping her. Her only chance was to shove it down, break through, or slide underneath — but there wasn't enough time. The first dart whined past her head. Placing her hand against the barrier, she decided to leap over it and hope none of the projectiles found their mark.

There was a stabbing pain in her forearm and Hannah thought she'd been hit. Was that all it took — one little dart — to blink her out of existence? The pain traveled to her thumb, and the toothpick from the attic slid out of her skin and into a tiny hole in the fence.

Instantly, the barrier crumbled. The empty space on either side of her solidified into walls. The spears and the darts were trapped in that dark place beyond. She was safe. She let out a breath.

"Everybody okay?" Her voice was shaky and weak.

"Uh . . . we're fine," Stefan said.

"Is something the matter, Hannah Silver?"

They really can't see what I see. "No. I'll just keep going."

Two more steps down and she was back in that endless cave. She had the sinking feeling that it didn't connect to the undercity at all, and wasn't exactly on any Institute map.

This time there was a rotten stench to accompany a far-off gibbering and scrabbling, as if two vicious armies of rats were fighting over scraps. The stink was searing her nostrils, making her dizzy. Her vision swam.

She felt something brush her leg.

It was a white, viney appendage. Beyond the walls, whatever disgusting thing it was attached to exhaled in satisfaction as it discovered prey. Hannah wondered how long it had been since anyone had ventured down here.

Steeling herself, Hannah grabbed the vine. Fungus from the subway station in Nusle Kruselskaya came pouring out of her thumb. The predatory thing's anticipation became a surprised yelp, then a keening whine. The vine began to wriggle. Hannah held on until the fungus stopped spewing out. It went slithering away, fading into the darkness. The staircase was whole once again.

"Are you hurt?" her mother's anxious voice called out.

"No," she said hoarsely.

"Let me walk beside you," Eri said.

Hannah steadied her voice. "I'm fine."

She took a few more steps before she realized the next trap had already begun. The walls hadn't disappeared; they'd become two complex puzzle pieces, full of unearthly geometry. Hannah could sense their desire to be together before they even started to close the gap. There was an ominous rumbling. She was going to be crushed, her spine snapped before her soul was taken. Desperately, she searched the patterns — labyrinths of angles that didn't quite make sense. She mashed her thumb against the walls at random, but they just kept pressing on, narrowing the stairwell so that she was forced to turn sideways. At the last second she spotted the missing piece: a rectangular gap the size of a —

Space bar.

She felt it exit her thumb and slot into place. The walls stopped. Hannah turned to find four worried-looking expressions.

"Did you see that one?" she asked.

Her father raised a bushy eyebrow.

"Never mind."

Now the door stood alone in the void. The stairwell had faded into oblivion. It was too far to jump — and besides, what would she land on? She thought for a moment, then placed her hand out over the emptiness and gave it an encouraging shake.

Water sprayed from her thumb. It smelled fishy and gross, like the floating canals of Caymiri. Instead of dripping down into the darkness, the water flowed across the void. A canal rippled into place.

With an awkward diving motion, Hannah pushed out into the water. She paddled hard to keep from going under (after all, there was no bottom). Her legs kicked down into the empty air, but she splashed her way across. Treading water, she reached up until her fingers gripped the doorknob. She pulled herself up onto solid ground.

Her mother and father held hands. Stefan shifted his weight nervously. Eri folded her arms. They all stood in front of the door. Hannah tried to think of something to say.

Charlemagne crawled up the handle of Eri's sword. *"Get on with it!"*

Hannah's father jumped. "That thing can *talk*?"

Hannah sent a silent thank-you to Albert, Nancy, and Belinda. Then she opened the door. . . .

Chapter Thirty-Six

They stepped out into the tall grass of a prairie. She watched her mother cross the threshold, followed by Eri and Stefan. Her father came through last, and the door slammed shut behind him.

With a surprised grunt he reached for the doorknob and grabbed nothing but empty air. Before anybody could stop him, he drove his shoulder into the space where the door had been and flopped into the grass. Hannah's mother rushed to help him up. He got to his feet, brushed off his corduroys, and picked a twig out of his beard.

"Guess that was a one-way trip."

Like a mime, he measured out the area of the door frame with his hands, slapping his palms against the air.

"Here, boy!" Stefan called out, agitated. "Over here, Charlemagne! Where'd you go?"

Hannah's heart sank. If Charlemagne was trapped on the other side of the vanished doorway, Stefan would be heartbroken.

"Lullaby!"

Hannah's mother recoiled in horror as Charlemagne bounded up her leg, across her stomach, and wrapped himself around her arm.

"Oh," she said, freezing in place, as if the paint-lizard were likely to sting her if she moved too quickly. "What do I do?"

Stefan scooped his pet away from Hannah's mother. "I think he wants you to sing him a lullaby."

Hannah began humming "Cork on the Ocean."

Her mother tried to dab the paint from her sleeve, gave up, and started singing along. The melody swam into Hannah's head and buzzed pleasantly, like a sugar rush.

"If only I had a guitar," her father said, shooting for a harmony line and ending up with something slightly off-key.

Hannah watched her mother skim a hand along the wispy tips of the waist-high grass. Her father studied the empty sky, a puzzled look on his face. It didn't have the brilliance of a lightday or the melancholy of a noonday, and it certainly wasn't dark. It was none of those things, and yet somehow it was *all* of those things, a perfectly neutral color that Hannah had never seen before.

Stefan was the first to ask the question on everybody's mind. "Where are we?"

Her mother took a deep breath. "It smells like . . . home. Like earth. Like we're *alive.* Is anybody else getting that?"

Hannah wanted to believe they had crossed back over into the world of the living, and considered how good it would feel to entertain that thought, even for a little while. But it would be a lie.

"I've never seen a sky like that back home," she said.

"Maybe it's Ascension," Stefan offered.

"I do not think so," Eri said.

"How do you know? Maybe this is it, a field with some grass and stuff. Maybe we're the first souls to ever make it here. Think about *that*."

"*Hannah* was the first soul to make it here," Eri said. "We just followed her."

Her mother swished through the grass in a lazy circle, bending stalks with her arms. "Hannah, it's the strangest feeling, being your mother right now. It's like I don't know anything about you. How did you know you could do that?"

"Because I think the city wants me to be a part of it. Ever since I crossed over, it's almost like it knows me. Maybe this is what dying is." She held her hand up to the light and gave it a long look. "Maybe I *am* dead."

Her mother pulled her in for an embrace. "We're together. It doesn't matter if we're in Cliff House, or the city, or . . . here, wherever this is."

Her father joined them. His big feet flattened entire clumps of grass. "Look at that, up ahead." The flatland unfurled like wall-to-wall carpet, as far as she could see. But then she noticed that what she'd taken for the haze of a distant horizon was really a long bank of fog. It wasn't much darker than the sky, but there it was, blocking her view.

She followed it with her eyes, turning her feet slowly, until she had made a complete circle. The view never changed. The field was encircled by fog. If they kept walking in any direction, eventually they would hit it.

She had never been in such a flat place before, and the sheer panoramic breadth was making her woozy. Looking down into the grass, she saw a black flower. Kneeling for a better look, she realized it wasn't a flower at all but a bulbous fruit about the size of an artichoke. She poked it and a little bit of dust puffed out. She picked it up and handed it to Stefan.

"Wow," he said, "I think it's —"

"Foundation," her father said. Gently, he took the fruit. He closed his hand into a fist, and when he opened it, the flower had been crushed. He was holding a pile of black grains. "Raw, unprocessed Foundation."

"Then we haven't gone anywhere at all," her mother said.

"Perhaps Ascension is built from the same material as the city," Eri said. "Foundation could exist here, too." She smiled — *smiled* — at Stefan. "As you say, nobody knows."

"I say we start walking," Hannah said.

"Which way?" Stefan turned in a circle of his own, gazing out at the fog.

"North," Eri said.

Stefan thought for a moment. "How do we know which way that is?"

"It was a joke," Eri said. "I was telling a joke."

Charlemagne cackled. Hannah's father shuddered.

"Let's go this way," Hannah said, leading her mother by the hand.

"Is this another one of your new skills?"

"No, I just picked a random direction."

They walked in silence. The only sounds were the hushed whispers of the grass and a faint hiss whenever someone trampled a Foundation plant.

Hannah pointed. "Look!" She could have sworn she'd spotted the fog thinning out.

"What is it?" her father asked, squinting.

She glimpsed the edge of a great city wearing the haze like a cloak: towers of glass, monuments of stone. A skyline on the horizon, suddenly exposed.

"It's —"

But the fog had already rolled back, and the city was gone.

"It's nothing," she said. "Let's keep going."

She didn't want to think about choked sidewalks and traffic. Somewhere out there, billions of souls went about their business. Here, five souls crossed a field, and it was peaceful.

THE END